AN APOCALYPSE TO REMEMBER

BOOK I - CHRISTMAS CAPERS

James T. Harper

This book was written for, and is dedicated to Tony Stupich; simply the best.

CHAPTER 1

A CHRISTMAS MORNING BANG

As was his nature, Kyle awoke first. His brain, Loyal Reader, brilliant as it is, has always been unable to let him sleep past about 7:00 am. This was a bittersweet trait; fantastic for the workweek, but admittedly slightly annoying for poor Kyle on weekends and vacations. Still groggy from a somewhat restless night's slumber (unfortunately par for the course of late), Kyle rubbed his heavy eyes, looked at his watch, grunted in dismay that it was barely 6:30 am (6:18 to be exact), tossed around for what seemed like an eternity (but was, in actuality, just under 14 seconds), and settled in for a quiet reflection on the day that lay ahead.

Knocking first upon his brain's door was the realization that it was Christmas Day - December 25th, his husband Chad's favourite day of the year. Upon meeting each other (back when meeting another person didn't involve guessing who was going to kill whom first over the last tin of Fancy Feast or cannister of gasoline), Kyle quickly realized Chad's borderline pathological love of all things Christmas. As the years wore on in their blossoming relationship, Chad would lovingly push the boundaries of acceptable protocol to find new and inventive ways to justify decorating their house as early in November as possible. Of course, if Chad has his way, Kyle knew that their home would be a perennial Christmas wonderland. Luckily for all parties involved, Chad did not get his way and their house, at least while they were still able to live there, never did resemble a permanent homage to one of Santa's wet dreams. As Kyle reflected on Christmases past, the festivities each year would inevitably bring, and the excitement Chad would display, a bittersweet smile crossed his face.

Those were simpler times, he reflected.

Hot on the heels of these heartwarming memories, was a sudden realization that he was ravenously hungry. It was difficult for Kyle to remember the last time he had eaten anything that could even remotely be considered something resembling a good meal. Last night's Christmas Eve dinner, for example, consisted of a can of creamed corn seasoned with an ancient McDonalds ketchup packet. This memory, though barely 10 hours old, was without any measure of hyperbole, enough to make a grown man cry.

A series of gurgles, all of slightly varying pitch and intensity, leapt from Kyle's stomach and filled the room. These resembled, rather amazingly, what you might expect to hear from the depths of some ancient and destitute plumbing system.

Perhaps of the Eastern European variety, Kyle mused to himself.

Chad stirred in the bed beside him, perhaps because of Kyle's body movements, but most likely because of the ensuing guttural chorus.

Two puppies (Boston Terriers, in case you were wondering, Loyal Reader) were doing their best imitations of freight trains under the covers, oblivious to the world that soldiered on around them. Truth be told, neither dog was a puppy. Bronx would be turning 13 in four short months and Brooklyn would be 12 years old just two months later. In their daddies' eyes, however, they would forever remain puppies.

All things considered, a Christmas morning cuddle fest, as Chad would often refer to it, with the cutest puppies in the known Universe was a very good thing.

Surprisingly, at least to the casual observer sitting at home stuffing Cool Ranch Dorito after Dorito into an awaiting orifice, Kyle's third thought of the morning was wondering what fresh Hellscape the zombie apocalypse would casually toss their way today.

A zombie apocalypse is a funny thing, Loyal Reader. Well, perhaps not literally funny to the billions of people that ended up becoming undead flesh cravers, but most certainly figuratively and in a playfully metaphysical sense.

Throughout human history, television, cinema, and scores of written works have used up pretty much every possible angle to portray the advent of insatiable zombie hordes. So much so, in fact, that the average person could end up thinking that had, for example, a secret government laboratory from a parallel Earth maliciously released a zombie-creating virus, that surviving the ensuing carnage might actually be within the realm of possibility. Fictional heroes have provided volumes of veritable how-to guides for avoiding certain death (or undeath, as it were). As it turns out, and as Kyle and Chad would become very, very painfully aware, every last TV show, movie, and doorstop-of-a-novel written by Johnny Down-The-Street got it wrong.

Survival, as it turns out, is pretty much all about being insanely fucking lucky and nothing more.

As of that fateful Christmas Day, Loyal Reader, no inhabitant of this planet we lovingly call Earth knows exactly how this whole apocalypse thing got started. Not the scientists working tirelessly in their labs, not the politicians standing on their podiums spouting calming platitudes, and most certainly not the most recent Academy Award winner for best supporting actress.

What everyone did know, however, is that roughly 8 months ago on May 22nd, 2017 zombies just appeared. On May 21st, life was proceeding just like it always had, and the next day the world was quite literally overrun with the undead.

Zombies seemed to appear simultaneously in all parts of the globe. There appeared to be no rhyme or reason as to who was infected and subsequently turned. Whatever caused people to become zombies affected everyone from billionaires and presidents to the destitute and homeless. It was as if instantaneously the world was simply overrun with billions and billions of the ravenous undead.

The actual number of zombies was, of course, never measured. In the first days of the apocalypse, those with some appreciable amount of time on their hands (Zombie Ecologists, perhaps?) estimated that roundabouts 75-80% of the world's population had been instantaneously transformed.

Total bummer, Loyal Reader.

To their credit, the creators of zombie fiction did get some undead characteristics right. Of course, no single television show, movie, or book was entirely correct, and when you think about it, that's to be expected. Reality is often quite different from what gets shoveled down our throats as entertainment. The undead that began to roam the land in search of super yummy flesh resembled kind of a greatest-hits amalgamation of what one might reasonably expect from the average television or film zombie.

For example, when first formed, a zombie is extremely energetic and exceptionally sensitive to sound and vibration in its environment.

Like, really annoyingly so.

It was as if someone force-fed them a shipping container's worth of amphetamines and set them loose on the world around them. They would run as fast as they possibly could with only one goal in mind, to mindlessly feast on any living thing they encountered. To be fair, the previous statement isn't exactly correct. It's not like you could distract one of these undead Energizer Bunnies by throwing a bag of broccoli at it.

Let us be quite clear, Loyal Reader, no problem in the world, undead or not, was ever solved by launching a bag of broccoli. If anyone has ever told you different then run and make sure you tell someone you trust.

Instead, these zombies were very predictably of the carnivore variety; any living animal would do.

As such, instead of throwing a bag of broccoli at a zombie, a much more effective approach would be for you to throw, for example, a bag of incredibly adorable kittens. Being adorable, as you have probably guessed by now, Loyal Reader, increases a kitten's yumminess by an order of magnitude.

Of course, if you did that Loyal Reader, someone named Meredith, or Susan, or Jeanette would be labelling you a goddamned soulless monster quicker than a zombie could bite the head clean off one of the aforementioned helpless kittens.

For roundabouts two weeks following *The Turning*, as it was called, this insanely metabolic blood thirst was the norm, and a lot of people died.

Like, a whole lot of people.

If the 75-80 some-odd percent of the population turning into zombies in an instant wasn't enough of a cosmic slap in the nards for humanity, then the ensuing fortnight's decimation of a healthy portion of the remaining humans certainly made up for that. Of those lucky bastards that were not affected by *The Turning*, the lion's share ended up being summarily devoured during those first blood-spattered two weeks.

Let this be a lesson, Loyal Reader, to never underestimate the efficiency of a carnivore that doesn't need to sleep and doesn't waiver from its need to feed.

After the initial feeding frenzy, the undead began to slow down and take a relaxed, rather lackadaisical approach to seeking out their food. Instead of partaking in a rush-hour surge to eat, they would stumble around their environment at a nice, almost leisurely pace.

The apocalypse, you could say, became just a little more civilized.

While this laissez-faire mode of flesh acquisition made it much easier for people to outrun the zombies' insatiable appetites, it did have the secondary effect of making them much more difficult to hear. It's not like they were stealthy by any stretch of the imagination, but they were definitely much quieter than the mad hatter approach they displayed during those first two nerve-wracking weeks.

Another fortuitous side effect of the zombies slowing down appeared to be that the seemingly supernatural auditory and visual acuity they initially displayed became somewhat dulled. They still responded to loud noises and large-scale, quick movements, but a sneaky human could navigate the environment somewhat successfully with enough patience and care.

This was a good thing.

Arguably the most egregious mistakes that popular culture made concerning zombies had to do with two situations: a) how humans can be turned into zombies, and b) how to neutralize a zombie. So, let's be perfectly clear, Loyal Reader. If a zombie bites you, or you manage to ingest zombie blood or some other unthinkable zombie effluent in some spectacularly unfortunate sequence of events, you will not become a zombie.

That's just silly.

The only event that ever made a human a zombie was *The Turning*, this seemingly magical instantaneous transformative event. No more zombies ever arose and perhaps no more ever will; who can say? In a post zombie-bite life, the biggest worry would, in fact, be some pustulous infection that manifests in the wound. Zombies, you see, are by nature quite disgusting. They have no sense of grooming or body care, most probably related to the whole being undead thing and not having the cognitive presence of mind to worry about showering, brushing their teeth, and scrubbing their pits. Of course, perhaps they do have the cognitive presence and they just don't give a damn.

Good for them.

Good for them, indeed.

If, though, you are unlucky enough to ever find yourself being killed by a zombie, take solace in the fact that you are only serving as a meal and will not be relegated to roaming the land in search of non-broccoli flesh.

There are a number of ways to neutralize a zombie, each with varying levels of satisfaction on the human's part. Damaging or cutting off an appendage or three is a good way to immobilize a zombie, but it still leaves the head to deal with. Let's be honest, Loyal Reader, that's the business end where all of the I-want-to-eat-your-flesh action is going to take place. It's difficult to conjure something more embarrassing in a zombie apocalypse than being eaten by a stationary, flailing zombie torso. One would rightly die quicker of the complete and utter shame of the situation rather than the actual undead doorstop munching away at your body.

To mitigate such ego-deflating situations, it is always a good idea to neutralize the zombie completely. And no, Loyal Reader, before you even begin to spout your TV-inspired drivel, you can't just shoot a zombie in the head or stick a knife through the skull or something über sexy like you would see in ultra-slow motion on *The Walking Dead*. Sadly, it is at least an order of magnitude more disgusting than that.

> *Editor's Note:* If, Loyal Reader, by some non-denominational miracle this book has managed to defy all reason and logic and still be something even remotely resembling a 'thing' many, many moons from now, that above reference to *The Walking Dead* may have whooshed just above your pretty little skull. If that is indeed what just transpired, be not alarmed. Luckily, our meandering story is choc-full of references to such pop-culture gems and like the above paragraph, we will always apply a liberal swatch of context and just enough overextrapolation to take down a charging and bloodthirsty Kardashian (See? Pop culture practically oozes from our every pore!) Armed with such information, not only will you be able to Nancy Drew your way to putting all the dots together, we can now safely euthanize this pathetic excuse for a paragraph.

As you likely have suspected, Loyal Reader, the head of the zombie is where you need to focus your attention. However, to reliably put a zombie out of its misery, you need to essentially pulverize its head into a bloody goop.

For some reason, simply penetrating the brain with some foreign object just will not do, you've got to get in the brain case and mash it up really good.

So Loyal Reader, let's review. Unless you are shooting a zombie in the head with enough firepower to decimate its contents, this has no more of an effect than shooting it in its left big toe. Simply cutting off the head will indeed displace it from the body of the zombie but said head will just keep on trying to eat any flesh that happens to be in its vicinity, as comically terrifying as this is. And make no mistake, it is quite comically terrifying. You really have to admire the zombies' conviction; they seek out food, they find food, they eat food, and they will apparently repeat these behaviours *ad nauseum* until their brains are gooified.

A few moments after Kyle awoke, Chad joined him in the land of the conscious; a pretty nice place to be when you are lucky enough to be surrounded by the ones you love. For the briefest of moments, life had all the characteristics of being something approximating what may be in the vicinity of what one might call normal. Brooklyn was absolutely loving every minute of the early morning cuddles with her daddies; she's always been good that way. Bronx, however, was horribly unimpressed by the whole affair, and this was not at all surprising. Bronx would growl and snarl at the very thought of being forced to engage in an activity that either disrupted his hard-earned sleep or that he did not explicitly instigate. Even when he acted like he wanted love and affection, the surly teenager in him often shuddered at the thought of excessive coddling.

This Christmas Day scene, as mentioned earlier, was perfectly characteristic of any such morning in the life of our heroes. Unfortunately, Loyal reader, life was, of course, not normal at all and this would turn out to be not like any other morning Kyle and Chad had experienced. This is saying quite a bit given what they had been through in the past seven months. *The Turning* had taken their idyllic life and quite completely turned it upside down and inside out. No longer did Kyle and Chad cavort around in their spacious home in the wilds of Greater Vancouver, British Columbia; no longer did they spend far, far too much of their time lazing about and watching their favorite digital distractions; no longer did they celebrate special occasions (or sometimes any occasion, really) by consuming anything from the McDonald's menu, or feasting on any of a selection of other carbohydrate-

and lipid-infused foods that they could get their grimy little hands on; and certainly no longer did Kyle and Chad venture out of the relative safety of their current abode without first fetching Betty and Veronica.

Oh, how life had changed, Loyal Reader.

Like any famous duo in history, Betty and Veronica had vastly different approaches to getting the job done and yet perfectly complimented one another in every single way. Unlike their familiar literary counterparts, Betty and Veronica were not two young women relentlessly pursued by the likes of Archie Andrews and Reggie Mantle, but rather two loving, affectionate, and efficient tools for disposing of any zombie threats Kyle and Chad should happen upon.

Betty, you see, was an axe. A Gränsfors Bruk double-bit felling axe, to be precise. With a 3lb head and 6 inches of cutting surface on each side, she could slice the head off of a zombie, lickety-split. Once liberated from the body, dealing with a chomping zombie head was all about Veronica. Being a 16lb Urrea octagonal sledgehammer with a rich, hickory handle, Veronica excelled at systemically bashing said zombie head into oh so much disgusting goop.

Gwyneth Paltrow, were she not resting uncomfortably in the digestive tracts of 61 different zombies, would be extremely proud.

Thus, Loyal Reader, it is safe to say that not only did pure, blind luck play a role in Kyle and Chad's survival thus far, but Betty and Veronica had also become an integral part of their beating the daily odds and surviving in the zombie apocalypse.

It wasn't too long until the Christmas Day laze-fest was quite rudely interrupted by the most unwelcome of unexpected guests - harsh reality. True to form, harsh reality decided on this festive morning to announce itself with a rather loud bang.

Back in the first days of *The Turning*, this sort of event would have been very much terror-inducing. A noise of that magnitude would have set off pretty much every zombie in a half-mile radius into a mad frenzy. The dwelling would most likely have been surrounded within minutes and all hope would effectively be lost. Luckily Kyle, Chad, and the puppies had two things going for them. First, they were seven months into this apocalyptic journey and any zombies in the vicinity were not nearly so sensitive to such loud noises. Second, the bang, as startling as it was at such an ungodly hour, was unlikely to have attracted the attention of any zombies.

You see Loyal Reader, Kyle and Chad were sequestered quite nicely in the middle nowhere, in northern British Columbia.

CHAPTER 2

ARE YOU THERE SANTA? IT'S ME, PUBERT

By any reasonable metric, Loyal Reader, May 22nd was supposed to be like any other day. Around the world, people were supposed to soldier through one more day in their boring, predictable lives. However, for somewhere around five-and-a-half billion of Earth's human inhabitants, their stories instantly came to an abrupt and rather undead end. It was very much a shit show of a planetary lottery that occurred, and if your number was drawn, well, it sucked big time to be you.

Like, really big time.

The Earth, of course, is quite large and quite round, with absotively posilutely not a single solitary apology to the dimwitted and moronic flat-earthers out there lucky enough to piece together these strange looking hieroglyphs and comprehend the words on this page. As such, due to time zones and the like, *The Turning* happened at different local times all across the globe. For example, it was mid-morning in jolly old London, it was just around dinner time in New Delhi, it was well into the evening in Melbourne, and smack dab in the middle of the night (3:42 am, to be exact) in Greater Vancouver. As the average three-toed sloth would hypothesize, those parts of the world that were unlucky enough to be experiencing daylight hours fared the worst, by a large margin.

How cruel was this day to the average human, Loyal Reader? Let us visit the unfortunate example of Pubert Llewelyn Cavendish. Hailing from none other than Manchester, England, his untimely demise illustrated this happenstance to a proverbial tee.

Poor Pubert just couldn't catch a break in life or in undeath. One might argue that a zombie apocalypse was not the first of life's bad hands that poor Pubert was dealt, and one would be entirely correct.

C'mon Loyal Reader, his name was Pubert, after all.

It is immensely challenging to put into words the level of teasing and adolescent harassment that poor Pubert experienced throughout his childhood. We can only assume that his parents would never admit it, but they must have unconsciously hated their son for there is, in actuality, no other satisfying explanation for why they would provide him with such a moniker.

Their naming choice and the plethora of childish schoolyard insults hurled poor Pubert's way aside, Pubert did actually lead a remarkably bland and average life. While it is true that every single person he met had something to say about his name, whether to his face or not, Pubert turned out to be painfully average looking, average height, average weight, average intelligence, had average amounts of hair in the general places that average men would expect to find them, and he was mostly tolerated to an average degree by the people who encountered him.

On May 22nd, 2017, 27-year old Pubert slogged out of bed at the perfectly average time of 7:30 am and set about to do all the flavourless and mundane things that average men in their late 20s named Pubert are apt do to when getting ready for whatever humdrum activities they would be partaking in that day. This involved consuming a breakfast that consisted of two hard-boiled eggs, dry whole wheat toast, ½ a medium-sized grapefruit (no added sugar necessary, thank you very much), and a glass of tepid water. Eventually, more often than not Pubert would manage to arrive at his tediously average job a mediocre three minutes early, at exactly 8:57 am.

Pubert worked at Chase & Killington a law office in the heart of Manchester. His job was that of a data-entry clerk, a deliciously average-paying job with no special skills requirement other than a heartbeat, vision, fingers, and a penchant for repetitive tasks.

Interesting fact, Loyal Reader, in no civilization in recorded history has data entry ever been considered an exhilarating, fulfilling, or noble career choice. For Pubert, though, it did pay the bills, which is really all someone who is excruciatingly run-of-the-mill could ask for.

On this particular day at 11:42 am, however, the all-seeing cosmic Tardigrade of Life (hitherto referred to simply as the Universe to avoid any controversy) finally provided Pubert's life with final moments that were both exciting and, in some sick way, quite fulfilling.

While exciting may not be the word that most people would use to describe the horrid bloodbath that was about to ensue in the law offices of Chase & Killington, it certainly would be one way to describe it, Loyal Reader, and we stand by this decision. Compared with Pubert's middle-of-the-road existence in life thus far, one could definitely argue it is an apt descriptor. Having said that, it is a much more likely scenario that some of our loyal readers could maybe find the use of the word fulfilling in this particular instance to be borderline psychotic.

Fair enough. The expression of that opinion, as wrong as it happens to be, is very much respected.

You see, Pubert worked down the hall from, and in the third cubicle on the left from, a 52-year old complete and utter waste of human flesh named Dallas Corduroy. Yes, Loyal Reader, that was his actual name.

You kind of want to slap him already, right?

It wasn't that 'The Cordster' [as he demanded he be called (ugh)], was necessarily pure evil; there could have been, for example, a shred of humanity still left in his bloated, capillary-bursting frame. If some microscopic shred of humanity was hiding in all that real estate, though, Pubert never discovered it. Where most adults found Pubert's name amusing and the stuff of good-natured ribbing, The Cordster was a first-rate fucktard of a dick about it. As in all aspects of his life, The Cordster took great pleasure in belittling and mocking others. Pubert's name, as you can imagine, provided him with an easy (and daily) target.

As we rejoin the morning in question at precisely 11:42 am, Pubert was innocently in the midst of retrieving billing information from none other than the aforementioned fucking insufferable Dallas Corduroy when nothing short of pure and unbridled chaos ensued. Pubert only managed to register two conscious and coherent thoughts before he was quite viciously and, commendations to zombies everywhere, ergonomically devoured.

Pubert's first thought simply registered as incredible confusion at all the sudden commotion and noise in what was usually a rather quiet office environment. To Pubert's untrained eye, it seemed as though everyone was running around the office in all directions and making sounds that one might realistically find comical if they weren't instantaneously accompanied by a chorus of blood curdling screams.

The Cordster was similarly transfixed, and this lasted a grand total of 6 seconds, culminating with his being abruptly tackled, killed, and eaten by Jenna Addington, that cute new partner the firm hired just last week. Pubert wasn't proud that, struck motionless with awe at what was transpiring before him, he took some small amount of schadenfreude at the second thing he registered - witnessing *Dallas Fucking Corduroy* becoming a high-cholesterol snack for poor, bloodthirsty, and completely terrifying Jenna.

It was with this final come-uppance floating through Pubert's brain and a smile plastered on his face that he met his demise at the hands and teeth of Penelope from accounting.

Sadly, the tale of Pubert Cavendish was repeated over and over and over and over and over and over and over and over again all around the globe. When a substantive amount of the population instantaneously becomes flesh-craving undead, those unsuspecting sods that didn't immediately turn into zombies were quite simply ripe for the picking. As unfortunate as it was, those that were trapped with others in buildings or walking the streets in cities were the ones most likely to find their eventual demise at the hands of the undead. The sheer numbers of newly transformed, insanely fast-moving zombies were just too much for most people to escape from.

The lucky few, if you could call them that, were those that were conveniently located away from the metropolitan areas of the world and those that were somewhat safely locked away in their houses, cars, or whatever type of sealed habitat they happened to be occupying.

As it turns out, Loyal Reader, two of those people safely locked away in a spacious and beautiful two-level chalet at Ridgecrest Pines in British Columbia at 3:42 am on May 22nd, when the world as we all knew it imploded in the most spectacular of ways, were none other than Kyle and Chad.

Lucky bastards?

"What the fuck was that?" Kyle shouted immediately after the bang.

Bronx, hearing the noise and Daddy Kyle's exclamation, contributed a few crisp barks for added effect.

"Shhhhh, Bronxie," Chad said to his little man in soothing tones. If someone or something was indeed outside, Chad knew it would be best not to advertise the fact that there were people in here. *That's how bad things happen,* Chad thought to himself, and then added, "That's not good."

For good measure, Bronx responded to the gravity of the current situation by adding three more barks.

Finding out what caused the holiday commotion was somewhat problematic, Loyal Reader. When one finds oneself in the midst of a zombie apocalypse, one realizes quite quickly that besides the aforementioned pure, blind luck that is involved, one of the keys to survival is the ability to stay safely out of harm's way. Harm, of course, being primarily the flesh-eating action of the zombies and the general kill-or-be-killed motto to which the vast majority of the surviving humans subscribed. Being currently sequestered in a cabin (not the chalet referenced just a few seconds ago, please do pay attention Loyal Reader) in the backwoods of British Columbia smack dab in the middle of winter, meant that both of these sources of harm were thankfully few and far between. Sure, there was always going to be some measure of zombie activity anywhere one would happen to venture, but not nearly as many were cavorting about in the woods as there were in cities and towns.

People were even rarer. At their best estimate, Kyle and Chad would agree that it had been quite some time, perhaps even a couple of months (no one was doing the math) since they last interacted with another living person. Given how that previous contact ended (perhaps a story for the next volume?), their solitude was a welcome companion.

Staying safely out of harm's way in their cabin was an exercise in trade-offs. Our heroes had to go to great lengths to not advertise the fact that the cabin was occupied. Should a person or a zombie happen to be in the area, there was no need to broadcast their location with unnecessary noises, activity, or other enticing environmental stimuli.

Some noises and outdoor activities, however, were necessary. This is the middle of British Columbia in the dead of winter, after all, so very cold temperatures are the norm. Without some sort of heat, our heroes' cabin stay would have been unbearable, even for an apocalypse; it's not like Kyle and Chase were tree people.

To afford them the pampered lifestyle they felt they deserved, Kyle and Chad had an electric heater powered by an outdoor generator that did make some noise, but it was a risk that they were willing to make. Having been in the cabin for the better part of seven months now and with no abnormally frequent zombie encounters during that span, all did seem to be working out just fine.

In addition to the sounds emitted by the generator, our heroes also had to venture outside at least twice daily to afford the puppies the chance to do the things that puppies need to do outside. The back of the cabin had a fenced in area that functioned nicely to keep the puppies contained when nature came calling.

Necessary noises and outdoor adventures aside, once all family members were inside the cabin, considerable effort was taken to minimize detection by the outside world. This of course meant that Kyle and Chad had barricaded and reinforced every possible ingress point to new, wonderful, and absurd levels. Windows were hammered shut with wooden boards and black garbage bags were taped over any crack or fracture in the wood that might allow someone or something to see into the cabin or for light to escape. All of this reinforcing and obsessive-compulsive fortification also had the secondary effect of making it difficult to immediately see what had caused the loud bang without opening up one of the doors or ripping the boards off of one of the windows and quite conspicuously peering outside. The sheer metabolic effort that would have been involved in that particular action was way too much. Given the quantity of wood and the obscene number of nails that went into barricading the windows shut, it would actually have been easier to get out Veronica and bash a new window into existence.

Regardless, old habits do die-hard, Loyal Reader, and it was Kyle that first showed signs of said metabolic fortitude, leaping out of the bed and to the window that faced the direction of the bang, pulling back the garbage bag, and peeking through a crack between the wooden boards to see what he could see.

"Can you see anything?" Chad asked, his voice slightly higher pitched than usual.

The crack was quite small, and it wasn't fully bright outside, but Kyle miraculously managed to see something moving away from the cabin.

Whilst Kyle began his wooden crack-based viewing extravaganza, Chad was busy trying desperately to keep Bronx from producing any further sounds. At their most basic, noises that suddenly appear out of nowhere are not the kinds of things that anyone with a sound mind wants to hear in the midst of a zombie apocalypse. One-off noises that are then accompanied by the barking of cute little puppies are even more so not the kinds of things that anyone with a sound mind wants to hear in the midst of a zombie apocalypse.

Why? Excellent question, Loyal Reader. We're glad you're finally paying attention and pulling your considerable weight around here. Noises, as it turns out, have a nasty tendency to be immediately followed by situations that lead to someone or something dying.

"What the fuck?" Kyle said incredulously.

"Please don't let it be a zombie horde," Chad begged to the Universe.

Kyle went silent and continued peering through the crack.

Chad grew even more concerned. "Well?" he asked.

Kyle turned back from the boarded window and looked at his husband. An expression of equal parts confusion, bewilderment, and dread crossed his face.

"Oh dear," Chad lamented. "This can't be good. What did you see?"

"You wouldn't believe me in, like, a million years."

"Just tell me what you saw!" Chad insisted.

"I think I just saw someone in a Santa suit being dragged down the path."

"You're shitting me!"

"I told you you wouldn't believe me! Have a look for yourself."

Chad made his way to the window and peered through the fissure. There was no sign of the alleged Santa-clad person, but the snow in front of the cabin was disturbed such that it supported Kyle's hypothesis that someone or something was dragged away.

"Oh shit," Chad whispered.

"Did you see Santa?"

"No," Chad replied, "but something was definitely dragged away."

"What should we do?"

The front yard of the backwoods cabin was actually quite picturesque, especially in the winter, when a fresh blanket of snow covers the ground. Chad would often imagine the cabin proudly featured on the cover of Apocalypse Weekly *or* Better Homes and Zombies.

"Ample green grass in the summer, and a bounty of coniferous trees provide a much-needed escape to nature from the hustle and bustle of surviving the daily rat race of the end of the world," the accompanying article would boast.

An escape, as it turns out, is exactly what this cabin provided, being quite well hidden and located very far away from civilization.

17

This was in sharp contrast to the chalet in Ridgecrest Pines where Kyle and Chad soundly slept at the time of The Turning. *Not that Ridgecrest Pines was the epicenter of all things in British Columbia, far from it, in fact. However, it is located just off of the Trans-Canada highway and is a very popular tourist attraction, so it can hardly be considered an isolated location. However, as we discussed earlier, as far as places to be when the zombie apocalypse hit, Ridgecrest Pines was definitely not the worst place in the world (see the aforementioned tale of poor, poor Mr. Cavendish for an example of one of the worst). All in all, as Kyle and Chad would attest, it worked out pretty well for almost everyone involved.*

Ridgecrest Pines nuzzles up quite snugglingly (yes, that is a word, so shut your festering gob!) between Mount Revelstoke National Park and Glacier National Park in southern British Columbia, Canada. The scenery is out of this world and both parks offer plenty of opportunities to enjoy everything that nature has to offer.

Ugh! This just sounds positively dreadful, doesn't it, Loyal Reader?

Luckily, Kyle and Chad also shared this appraisal of the situation, so we can continue to tell their story rather than abandon it in complete and utter disgust.

No, our heroes were not in the wilds of British Columbia to take selfies in front of glacial lakes or do yoga poses in front of perverted squirrels or the like. Kyle and Chad would leave those activities in the more than capable hands of the booming west coast hipster population. Rather, our heroes had grand plans to use Ridgecrest Pines as a home base while they spent the weekend riding The Mountain Coaster in neighbouring Revelstoke as much as they possibly could.

If you haven't heard of this particular amusement ride, then really what does it matter? The world is basically gone now and you're never going to ride it, so let's just assume that you would have loved it as much as Kyle and Chad would have and your life is certainly less for never having experienced it.

Bottom line? It sucks to be you, Loyal Reader.

When Chad first ventured onto the interwebs to find a place for him, Kyle, and the puppies to stay on their Mountain Coaster Trip of Love and Lovingness, *the plan was as simple as it was elegant - to find a reasonably priced, but somewhat sanitary accommodation smack dab in the middle of Revelstoke. This would mean that they wouldn't be travelling too far from the puppies whenever they left, which was, in reality, the only critical requirement. As Chad was innocently web-surfing the accommodations offerings in Revelstoke proper*, he noticed an ad for an interesting place called Ridgecrest Pines.

Making his way to their website, Chad found out that it wasn't too far from Revelstoke (under 10 km), and, if the pictures on their website were any indication, it was a very cool location. A quick perusal of their offerings led Chad to the magical discovery of pet-friendly chalets at somewhat reasonable rates (these are chalets, after all, not tree-people accommodations, so you can't expect bargain basement prices). Not only would Kyle and Chad have their very own palatial chalet to stay in, but Chad would feel like a princess, the puppies could come, and based on the map of the grounds, the chalets were set apart from the rest of the cabins and peasant-type rooms, so some element of privacy would be assured.

Had Chad not glanced at that cool-looking ad, they may well have ended up staying in a much more populated location and this particular story you are reading about right now, Loyal Reader, might well have ended before it even began.

CHAPTER 3

MUSINGS OF THE REINDEER AND JUGHEAD VARIETIES

Comprehension can be a finicky bedfellow, Loyal Reader. As anyone who has ever lived will tell you, there are just some instances during your life that make you realize you are not fully prepared to understand what has transpired before you. This certainly was the case in 2017 when Kyle and Chad awoke in their chalet in the early morning hours of May 22nd to the horrifying chaos that would soon become the new normal, and it was certainly the case again, seven months later, when they found nine confused and surly reindeer tethered to a surprisingly small sleigh on top of their cabin on the morning of December 25th.

First off, no need to worry, Loyal Reader, the reindeer were just fine. Let's be realistic here, they were presumably just flying through the air at who knows what incomprehensible speed and towing a sleigh containing a morbidly obese man dressed in red velvet. So, we can all rest easy knowing that reindeer can certainly handle being stranded on the roof of a cabin in the middle of the woods.

Were they generally pissed off at the world around them because of the absence of said aforementioned scarlet gift-giver? Perhaps, but who can say?

Once our heroes' minds had suitably wrapped themselves around the apparent abscondage (we're pretty sure that should be a word, Loyal Reader), the first order of business was to try and get to the bottom of this Scooby-Doo mystery. It would take someone with absolutely no shred of a soul to be able to resist at least a cursory investigation into what the Hell was going on. It would require, in fact, the living personification of Buzz Killington to resist such an adventure.

It wasn't long before Kyle and Chad were all bundled up like extras from *A Christmas Story* and making their way out to the front yard to try and figure out what had transpired.

Kyle was completely transfixed by the abduction he witnessed and made his way directly to the path around front. Chad, on the other hand, had the dubious distinction of being the first to notice the reindeer, and in his defense, he remained remarkably calm about the whole event. It only took an instant of shouting, "What the fuck is that?" in Kyle's general direction to get his husband's attention diverted to the cabin's rooftop. And so, they both began the process of trying to comprehend the sight before them. It's a very good thing the puppies were still in the cabin; the presence of nine large mammals would only have served to exacerbate the already skyrocketing stress levels of the situation at hand.

Kyle and Chad stood in the front yard, motionless, staring at the reindeer and the sleigh. Try as they might, they just could not imagine a situation where they weren't witnessing quite compelling evidence for the existence of Santa Claus. Let's forego the blabbering that ensued between our heroes. Suffice to say that the phrases 'what the fuck' and 'this can't be real' were uttered multiple times. Instead, Loyal Reader, let us review the evidence at hand:

- *Nine reindeer?* ✓
- *Santa's sleigh?* ✓
- *Fat, bearded man in a Santa suit? Abducted, mind you, but still a possibility* ✓

To be fair, Kyle couldn't tell if he was bearded or not, but really, that's not going to be the detail that makes this whole thing fall apart right now, is it? Like it or not, all the evidence seemed to be pointing in one very obvious direction - yes, Kyle and Chad, there is a Santa Claus, and he's been kidnapped.

Given that you have already come to accept that zombies actually exist, Loyal Reader, it really shouldn't come as too much of a surprise to find out that not only is there indeed a Santa Claus, but that his reindeer were currently occupying prime real estate on the roof of Kyle and Chad's cabin.

Further, you shouldn't be too astonished to find out that something or someone had dragged the very real and genuine Santa away from the cabin that Kyle and Chad had been calling home for the better part of the last seven months in this wacky and wild undead-filled world.

That is all.

Faced with recent events, it would be rather impossible to cover the myriad of questions popping around in our heroes' heads. A few of them were logical, expected, and relevant to the situation at hand. For example:

- *Who abducted Santa?*
- *Why was he abducted?*
- *To where was Santa being dragged?*
- *Does this mean there is also a Mrs. Claus and elves?*
- *Is there a North Pole workshop?*

Other questions that batted around were slightly more esoteric, but still very much relevant.

- *Chad wondered what the Hell Santa was doing in nowhere, British Columbia on Christmas morning.*
- *Kyle wondered what the hell could have possibly dragged away a full-grown man.*
- *Both Kyle and Chad, interestingly enough, wondered that if Santa was indeed real, why the fuck he didn't get them any of the presents they asked him for when they were kids.*

Eleven-year old Chad had his sights set on *Star Wars* action figures while Kyle, at the same age, wanted nothing more than the *Mountain Monster* - a vehicle that could climb vertical surfaces! In a cruel twist of fate, neither of them received their respective gifts and Santa, now apparently very much real, would have some serious, serious explaining to do when our heroes found him.

23

Kyle and Chad found it astonishing that the commotion of a reindeer-pulled sleigh smashing down onto the roof of the cabin followed by the unfettered kidnapping of Santa didn't attract any of the undead. One would think even the slowest and most oblivious of them would have shuffled on over to inspect the situation by now. The yard, however, was remarkably zombie-free. This was fortuitous, not only because it meant that Kyle and Chad didn't have to worry about being eaten right this second, but also because it provided a stress-free environment to begin putting together what had actually transpired and where our heroes would go from there.

Based on the disturbed snow around the sleigh on the roof and the rather large white crater beside the cabin, Kyle and Chad surmised, quite correctly as it turns out, that the details played out like this:

> - *For some reason or another, Santa experienced a post-landing fall out of the sleigh.*
> - *There was a brief and violent pause on the roof of the cabin.*
> - *Events then culminated in what Kyle and Chad hoped was as painless a greeting from the snow-covered yard as possible.*

It had been quite a while since Kyle and Chad had been in the front yard of the cabin. As such, the winter's snowfall provided a beautiful forensic layer of smooth whiteness to document any movements that would have occurred after Santa took his tumble from the roof.

As fortunate as this was, it unfortunately didn't make one iota of a difference. The tracks our heroes made from the front door to the middle of the yard were pristine and easily differentiated. However, most of the rest of the front yard still existed as flat and undisturbed blankets of snow. The exception, of course, was the area of the front yard leading from Santa's impact point to the path that lead away from the cabin. This area had all the signatures of someone, or something being dragged through the snow, which correlated quite nicely with what Kyle saw between the slits in the window boards.

Now that the yard had been inspected, Kyle and Chad had a pretty good idea as to what had happened that morning, but the question remained as to what, if anything, they were going to do now.

Armed with what they knew, Chad suggested it might be a good idea to somehow coax the reindeer down off of the roof, somehow commandeer the sleigh, somehow convince the reindeer to fly, and somehow go find out what happened to Santa.

In case you hadn't noticed, that is a large amount of somehows, Loyal Reader.

Kyle picked up on Chad's liberal use of the word somehow and advocated what he thought was a more pragmatic and, unsurprisingly, technological plan - stay within the safety and confines of the cabin's yard and use their trusty drone Jughead to search the surrounding areas for clues to the Christmas Day mystery.

So, Loyal Reader, at 7:47 am on Christmas Day, our two heroes found themselves facing quite the conundrum.

Believe me when I say, Loyal Reader, that reindeer are notoriously difficult to work with. Santa, of course, knew this, far more than most anyone else on this planet. This was, perhaps with the notable exception of Alexei Zhernakov, a delightfully eccentric man who, in believing he was a living reincarnation of a playful reindeer named Sascha, spent every waking hour since he was a young man amongst a wild population of reindeer in northern Siberia.

Little known and unsurprising fact? Alexei, the poor sod, ended up dying a virgin.

John D. Hancock of Kansas City, Missouri was also painfully familiar with the pitfalls of working with reindeer. Who is John D. Hancock, you say? What an uncomfortably obvious question. You, Loyal Reader, would find yourself to be in fine company not knowing the answer to that particular query. In fact, prior to *The Turning*, we estimate that a grand total of only 4,164 people on Earth even knew he existed, and, to be perfectly honest, and as is the sad case for most people on this planet, far fewer than that even cared.

Poor John.

But why would Mr. Hancock have anything to say about the notoriously churlish reindeer? The answer, as is usually the case, is surprisingly simple - he helmed the filming of the visually mediocre distraction that would become the movie *Prancer,* featuring, as its title implies, a reindeer in many of the emotionally pivotal scenes.

And that is an amazingly liberal use of the word emotionally, we might add.

As Christmas Day would progress, our heroes would join the illustrious ranks of Santa, Alexei, and John amongst the ranks of those unfortunate enough to know what righteous asshats reindeer can truly be.

Dealing with the reindeer that currently adorned the cabin roof was perfectly avoidable, you see, and this avoidance was the course of action that Kyle and Chad ended up pursuing. Yes, the reindeer seemed precariously perched and yes, the reindeer didn't appear to be at all interested in going anywhere, but that didn't mean Kyle and Chad had to deal with them. In theory, one could just leave the reindeer be and see what trouble they get up to. Given the current hypothesis that the reindeer could fly, one would think that they'd be perfectly suited to going off and doing whatever it is that reindeer would need to do whenever it is that reindeer needed it to be done.

Or something like that.

Who can say?

Fate, however, had other plans for our heroes and indeed Christmas Day was going to eventually revolve very heavily around the reindeer on the roof.

It was with the aforementioned reindeer avoidance in mind that Kyle advocated using Jughead the drone, leaving the reindeer to their own devices and try and figure out what happened to Santa. Chad, true to form, was all about the reindeer. He desperately wanted nothing more than to tame the reindeer, earn their trust, fly acrobatically through the air with them, and become part of some *Technicolour Christmas Mystery Reconnaissance Adventure Team* with them.

This, Loyal Reader, is what Kyle had to deal with in their marriage.

Since *The Turning*, Kyle and Chad had come up with a fail-safe method of breaking any deadlocks when it came to deciding all major life decisions - a rousing matchup of best-of-three rock/paper/scissors. This day, Kyle emerged victorious and the pair headed back inside to begin Jughead's preparations.

Bet you thought we were going to give you the play-by-play, right? Don't be silly, Loyal Reader, that would be as boring as watching gooified zombie slurm dry.

It was quite fortuitous and not at all surprising that Kyle and Chad had Jughead with them at the cabin. Jughead came equipped with his very own high-resolution camera (affectionately referred to by our heroes as Jellybean), which would have been useful given that the journey to Revelstoke back in May had promised to be an excellent opportunity to get some very cool mountain footage. Although getting said footage was ultimately not meant to be (thank you very much, zombie apocalypse), Jughead and Jellybean had continued to be the most loyal of companions, serving Kyle and Chad well over the past seven months.

Do not underestimate, Loyal Reader, the usefulness of a flying machine that can record video of an outside world rife with the undead. Why take unnecessary risks with your life when a robotic pawn is more than happy to take one for the flesh-covered team?

Maintaining a drone (or any piece of electronics for that matter) in an apocalyptic wasteland is actually quite simple if you are someone who knows her or his way around all things technological. Luckily, Chad was married to just such a man. This meant that that Jughead's batteries were charged and ready to go. We could, at this juncture, bore you even more, Loyal Reader, with the details of how our heroes managed to keep everything charged and how they managed to incorporate technology into their apocalyptic existence, but these details are so very excruciatingly mundane in comparison to getting to the bottom of this Santa-themed Hardy Boys mystery. Besides, one must leave something to the imagination, no?

Exactly!

It didn't take long for Kyle to get Jughead ready to go. He took Jughead out to an area of the font yard where Chad had cleared the snow away and put down an old piece of plywood as a take-off and landing pad. Given that a Santa-sized object had been dragged along the otherwise undisturbed snow, the general direction of the Santa-knapping trail was clearly visible from the cabin. The problem with figuring out what happened to the jolly old alcoholic was that the trail very quickly turned out of view as the cabin is connected to a dirt road by a lovely and lengthy walking trail that snakes in and around various stands of trees. This, of course, meant that Kyle would not be able to navigate Jughead along the trail as the chance of hitting tree branches was far too high. Instead, Kyle had elected to have JellyBean record aerial footage of the whole area around the trail and down to the road in hopes that some details would emerge. The tree line wasn't too high around the cabin and surrounding areas, so Jughead wouldn't have to fly at an obscene altitude, making the chances of figuring out what happened at least a little bit higher.

The flight itself was short, sweet, uneventful, and lasted less than 10 minutes. There is always a chance that the sound of the drone will attract zombies, so Chad spent the short time it was in flight with Veronica in hand, patrolling the perimeter of the cabin for unwanted visitors. Interestingly enough, the reindeer, still happily standing on the cabin's roof, were utterly unfazed by Jughead. Kyle even flew above them out of a perverse need to see if a response could be elicited, but to no avail. While neither of our heroes were experts on reindeer behaviour, one would expect at least a casual recognition of a drone flying right above their heads.

Stupid, oblivious reindeer.

When the flight had been completed, Kyle collected Jughead from the landing pad and brought him inside to download Jellybean's footage onto their computer. Close inspection of the video feed revealed two items of note. First, Kyle's skill at piloting Jughead was, as usual, phenomenal. He managed to get an excellent overview of the path and surrounding area all the way to the road. Second, and more surprisingly, was that the video resulted in more questions about what happened to Santa than it answered. The drag marks in the blanket of snow were clearly visible as they ran away from the cabin's front yard and down the path, but they abruptly stopped just short of the snow-covered dirt road. There appeared to be no footprints or any other discernible marks in the snow cover. In fact, the snow all around the end of the drag marks was rather pristine, save for a single red hat that our heroes surmised clearly belonged to Santa, sitting in a snow bank off to one side.

Consequently, Kyle and Chad concluded that Santa was indeed taken by something or someone. Further, this something or someone managed to disappear from the edge of the road without a trace.

As if sensing that something was amiss, the reindeer chose this particular moment to begin causing a commotion on the roof.

CHAPTER 4

LADIES & GENTLEMEN: UNDEAD MARTIN

*D**are we say that the commotion of nine reindeer on a roof paled in comparison to the commotion that Kyle and Chad witnessed whilst driving on the morning of May 22nd?*

Yes, yes, we do, Loyal Reader.

Our heroes were blissfully ignorant of The Turning *when it occurred at 3:42 am. Both Kyle, Chad, and the two puppies were sleeping quite comfortably and continued to do so until they woke up that fateful morning. This, Loyal Reader, is where the first of the lucky breaks visited Kyle and Chad - neither of them had turned into a zombie. The odds were clearly stacked against this happening, given that there was apparently a 75-80% chance that they would be turned, but it seems that fate had other, ultimately more nefarious plans for our heroes.*

The morning started as pretty much all mornings do. Kyle woke up, as expected, at the ripe and ungodly time of 6:16 am. He put on a pot of coffee and melted into a comfy chair while Chad and the puppies continued their discordant snoring contest in bed. Chad had booked three passes for each of them for the Mountain Coaster that day and since it didn't open until 9 am, they had a good portion of the morning to laze about before heading off to the mountain. It all promised to be the most civilized of days.

And laze about they did. Kyle and Chad had agreed at the outset that their weekend getaway would be technology-free. Phones, iPads, computers and such were brought with them for emergencies, but once they arrived at

29

the Chalet, our heroes had decided to unplug and relax without having to connect to the outside world. This was not easy, Loyal Reader, as Kyle and Chad were just like every other average human being, used to relying on the internet to amuse them.

Chad got up shortly before 7:00 am and walked the puppies around the chalet so they could sniff everything in sight and find the perfect spot to do their business. Nothing appeared out of the ordinary. The chalet was sequestered quite nicely away from the other accommodations, so if there were any noises being made by the zombies loose inside the other buildings, Chad couldn't hear them.

Our heroes had their breakfast - crumpets with smooth peanut butter for Kyle and crumpets with smooth peanut butter and raspberry jam (with seeds, thank you very much) for Chad - and puttered around before showering and packing up for their day of fun-filled excitement racing down a mountainside.

The puppies were fed and then given good-bye pats and left safely on their favourite blankets on the spacious chalet sofa. Kyle and Chad packed up their stuff for their day of adventuring, got into the car, and came oh so close to making it out of the resort and onto the highway before encountering their first zombie, one Mr. Martin Emerson.

Martin Emerson, along with his wife Vanessa, occupied a family suite near the entrance to Ridgecrest Pines. At 3:42 am, whilst sleeping beside her, he unceremoniously transformed into what we will lovingly call Undead Martin, much to his wife's chagrin. We won't go into the gory details of what unfolded in the next few flesh-eating minutes, suffice to say that the suite's bedroom strongly resembled the set of a Wes Craven film shortly thereafter.

Once he had finished binging on the corpse of his wife, Undead Martin, as was the case with all of the newly turned zombies during their first two weeks of undeadedness (yes, that's a word now too), spent the next few hours running frantically around the suite searching for more food, bouncing around like a veritable pinball.

This scene was repeated all over the occupied suites of Ridgecrest Pines; the brand-new zombies were locked in their accommodations and, as one would expect, didn't have the wherewithal to unlock doors, let alone open them. Instead, the inhabitants ran and ran and ran around whatever space they happened to be occupying, and then ran some more, all in a frenetic search for food.

At exactly 8:47 am, Undead Martin, as stupid-ass luck would have it, managed to lose his footing and fall headfirst through his suite's bay window, freeing himself of the confines of his abode, into the outside world, and smack-dab into the passenger side of Kyle and Chad's car.

It should go without saying that Kyle and Chad were somewhat surprised at the sight of a bloody person running at full pace towards their car. Kyle's cat-like reflexes did allow him to slow down a fair bit as Undead Martin approached, which is commendable given that both he and Chad were not quite able to process what was unfolding.

Undead Martin slammed into the driver's side at breakneck speed and with such uncanny force that it knocked him to the ground a clear five feet away. As luck would yet again have it, before Kyle or Chad had time to open their doors to inspect what in the name of Sarah Jessica Parker was going on, Undead Martin was once again on his feet and clamoring all over the car, adding liberal amounts of blood and other chunky bodily fluids to the appreciable dent he had just forged in the door.

This is why we can't have nice things! *Chad thought to himself.*

Not really knowing what the proper protocol would be in such an instance, and who could blame him, Kyle plastered his foot to the gas pedal and sped away down the road as they both attempted in vain to grasp what was happening. Undead Martin did manage to chase the car with his uncanny speed for a fair distance but was of course no match for the car and quite soon Kyle and Chad were out of Undead Martin's sights. Finally making it out of Ridgecrest Pines and onto the highway, Kyle pulled the car over to the side of the road to take a moment and figure out what the hell they were going to do.

The first couple of minutes consisted of both Kyle and Chad being shell-shocked. There were very few words that could adequately express the confusion they were experiencing, but once the adrenaline stopped pumping, they decided a friendly call to 911 was in order. This, however, was fruitless. No one answered.

They tried again.

Again, no one answered.

This went on for a length of time some might consider comical under different circumstances until our heroes realized that no one was going to answer.

As luck would have it, Chad took that moment to notice that a car had gone off the road and squarely into the ditch a fair distance ahead of them on the highway. Kyle pulled up to where the car had careened off the road and our heroes bore witness to a gruesome, gruesome discovery.

The car was still running, which was quite weird, and appeared to have been the scene of something just really, really awful. The windows were streaked with blood - a lot of blood. Our heroes could make out what appeared to be two people in the car, but they were hunched over and preoccupied with something.

Unbeknownst to Kyle and Chad, the two people in question were zombies that happened to be in the throes of eating the third person that happened to be in the car and not of the zombie variety.

Gross.

Erring on the side of safety, Kyle and Chad decided it was best to go back to the chalet and try to contact the local authorities, rather than stay sitting in their car on the side of the highway.

The drive back to the chalet was blissfully uneventful. Undead Martin was nowhere to be found, and the duo made it safely back to their chalet without any further bloody encounters. The puppies, of course, were very excited that daddies had come back, and as Kyle and Chad sat down on the couch beside them, opened their computers, and brought up various news websites, they realized that things were far worse than they could have ever possibly imagined.

This is saying something, given how imaginative Kyle and Chad are known to be by people who take note of such things.

CHAPTER 5

OF BLARFENFÜGERS AND PLÜRFENSCHNOOKS

Early reviews are in, Loyal Reader, and as one would have reasonably guessed, the cacophony of sound from nine surly reindeer causing a fuss on the roof of the cabin was somewhat loud. It had been over a month since Kyle and Chad encountered another person and just under a month since they had seen their last zombie in the cabin area, so the very last thing they needed was for reindeer noises to begin attracting some very much unwanted attention.

Unfortunately for Kyle, Chad, and the nine reindeer, that is exactly what happened.

The debate about what to do with the nine antsy ungulates didn't last long. The more Kyle and Chad debated in the cabin about what to do, the noisier they seemed to get. A number of options were floated about, ranging from scaring or forcing them off the roof and letting them do their own thing, whatever that may be, to corralling them all and somehow keeping them safe, however that may be. Both of these plans, regardless of how bursting at the seams with 'whatever that may be' they were did require finding a mechanism for getting said reindeer off of the roof, so it was decided this would be the first order of business.

Our heroes went outside to the front yard and inspected the situation. Indeed, the reindeer were not happy. They were stomping about quite rudely all over the cabin's roof, causing Kyle and Chad to remark that it seemed to be yet another genuine Christmas miracle they hadn't broken through yet.

Yelling at the reindeer turned out to be horribly inefficient, and only seemed to exacerbate the current situation. No verbal cues or commands got their attention. In fact, Kyle was positive that the reindeer were actively ignoring anything they hollered at them.

Next on the list of things that just didn't work was to try and throw snowballs at them, perhaps eliciting a survival response or something like that. Kyle and Chad found out rather quickly that reindeer are not only oblivious to verbal harassment, but to snow-based assaults as well. Snowball after snowball after snowball hit them and they didn't seem to give a flying fuck. In fact, Chad was certain that the reindeer were enjoying the attention.

Asses!

Kyle suggested that he climb onto the roof and try to physically get them to come down, but Chad put an end to that idea before Kyle barely managed to verbalize it. A swift reindeer kick to Kyle's face (or other sensitive parts of his body it would be prudent to point out, Loyal Reader) was not on the agenda for this particular Christmas Day. Quickly running out of options, Chad even managed to convince Kyle to sing some Christmas carols with him to see if that would have any effect. These were Santa's reindeer after all; perhaps the magic of Christmas in an incredibly off-key musical format would show some level of success at coaxing them to the ground. Sadly, this pretty much seemed to have the opposite effect, as they seemed to stomp and huff louder with every note that our heroes produced.

Bastards!

It was then, after a good 30 minutes of futility, that Kyle had the brilliant idea to use the one thing that very few animals can resist - food. Chad, with years of watching nature documentaries under his hefty belt, had a very good idea of what reindeer liked to eat - grass and lichens. Further, our heroes' cabin was in the middle of nowhere, British Columbia containing an abundance of forested areas with trees and dead logs galore - prime real estate upon which lichens could grow. During the summer, there would be an abundance of grass too, but this was the middle of winter and any grass from the summer and fall would be covered by a profuse amount of snow and realistically not all that appetizing to your average discerning reindeer.

Chad recalled that one species of lichen, somewhat aptly named reindeer moss, is especially favored by these beasts. His hunch was that a quick jaunt into the wooded area around the cabin would result in enough tastiness to tease the reindeer off of their perch.

Chad was correct.

Interesting fact, Loyal Reader - reindeer moss is composed of neither reindeer nor moss.

Stupid people with their stupid names for things.

Kyle stood watch at the cabin while Chad and Veronica made their way into the woods. It made sense to have one of them stay behind in case someone or something, attracted by all the commotion, showed up for a surprise visit. Since Chad knew exactly where to look for the lichens and, perhaps more importantly, what the lichens looked like, it was logical that he be the one to go.

As it turned out, Chad's trip was equal parts short and fruitful. It didn't take him long to find a few good stands of the lichens and he encountered zero zombies or people on his 18-minute and 32-second trip. Just to be safe, Chad also collected a number of other lichen species to spice up the nutritional offerings to the nine righteous roof assholes.

As if to mock the previous efforts of our heroes, it took a grand total of 25 seconds for the reindeer to realize that Chad had returned with food and delicately floated their way down to the front yard.

Have we mentioned lately, Loyal Reader, that reindeer are asses?

It was quite mesmerizing, to be honest, witnessing the grace and form the reindeer displayed in getting to the ground. Still harnessed together in pairs (save for the lead reindeer, of course) and pulling the remarkably small sleigh, they lifted off of the roof in a perfectly choreographed sequence and drifted effortlessly in a gradual, downward spiral around Kyle and Chad. As soon as the nine hungry beasts reached ground level, Chad was summarily accosted by the herd.

This scene, if it were to be witnessed by a third party, would have looked quite hilarious.

With the reindeer all tethered together and a sleigh being towed behind them, there was no realistic way for all of them to have access to the lichens at once. Instead, they kept walking around Chad in circles, each waiting patiently for their turn in this conveyor belt of yumminess. It seems that reindeer (or at least those belonging to Santa anyway) always display some level of choreography when they do the things that reindeer do.

The reindeer were smaller than Kyle and Chad expected. When one sits back, relaxes, closes one's eyes, and thinks about a set of magical, glorified caribou pulling a sleigh that contains not only a fat, red-suited man and what should be a sack of about two billion presents, one might quite rightly assume that these critters would be of the large variety - big, strapping reindeer, perhaps descended from tough, Norwegian or even Russian stock.

Not so, Loyal Reindeer.

These animals were no taller than Chad (which, to save him from any embarrassment, we will simply describe as not very tall at all) and surprisingly lean. They all did, however, possess some seriously large antlers for their head size - majestic antlers, even. Given these were Santa's reindeer, Kyle and Chad expected the harnesses and reins to be a luxuriously velvety-like material adorned with bells and ribbons of red or green. In reality, they were made of a very thick, very tough, and very bland brown-colored rope.

Not very Christmassy at all.

Lame.

However, each of the nine reindeer did have a dark green collar with a name embroidered upon it in gold, and those names did not come as any surprise to our heroes, and unless you have spent the entirety of your life in a cave, they should not come as any surprise to you either, Loyal Reader.

Though there does remain a not insignificant amount of debate on the topic, most historians worth their weight in Roasted Daggertooth Pike Conger would argue that in 1823, Clement Clarke Moore authored the now iconic poem *A Visit From St. Nicholas* wherein he recorded the traditional names for eight of Santa's reindeer.

Heathens across the globe (mostly lazy, obese bipeds of the North American variety, as it turns out) now commonly refer to this work of literature by its first line of text - *Twas The Night Before Christmas.*

Regardless of where you stand on some people's children's penchant for renaming things that were already quite adequately named in the first place, this is not the focus of our current conversation, Loyal Reader. You see, as it turns out, Clement Clarke Moore did not, in fact, write this poem. Rather, it was the handiwork of Squillywig Blarfenfüger, one of Santa's most dutiful and faithful elves. To be more precise, Squillywig was (and still is) Santa's *Chief Word Manufacturer, Poetry Section.*

Tens of thousands of elves live at the North Pole, all working harmoniously to ensure that Christmas goes off without a hitch. Being one of Santa's Chief elves was, as you could imagine, one of the greatest honours a hard-working elf could ask for, and Squillywig was no exception. One can only imagine the sheer ecstasy and delight that Squillywig felt when Santa approached him in the early Spring of 1823, tasking him with writing a poem that would mesmerize the masses, revitalize the Christmas spirit, and most importantly, rhyme. The final product, as we all now know, was as flawless as it was beguiling, a trademark of all Squillywig's works.

As he had done from time to time throughout human history, Santa decided on the perfect method to introduce this poem to the people. Using liberal amounts of what we will simply call Christmas magic, Santa chose the American poet Clement Clarke Moore of the still embryonic United States of America to be his poetic vessel.

One night whilst Clement slept peacefully in his bed, Santa gingerly slid a hand-written copy of the poem (in Clement's hand writing, naturally - thank you Ipsy Plürfenschnook, Santa's *Chief Calligrapher, North American Division*) amongst the array of papers on Clement's desk and then lightly touched the snoozing wordsmith on the tip of his nose, implanting magical memories of the poem's composition in his brain.

And so, Loyal Reader, Clement Clarke Moore loudly and proudly announced to the world the now iconic reindeer names we have grown to love - Dasher, Dancer, Prancer, Vixen, Comet, Cupid, Donner, and Blitzen.

But what of Rudolph, you ask? Though Santa never had any need for more than eight reindeer to pull his sleigh, all of that changed on Christmas Eve, 1938. While emerging from delivering a bevy of presents to a tiny house in the small town of Merijärvi, Finland, Santa returned to his sleigh to find a ninth reindeer standing next to the others.

This was, in actuality, not that surprising, Loyal Reader, as a good 15-20% of the Earth's surface is covered by boreal forests, the preferred habitat of reindeer. Once every now and then, curious reindeer would pop in for a quick sniff and visit.

This particular visiting even-toed ungulate, however, was different. First and most conspicuously, his nose had a distinct reddish tinge to it. The nose didn't actually glow red, as you might have been led to believe (that was artistic license and made for the perfect heart-warming Christmas story) but it was noticeably red in hue. This nasal feature alone wasn't that unique, of course - reindeer do tend to come in all shapes and sizes and in a few different colors (even their noses), but red was one that Santa did not have the occasion to have witnessed before.

Chocking this curious visitor up to an interesting story to relay to Mrs. Claus and the elves, he and his reindeer set off to their next destination only to find that the red-nosed reindeer was flying right along beside them.

Now this, Loyal Reader, this was very unique.

It was so unique, in fact, that this was only the ninth time Santa has ever seen it happen. As he had done eight times before, Santa let the red-nosed reindeer continue to make his way with the pack for the rest of the night and once back at the North Pole, he became the newest member of the sleigh-pulling team, named Rudolph by Mrs. Claus.

Much like the radiance of a brightly glowing red nose, the story of how Rudolph came to be Santa's lead reindeer was yet another cherished poetry composition by our good friend Squillywig. True to his form, the poem functioned as a most clever and, as it turned out, extremely popular way of introducing Rudolph to the world.

If you count yourself amongst the exactly 636 people in the world that have ever cared about such things, Loyal Reader, then perhaps you have led your life up until this very point thinking that Robert L. May authored the poem that described Rudolph's origins. If, however, you are not part of that particular collective, you can now rest easy knowing that not only has pretty much all of the world's human population been decimated by a zombie apocalypse, not only has Santa been unceremoniously kidnapped in the wilds of British Columbia, not only are Kyle and Chad currently discovering more than they ever wanted to know about the churlish nature of the average flying reindeer, but you now also know that not only did Robert L. May exist, but he was chosen by the jolly old man himself to inform the world of Santa's newest reindeer addition.

Phew!

What a productive day, Loyal Reader!

And we're just getting started.

CHAPTER 6

UNDEAD LUCIE'S REINDEER GAMES

Finding a solution to the current problem presented by the nine disagreeable swirling ruminants was the most pressing concern for our heroes. They valiantly trudged through the nipple-deep process of trying to figure out what in the name of Ellen Degeneres to do with them as best they could. Perhaps it was that both Kyle and Chad were deep in thought and not paying attention to the world around them. Perhaps it was the hypnotic spiraling of the reindeer around Chad that was providing ample distraction. Perhaps it was the visual static of snow as it began to fall, creating a beautiful veil of white. Perhaps it was a just a little bit of all three.

Who can say?

Regardless, Loyal Reader, the sad and heart-wrenching fact is that our heroes' collective attention was suitably appropriated, with the direct and unfortunate consequence that neither Kyle nor Chad nor any of the nine reindeer noticed the approaching zombie until it was much, much too late.

Truth be told, it wasn't until poor Prancer let out an ungodly sound that everyone who had a stake in these proceedings realized quite quickly that something was very, very wrong.

And that, Loyal Reader, is an understatement.

Unbeknownst to Kyle and Chad, the zombie was attracted by the earlier sounds of the reindeer on the roof and managed to get a glimpse of Chad while he was collecting lichens in the forest.

Ready for a fun fact, Loyal Reader? We thought so.

Before *The Turning,* the reindeer-feasting zombie was none other than Lucie Stewart, a 24 year-old hiker from Casper, Wyoming. Though she never admitted this to another soul (and, might we add, rightly so), young Ms. Stewart had her sights set on becoming a household name in Casper's surprisingly bustling improvisational comedy scene.

Gross.

For Undead Lucie, however, this dream, almost as difficult to comprehend as the bloodbath that was about to unfold, was now lovingly replaced by the visceral and unquenching need to consume warm, moist, animal flesh.

It took Undead Lucie a fair bit of time to finally arrive at the cabin, but when she did, blind luck saw fit to ensure she approached along its east wall. This, fittingly, was not only the one spot that provided some element of cover, but also happened to be both the single furthest point of ingress from our heroes and the closest edge of where the nine-reindeer-long spiral reached.

As Undead Lucie emerged from beside the cabin, it was Dasher who had just rounded the corner, leaving poor Prancer to be the unlucky one to amble right into her path.

Undead Lucie, now a roughly seven-month-old zombie, moved a whole slower than she did during her first two weeks of flesh-eating existence (we covered this back in Chapter 1, Loyal Reader, please do try pay attention). Though now plodding along at a leisurely pace, Undead Lucie still managed to move with some degree of speed over short distances. Consequently, she wasted no time latching on to Prancer and ruthlessly and efficiently ripping that pesky flesh away from his neck.

Soon blood was flying everywhere and so soon were the reindeer. Perhaps as a magical evolutionary escape mechanism, as soon as the other reindeer realized one of them was hurt, they immediately took to the sky and flew a rapid and irregular pattern above the cabin and surrounding area. Undead Lucie tried her hardest to remain attached to Prancer, with very little success. After a miniscule three seconds in the air, she fell hard to the ground somewhere behind the cabin.

Wasting no time, Kyle grabbed Veronica and made quick work of poor Undead Lucie.

What happened next, however, was utterly heartbreaking.

Let us take a moment to pause whilst you go grab some tissues, Loyal Reader; you are most certainly going to need them.

Unless, of course, you are a heartless husk of a human. If that is indeed the case, Loyal Reader, we would like to share, with all the honesty of a douche canoe named Tyler who's just 'too honest' for his own good, that we have never liked you.
Not one little bit.
Nada.
Zilch.

The remaining eight reindeer stopped flying as soon as the zombie had been neutralized. They returned to the front yard where Chad was still standing, mouth agape and in complete shock. As Kyle returned from gooifying Undead Lucie's brains, Chad asked him to fetch some towels to try and stop the copious amounts of blood that were currently gushing from Prancer's neck.

Regrettably, by the time Kyle made it back outside (only 63 seconds later, we might add) it was too late. Poor Prancer had lost too much blood. Undead Lucie had severed pretty much all of the major vessels in Prancer's neck, and our heroes had neither the knowledge nor the tools to fix such a gaping wound.

Chad, in tears at this point, held out hope that Christmas magic would somehow fix Prancer and make him all better.

It didn't.

That, apparently, wasn't the way the wonder and magic of Christmas worked.

Of course it wasn't.

Prancer, perhaps sensing his fate, lay calmly and quietly on his right side in the snow as Chad pet his snout gently and Kyle kept pressure on his neck. The other reindeer were eerily calm and kept their gaze squarely on their companion, who slipped away a few moments later in a magically morbid display of a bright, glowing, blue light.

It had been Kyle and Chad's experience that when one zombie makes an appearance, the odds were greater than average that others could be just around the corner. To that end, our heroes decided that the quickest and easiest way to prevent another reindeer from being killed and to prevent a Kyle or a Chad from being killed, was to get the reindeer into the cabin until any potential risks had been evaluated.

Kyle went back into the cabin to lock Bronx and Brooklyn in the upstairs bedroom (the puppies and animals of any other kind unfortunately did not mix all that well). Seeing as the reindeer were tethered to the sleigh, uncannily small as it was, there was absolutely no physical possibility of getting them all into the main floor of the cabin in that particular configuration. So, once the puppies were secured, Kyle set about undoing the harnesses and reins, freeing the reindeer, one by one. As each of the reindeer were liberated, Chad would usher each one into the cabin. All this managed to get completed with only just a minimal amount of fuss on the part of the reindeer.

Thank goodness for small miracles, Loyal Reader!

By the time all eight reindeer were in the cabin (being rather well-behaved, all things considered) and Kyle and Chad had joined them, the realization of their current predicament hit home very quickly - there was virtually no room to maneuver in the main floor of the cabin. All of the furniture had been pre-emptively moved to the walls, creating as much of an open space as possible. While this was just enough room for eight reindeer and two grown men to move past one another, it definitely was not a permanent solution.

Reindeer, as you may probably be aware, Loyal Reader, are not indoor pets. They like to move around quite a bit and they don't wait until you decide to let them outside to do their business. In fact, this was ever so poignantly displayed within 3 minutes of the reindeer being sequestered in the cabin. Three of them had urinated, two of them had taken dumps, and all eight of them were pacing around the main floor and liberally spreading their waste to every available square centimeter.

Kyle and Chad decided the quicker they could get them to agree to go back outside the better.

Our heroes held out hope that once the reindeer were led outside, they would return to their perch on the roof of the cabin, removing all possibility of any more zombie-related deaths in the family.

To that end, our heroes ventured out to do a sweep of the surrounding areas and made sure there were no more unwanted guests loitering around the cabin's property. Finding none, Kyle and Chad returned to the cabin and led the reindeer back to the front yard where, it was assumed, they would once again make their way up to the roof.

However, as we learned earlier, Loyal Reader, reindeer are notoriously difficult to cope with and are not known for their ability to follow directions from anyone other than Santa. It should, then, come as no surprise that Kyle and Chad could not coax the reindeer back onto the roof. Not even throwing lichens up there worked. One or two of the reindeer would indeed fly up and land on the roof, but only long enough to grab the thrown lichens and return back to the apparent comfort of the ground.

Asses.

Complete asses.

As is turned out, the only remaining realistic place for our heroes to stash the reindeer was the back yard of the cabin. No matter how much of the adjacent terrain had been checked for undead, the sad reality was that the reindeer would always be in danger if left out in the open. The back yard provided as good a solution as any to this conundrum, being that it was partially fenced off. To be precise, Loyal Reader, the word partially doesn't indicate that there wasn't a fence surrounding the entirety of the back yard, there certainly was. However, it's just that this particular fence wasn't all that great at performing its fence-like duties. You see, approximately one-fifth of this structure was in a magnificent state of disrepair; so much so that it was almost completely toppled over.

That just wouldn't do, Loyal Reader.

Not at all.

For those keeping track at home, it had been about six hours since the now infamous *Christmas Bang* and our heroes realistically only had about four hours of sunlight left to get the fence reinforced so the reindeer could continue amassing bodily wastes in a location other than the cabin's main floor.

Ordinarily, this job would take much longer than the afternoon afforded to our heroes, but Kyle and Chad had devised a plan that would exploit the advantage of having these large visiting helper mammals. All of this was, as you have probably already surmised, predicated upon the assumption that the reindeer would take a constitutional respite from being complete asses and cooperate with their hosts. If not, then there wasn't much that Kyle and Chad could do; Rudolph and company would just have to take their chances in a back yard that was in no way completely protected from the undead.

In our heroes' minds, all that was required to reinforce the fence into a functional zombie barrier was to get the toppled parts of the fence back to a vertical position. Raising the fence up and getting some pieces of wood to support both sides of the fence could easily accomplish this.

Luckily, Loyal Reader, Kyle and Chad knew of just the place to get the wood that they needed. It was quite a distance away, about 20 kilometers as the average crow might care to fly on any given day, and located just outside of a little village called Mica Creek. It would take far, far too long to go by foot, but it would be a quick and easy trip using the reindeer and Santa's sleigh.

Leading the reindeer from the back yard, through the gate in one of the undamaged parts of the fence, and out to the front yard was facilitated by using the now tried and tested method of the promise of food. All Chad had to do was go grab some more lichen and the reindeer would follow him wherever he went. It was actually quite cute, if you enjoyed that sort of thing.

Like the well-trained beasts they were, the reindeer exited through the gate in single file and remained in this formation all the way to the front yard. Once the reindeer saw the sleigh, they automatically lined up in pairs, ready to be harnessed in place. With Prancer gone, Rudolph and Dancer formed the lead pair and the remainder of them lined up similarly behind them. Kyle and Chad fastened their harnesses and made their way into the cabin to grab Betty, Veronica, and the puppies. Their destination was a secure site, which would afford the puppies the chance to run around and stretch their legs. Betty and Veronica, of course, always joined our heroes when they left the relative safety of the cabin.

Once everything was properly stowed in the back of the sleigh, Chad held the puppies tight while Kyle grabbed the reins and wondered exactly how the Hell he was supposed to get the reindeer to fly.

Kyle and Chad dreaded a repeat of the *getting-the-reindeer-off-of-the-roof-of-the-cabin* fiasco of earlier in the day, but unfortunately, that is exactly what transpired. Unsurprisingly, commands like "Mush!" and "Go!" and

"Fly, you fucking furry bastards!" were thrown about with much gusto, but sadly to no avail. Chad tried pleading with the reindeer, but they just looked back, blinked, and continued to busy themselves by doing absolutely nothing.

As frustration began to turn into stationary road rage, Chad had the brilliant, if not abashedly reductive idea of using Santa's command from *Twas The Night Before Christmas*. Given the generally fucked-up stuff that had occurred already today, it wouldn't be surprising at all to anyone involved if that worked. So, Chad cleared his throat and, as loud as he could, yelled "Now Rudolph, now Dasher, now Dancer, now Vixen! On Comet, on Cupid, on Donner, on Blitzen! Now dash away! Dash away! Dash away all!" As each reindeer heard their name, their ears perked up and their bodies tensed with cat-like readiness. As the last words of the verse escaped Chad's vocal cords, they began to run forward and almost immediately lifting up and off of the ground at a fairly steep angle until they and the sleigh that carried our heroes were spiraling around the cabin area and above the tree line.

As was the case when the reindeer and sleigh came down from the cabin rooftop, Kyle and Chad sat in utter amazement that the sleigh maintained a perfectly horizontal pitch behind the reindeer. It was as if the sleigh was riding a set of rails jutting out from behind Donner and Blitzen. Whatever the magical mechanism at work, the sleigh was kept perfectly level and remarkably balanced. There were no seat belts in the sleigh, but the front did curl back upwards towards the seating area, at least providing a roller coaster-esque riding experience while the reindeer gained altitude and made some rather sharp turns.

Kyle, as it turned out, was a natural at directing the reindeer. So much so, in fact, that Chad wondered if there was some unconscious connection between them. Before too long they were on their way and hurtling towards Micah Creek.

Chad found it strange how warm it remained at the front of the sleigh during the flight. The sled had no enclosure or windshield-type structure to speak of, and yet he and Kyle didn't feel any wind chill at all while flying. This was especially remarkable considering how fast they seemed to be going, and to be honest, there appeared to be barely any breeze at all. Kyle and Chad chocked it up to more of that good ol' Christmas magic, something that was becoming an umbrella excuse to explain whatever was currently happening that they were otherwise not able to wrap their puny brains around.

Our heroes, of course, had no idea how fast they were actually travelling at the time. Kyle thought it felt like they were going 50 or 60 kph (that's *kilometers* per hour, for our American metric-challenged sods out there; you poor fuckers), and he was remarkably close in that estimation, given that it took them just over 25 minutes to make it to the picturesque village of Mica Creek, British Columbia.

CHAPTER 7

HARD MICA CREEK WOOD

Given that you may not necessarily really care about such things, Loyal Reader, we shall be brief. Before the vast majority of people in the world met their untimely demise, Mica Creek, founded upon the banks of the majestic Columbia River, was not only a critical site for hydroelectricity production in southern British Columbia, but also possessed a rich and storied history as part of the Bend Gold Rush of the 1860s.

See? Learning is fun!

As had been repeated over and over again in countless rural locations across the globe, Mica Creek saw a steady and impressive increase in population in the 20th century, only to hit its zenith of about 4,000 inhabitants in 1973. This, not coincidentally, was when the Mica Hydroelectric Dam (located about 6 km north of the town) officially opened. Following that local monumental achievement, the population dropped pretty much overnight and continued to diminish at a relatively steady pace.

To be fair, once the dam was constructed, there was nothing left for the workers to do but pack up and find work elsewhere. By the time of *The Turning*, the population hovered at about 400 people (431 to be exact), a good portion of those being workers assigned to maintain the dam.

At 3:42 am on May 22nd, 312 of those 431 people became zombies. Of the 246 workers that were housed in the Chief Kinabasket Lodge, 182 of them turned. Of those that were lucky enough to remain human, the majority of them were quickly devoured by their newly formed zombie bunkmates, becoming one of the textbook examples of how deadly *The Turning* was for those trapped in enclosed spaces in the middle of the night with the ravenous undead.

Taking into account those people that perished in the Lodge, only a total of 32 people living in other accommodations in Mica Creek weren't turned into zombies and in the seven months since that fateful event, only six of them are still alive today, all having the wherewithal to flee Mica Creek in search of greener, more zombie-free pastures.

Kyle and Chad had been to Mica Creek a number of times since settling into their 'cabin in the woods' - which just happens to be the title of a magnificent movie, Loyal Reader.

Let's pause now whilst you go watch it.

... *tap, tap, tap* ...

All good? Then go watch it again; there's plenty of references and details we know for a fact you missed out on the first time.

... *tap, tap, tap* ...

Well done, Loyal Reader! Back now to the story so very much at hand.

Since living in their cabin in the woods, Mica Creek had become Kyle and Chad's primary source of tools and equipment. The location itself was remarkably devoid of free-range zombies. During their last visit in late October, a quick pop in to retrieve the last of their previously hidden foodstuffs, our heroes only encountered two undead, both banging their bodies against the front doors of the lodge, attracted by the muffled thuds of the hundreds of zombies still trapped within its walls.

The wood used to barricade the cabin windows was liberated from a rather large shed located on the easternmost edge of the settlement, and it was there that Kyle was currently directing the sleigh.

Landing, as was the case with taking off and flying, was a blissfully simple task. Again, it seemed like the reindeer knew exactly where Mica Creek was located and where the closest appropriate area to land the sleigh would be found. Kyle didn't have to do much of anything in particular with the reins, just small, focused pulling to guide the reindeer in the directions he wanted them to go.

As fixing the fence would require more of the wood that Kyle and Chad had helped themselves to before, Kyle had the reindeer set down on a flat, circular area adjacent to the large shed that contained the wood they were looking for. Unfortunately, there was no fence surrounding the shed, so Kyle volunteered to grab the wood while Chad and the puppies remained outside to guard the reindeer.

Normally, entering a large shed in the zombie apocalypse would be a rather stressful endeavour. These dark, enclosed spaces often seemed to be rife with the undead. Kyle, however, wasn't worried. He did a visual inspection of the perimeter, confirming that there was no damage to the shed's walls and therefore no ingress points for any zombie interlopers. Further, the front doors to the shed were chained and expertly padlocked shut, just as Kyle and Chad had left them the last time they were there.

This was one of our heroes' proudest post-apocalyptic moments, Loyal Reader; the doors were chained to ensure that, a) only humans could get inside, and b) only humans who were willing to put in serious effort would gain entry. Kyle reached into his jacket pocket, grabbed hold of a large key, gingerly opened the padlock, deftly removed the chains from the door handles, turned on his flashlight, entered the shed, and began fetching the wood they would need to fix the back-yard's fence.

The amount of wood our heroes required was not overly extensive. Kyle estimated that he wouldn't need more than 20 pieces of wood, and there were plenty in the shed. All in all, it took him about 15 minutes from the time he entered the shed until he was finished getting the wood, placing it in the back of the sleigh, and chaining the shed door shut once again. If this were a scene in an episode of *The Walking Dead* or some such dramatic show, there would have been zombies lurking behind every corner and our heroes would have had to fight their way out of some hellish and barely escapable situation, but the reality of the zombie apocalypse was not nearly so eventful most days, and this was a very good thing.

As Kyle and Chad were about to find out, though, all good things do eventually evaporate into nothingness.

Once all the wood was secured in the sleigh, all that was left was to make a quick stop at the tool shed, as Kyle wasn't convinced that they had enough nails at the cabin to fully support the fence. The good news was that the pair had also been to the tool shed before and locked its front doors, much like they did the woodshed. The bad news, however, was that the tool shed was located clear on the other side of the village. With the reindeer and sleigh, our heroes would be there in under a minute, but, as you can imagine, adding a stop always came with a certain element of risk.

As predicted, once everyone was in the sleigh, Rudolph and crew got our heroes to the tool shed in 46 seconds - not too shabby.

The tool shed was nuzzled all the way in the northernmost section of the village, right beside the humongous parking lot that once served the lodge, providing a nice, smooth area for the reindeer to set down. Chad was going to volunteer to go into the tool shed and fetch the nails so that Kyle didn't feel like he was doing all the heavy lifting, but both Kyle and Chad knew that Chad's knowledge of all things carpentry and construction was sorely lacking. Kyle knew what nails they needed and where the nails were located in the tool shed, so it was logical that he would be the one to go collect them.

Up until a small gaggle of zombies emerged from the tree line behind the tool shed, everything was going according to plan. Kyle followed the same protocol that he did for the woodshed - check the perimeter, go inside, and get the goods. While he was in the shed rummaging around, Chad took this opportunity to walk the puppies around the perimeter of the parking lot so they could stretch their legs and do their business. As if mocked by fate, it was at this exact moment, Kyle in the relative safety of the shed and Chad walking the puppies along the trees directly behind the shed, that Bronx once again decided to bark.

Bronx, delightful little dude that he was, didn't bark very often these days. His vision had been getting progressively worse over the last year (thank you very much cataracts), so movements generally didn't usually startle him. His hearing, however, was still sharp as ever and when he barked, Kyle and Chad knew that something was amiss. Chad couldn't hear what was causing Bronx to become agitated, and he wasn't eager to find out; these sorts of situations rarely ended well. At this point, Brooklyn began barking as well, not because she saw or heard anything, but strictly because she found the very thought of Bronx barking to be a personal affront to her very delicate nature.

Luckily, by the time Kyle heard the barking from inside the tool shed, the nails had already been located and he was in the process of stashing some in his bag. By the time he made it to the door of the shed, Chad was making his way there to collect him and make their seamless getaway. As Kyle emerged, the four zombies had managed to make their way out of the forest and were heading straight for the shed. Though the zombies were taking their sweet time, our heroes decided there simply wasn't enough time remaining to re-chain and padlock the doors. Though Kyle did have Veronica with him, in the interest of not endangering anyone's life, Kyle shut the door to the shed, our heroes picked up the puppies, and promptly hurried back to the sleigh.

As one would expect, the sight of zombies ambling towards them was getting the reindeer pretty antsy. To their credit, they did not abandon our heroes. Instead, once everyone was safely in the sled, they wasted no time in getting out of there. The zombies were still about 20 feet away when the sleigh was airborne, so the whole situation felt a bit more dramatic than it actually was. Still, though, any encounter with a pack of zombies, no matter the size, was enough to get the adrenaline pumping.

Twenty-three minutes later our heroes arrived back at the cabin, got the puppies safely back inside, did the requisite perimeter check for pesky zombies, and set about fixing the sagging portions of the fence in the back yard. Propping up the portions that were still in good shape took very little time, which was fortuitous, given that there was only about an hour or so of sunlight left in the day. The two remaining sections, however, required a bit more care to get them up to snuff. Our heroes did manage to get the job done just as twilight was approaching.

Fixing the fence this way wasn't a long-term solution by any stretch of the imagination. It was, however, tall enough and stable enough to stop an individual zombie or at least a small group of zombies from making their way over it or pushing it down. However, should the Universe in all its wisdom decide to send a horde of zombies to the cabin that night, then there would most definitely be larger issues to deal with than the possible untimely demise of the eight reindeer in the back yard.

With the animals safely unlatched from the sleigh and corralled in the yard with the remainder of their lichen goodies to munch on, Kyle and Chad retired to the safety and comfort of the cabin to decompress and reflect on the shit-show of a Christmas Day they just experienced. Our heroes' food stores were getting dangerously low. Their trip to Mica Creek in October exhausted their stored food supplies and provided them with a bevy of canned goods that Kyle and Chad had estimated would last them, if they rationed appropriately, until early January. This night, however, was not the time to continue brainstorming about where to forage next. Rather, Kyle and Chad decided a few weeks ago to have a proper, relaxing Christmas Day dinner.

Chad went to the cupboard and took out the cans they had set aside. Bronx and Brooklyn would each be enjoying a can of Maple Leaf flaked chicken while our heroes would feast on Dinty Moore beef stew. Compared to last night's creamed corn and ketchup, this was five-star cabin dining at its best.

The stress and turmoil of the day took its toll very shortly after everyone's Christmas dinner was safely in the confines of their tummies. Kyle and Chad soon joined the already snoozing puppies on the couch and though they had plans to sit down and have a good talk about the insane things that happened this day and what exactly they were going to do about the reindeer (not to mention Santa's abduction) our heroes were both sound asleep within minutes. And boy, what a deep slumber it turned out to be.

So deep, in fact, that the blood curdling noises from the back yard at 4:26 am almost didn't wake them.

Almost.

CHAPTER 8

BRONXIE WONXIE WOO, WHERE ARE YOU?

Harnessing all the powers of his auditory acuity, Bronx was the first to react to the middle-of-the-night screams. It shall, however, remain a matter of debate for the ages as to whether or not it was the screams that woke Kyle and Chad or the barking of their little boy. Regardless of this fact, Kyle, Chad, and the puppies were now wide awake and wondering what manner of horror story awaited them in the back yard.

Occurring smack dab in the middle of winter, 4:26 am on December 26th in southern British Columbia is quite a dark time of the morning; the sun wouldn't be fully poking its head over the mountainous horizon for another three and a half hours. Kyle and Chad considered grabbing their flashlights and heading out to the back yard to see what (or, as is usually the case, who) was responsible for the noise that woke them. Neither of our heroes actually managed to process the fact that the sounds that awoke them were screams; Kyle and Chad were busy wading through the sludge of slow-wave sleep to integrate exactly what the noises were. With such confusion abounding, our heroes decided that it was best for everyone involved if they waited until the sun was up before venturing out into the unknown of the outside world.

Helpful hint #428 of the zombie apocalypse: darkness is not your friend.

The decision to wait for daylight was painful. The reindeer had been quite noisy for some time after the screams, but eventually either calmed down or flew away. Not knowing what caused the ruckus and having no clue as to the details of its aftermath prompted rounds and rounds of speculation, each one more elaborate and gruesome than the last. Waiting, though, did provide the opportunity to prepare, and for this our heroes were thankful.

When daylight did finally manage to make an appearance, our heroes would head out into the yard, ready for whatever was thrown their way. Postulating as to what may await outside allowed Kyle and Chad to consider what their reactions would be and how best to approach each and every situation. They knew, however, that reality rarely conforms to expectations.

If nothing else, though, it did help to pass the time.

Morning did eventually come, and with it a most grim discovery in the back yard. So as not to be completely taken by surprise by the presence of any possible zombies or nasty humans, Kyle and Chad left through the front door, clutching Betty and Veronica, and stealthily crept around the left side of the cabin.

As anticlimactic as it turned out to be, there were no zombies or humans to be found anywhere; not in the fenced off portion of the yard with the reindeer and not in any of the surrounding areas out to the tree line. Once all parts of the property had been declared zombie and human free, our heroes opened the gate to the yard, only to be greeted by blood-spattered snow.

There wasn't a huge amount of blood, mind you, but it was noticeable and covered a pretty sizeable portion of the snow by the gate.

This was disconcerting.

Kyle and Chad went through the reindeer, one by one, looking for any signs of damage, but found nothing out of the ordinary. Fortunately, at least the reindeer were no longer acting stressed and didn't seem to mind the poking and prodding that ensued.

As if the mystery of who kidnapped Santa wasn't enough of a mind-bender, our heroes were now faced with the conundrum of who or what had bled all over the yard and who or what had made the noises that so rudely woke them early this morning.

This was, oddly enough, even more disconcerting.

Whatever happened, Kyle and Chad now knew that the fenced in yard was just not going to cut it as a method to keep the reindeer safe. In the interest of completing a more thorough and reindeer-free inspection of the yard, Chad retrieved the harnesses and reins so the animals could be tied up to the outside of the fence. As they do every time, the reindeer dutifully lined up for harnessing. It was only then that the Universe impressed upon Kyle and Chad the importance of not being able to see the forest for the trees, as only then did anyone notice that Cupid was missing.

Full marks to Kyle for being the one to notice Cupid's absence in the lineup, but very few marks to our heroes for apparently not being able to count to eight.

How very disconcerting *and* embarrassing.

Missing a reindeer, though a traumatic event on a number of levels, didn't change what needed to be done. Kyle and Chad moved the reindeer out of the back yard and began taking a closer look at the area with the hope that a clue would somehow magically appear.

None did.

The fence didn't appear to have suffered any large amounts of damage, at least no more than what was present when our heroes went inside the previous evening. There were a few holes and broken boards that could have been new, but to be honest, there was enough residual minor damage to the fence that Kyle and Chad were unable to fix yesterday that these small blemishes could easily have been there already. One of the holes did appear to be larger than the other ones, but it certainly was not large enough for a full-grown reindeer carcass to be squeezed through. At least not in one piece.

Without any hint of what might or might not have happened to poor Cupid, our heroes were at a loss as to what they should do next. The presence of the blood seemed to indicate that something untoward did indeed happen and Cupid didn't just fly off for kicks. The events of Christmas Day had contributed to a huge amount of disturbance to the snowpack all over the property, so there were no trails leading to or away from the back yard to indicate what might have transpired last night. Clearly something or someone had made off with Cupid.

Seeing as the gate was closed this morning, Kyle and Chad surmised that the culprit would seem to have been a human; someone with the wherewithal to open a gate, do something awful enough to a reindeer to liberate the amount of blood that was spattered everywhere, remove said reindeer from the yard, and close the gate behind them.

There were, of course, more magical and supernatural ways one could imagine a reindeer seemingly evaporating from the back yard, but our heroes were not inclined to go down those particular mental pathways until faced with no other viable options.

Life was fucked up enough already, thank you very much.

After a few moments of debate, it was decided that our heroes would take the remaining seven reindeer and do an aerial survey of the surrounding areas to see if there was any indication of where Cupid had magically disappeared. Unfortunately, the weather had begun to deteriorate as the morning light arrived. Given the current rate that the snow was falling, it wouldn't be long before the visibility would be complete and utter crap.

As Kyle began fastening the reindeer to the sleigh for their reconnaissance mission, Chad let the puppies out in the back yard for their morning constitutional. In wintertime, this is usually the briefest of affairs; neither puppy particularly liked the cold, but they both found the snow to be interesting enough to be worthy of attention, especially in early winter when the experience is still novel. As we have already discussed, Loyal Reader, Bronx's vision had been getting steadily worse over the past year. Fittingly, perhaps, Brooklyn's vision was just peachy; it was her hearing that was piss poor. They made a great pair and complimented each other wonderfully; one couldn't see and the other couldn't hear.

As a direct consequence of his deteriorating vision, when Bronx ventured outside, he would often hug the fence line. Not only did he find comfort in being up close and able to feel the wood, he also enjoyed, as puppies do, having a solid object to pee on. As such, Chad wasn't particularly concerned about the puppies and their bathroom adventures, but instead occupied his mind with cerebral musing related to Cupid's disappearance.

In retrospect though, Chad should have been concerned. Had his brain not devoted as much neural energy thinking about reindeer snatching, he might have caught a glimpse of unexpected movement out of the corner of his left eye and he might have recognized this movement as his little boy bolting across the field beyond the yard and into a stand of trees.

As would have been part of any reasonable prediction in such a situation, Chad's digestive system flexed its gymnastic muscles; his stomach lurched and perform five consecutive flips, all perfectly choreographed. The net effect, of course, being that Chad was sure he was going to pass out. Though it seemed like an eternity, in actuality, Chad paused for only 1.2 seconds before screaming at Kyle that Bronx was currently running into the forest. Chad called after Bronx as loudly as he could, but it was too late; Bronx had already disappeared into the woods.

This was not good.

Kyle, busy with the reindeer and sleigh, didn't notice Bronx's escape and was suitably confused by Chad's screams, taking a similar amount of time to process what Chad was yelling at him. Kyle dropped the harness he was fastening to the sleigh, grabbed Veronica, and headed to the yard. Chad wasted no time in picking up Brooklyn, who was very confused by all the commotion, placing her in the cabin, arming himself with Betty, and meeting Kyle at the back gate.

At this point in our relationship, Loyal Reader, I think we can rummage around the pantry and find some common ground. Most everyone, we posit, would agree with us that anyone with even a shallow, pedantic, and rudimentary understanding of what actually constitutes the quality of prettiness would, in fact, find snow to be pretty. In fact, we would vociferously argue that fresh snowfall is a fucking visual delight.

Among those that are proud card-carrying members of the *Disagree with Everything For No Good Reason Club* are none other than the residents of Bastardstown, County Wexford, Ireland. Word around the water cooler is that they're a bunch of petty heathens who wouldn't know a fucking visual delight from the hole in the ground they dug five minutes ago. We've never been to Bastardstown, so we are unfortunately not qualified to weigh in on this particular topic.

But we digress, Loyal Reader, as we tend sometimes to do.

And that's okay.

As pretty as it may have been on this particular December 26th at 9:32 am, snow was definitely no friend to Kyle and Chad. With Bronx having run into the forest behind the cabin a moment ago and the snow falling now quite heavily, odds were that any tracks their little dude left in open areas would be disappearing rather quickly. The terrain surrounding the cabin was forested, but unfortunately there were a good number of open spots. Though the tendency was for our heroes to go full tilt into the forest on foot, Kyle came up with a brilliant plan that sounded just insane enough to work, as most brilliant plans tend to.

What if, Kyle thought, *they each rode on the back of a reindeer into the forest?*

The logic being that they could cover more ground and have the potential advantage of a higher perspective while searching, being on top of full-grown reindeer backs and all.

Chad pointed out, quite correctly, that there were exactly 246 things that could possibly go wrong in this scenario, first among them that the reindeer might not be amenable to being ridden in such an unsophisticated manner.

This did seem to be a likely possibility given how generally disagreeable the reindeer had been over the past day.

As usual, Loyal Reader, it is once again worth pointing out that no reasonable inhabitant of this fine hunk of space rock in their right mind could blame our heroes for thinking such a thing. Since meeting Kyle and Chad just shy of 28 hours ago, one of the reindeer had died, whilst another had suffered what appeared to be an untimely demise at the hands of some bloody and mysterious vanishing act.

If you were an unsuspecting reindeer, Loyal Reader, you too would be rightfully wary of any plan these two wingnuts had devised.

Still, Kyle thought, to which Chad would most certainly agree, *it was worth a try.*

Time, of course, was of the essence. Every second that our heroes spent not looking for their little boy was one more second for him to get further away or, more critically, run into trouble of the zombie variety. It also didn't help that the aforementioned snow was ruthlessly and efficiently blanketing the surroundings areas. With that in mind, Kyle prepared two of the reindeer - Donner and Blitzen - for the rescue mission while Chad went inside to get Brooklyn settled, fetch some rope, fill a back pack with some towels and a blanket for when they found their little dude, and grab the walkie-talkies in case they got separated during their rescue mission.

We know what you are thinking, Loyal Reader, but in reality, there was no rhyme or reason as to why Kyle chose Donner and Blitzen for this mission. Rather, it was a simple matter of convenience - Donner and Blitzen were at the end of the tethered line of reindeer, making it the path of least reindeer-asshole-resistance to get them loose. Kyle quickly removed the pair from the rest of the group, being careful to leave the remaining five still tied to the fence inside the yard. He was amazed at how remarkably easy this task was.

Harnesses still in place, Chad arrived and handed Kyle the rope and his very own walkie-talkie. Kyle fashioned two makeshift reins, knowing full well that they wouldn't be perfect, but desperately hoping against all hope that they would work for as long as our heroes needed them to.

In the history of life on Earth, a grand total of 24 people tried to mount and ride a wild reindeer. Virtually all of these attempts have involved copious amounts of alcohol or dimwitted males, usually of the Swedish, Norwegian, Finnish, Russian, or redneck Alaskan variety. More times than one might care to admit, though, it was a hilarious and unfortunate combination of the two. Now, Loyal Reader, of those two dozen troopers who gave it the ol' college try - and this should come as no surprise whatsoever - very, very few, managed to approach a result that would come close to approximating anything resembling success.

There were so very few, in fact, that only one person has ever effectively completed anything even in the remote vicinity of resembling what some people might consider maybe one day calling riding a reindeer.

The one successful rider, Reidar Aalberg of Sodankylä, Finland managed to stay on a reindeer's back for 36 seconds - 34.6 seconds longer than anyone else. While this came as a complete surprise to his inebriated friends that looked on in complete and utter amazement, it came as no surprise to the reindeer. You see, Loyal Reader, Reidar Aalberg was the 438th Earthly reincarnation of the Finnish God *Tapio* - God of the forest. Reidar's powers, having been diluted over the millennia and therefore almost completely dormant though they were, did manage to afford him some degree of patience from the usually standoffish and unwilling reindeer; enough, at least, for him to become a living legend amongst his friends.

At the end of the day, isn't that all that really matters?

Once the reins had been fastened to Donner and Blitzen's harnesses, Kyle and Chad had to figure out how exactly how they were supposed to mount these beasts with any degree of success.

Anyone who knows anything about reindeer or has access to the internet will be quick to tell you that an adult will stand somewhere between 85 and 150 cm tall at the shoulder. As with most species of mammal in nature, the males tend to be somewhat larger than females, and this was true for Donner and Blitzen; Donner was 142 cm (about 4.5 feet) with Blitzen being only slightly shorter, at 138 cm. While not gargantuan in size, their vertical fortitude did require our heroes to manufacture a quick and dirty, yet relatively easy, mounting plan.

This, as has been painfully par for the course as of late, was much, much easier said than done.

How many quick and dirty, yet relatively easy reindeer mounting plans has anyone ever come up with in the history of humanity?

Precious damn few, that's how many. And we don't see you coming up with any at the moment either, Loyal reader, so stop being so fucking jugdy.

Sometimes we wonder, Loyal Reader, we really do.

If you had asked Kyle and Chad at some point before these Christmas escapades unfolded what the odds were that they would someday be riding two majestic and magical reindeer into the forest, they might rightly have thought you were high as balls.

Funny how life works out, no?

Kyle and Chad sidled their respective reindeer up to the fence, Kyle taking Donner and Chad taking Blitzen. The plan was as elegant as it was seemingly impossible - tie the creature to the fence with the makeshift reins, climb the fence, get on top of the reindeer, untie the reins, and hope to Kathryn Janeway it all works out.

And that's exactly what happened.

Donner and Blitzen, perhaps using their Christmas magic to sense the gravity of the situation, were perfect gentlemen during the whole affair. Within seconds, our heroes were mounted on their backs and making their way toward the section of the tree line where Chad spotted Bronx sprinting away. Though neither vocalized this fact, both men were terrified that they may never see their little man again.

The past seven months had their fair share of terrifying moments, Loyal Reader, but Kyle and Chad had not felt this level of fear and dread since that first day of *The Turning*.

CHAPTER 9

THE CHASE

*I*t probably won't come as a complete surprise, Loyal Reader, to learn that words continued to fail Kyle and Chad.
    Not only did they witness two horrific, bloody scenes on their short drive that sunny May 22nd morning, but as they sat in their chalet reading website after website and watching video after video, their puny little primate minds were incapable of processing the sheer magnitude of the events they were experiencing. Without going into the details of every story they read and every image and video they saw, suffice to say that the beginning of the zombie apocalypse was quite well documented. Not knowing for how long the Internet and cellular service would still be available (digital communications of all kinds were broken down in various places all over the globe; it was, therefore, only a matter of time before Western Canada joined that particular club), Kyle and Chad tried to piece together as much as they could about their current situation.
    Based on what they were able to find concerning the advent of the zombie apocalypse, they knew that, a) a very good chunk of the humans all over the world appeared to have instantaneously been converted into zombies, b) these zombies were remarkably fast, feral, and craved loads and loads of human flesh, and c) completely destroying a zombie's brains seemed to be the only way to neutralize it.
    One doesn't ever really expect to wake up one fine May morning to find themselves in the midst of a zombie apocalypse, Loyal Reader. Well, perhaps some of the more annoying people on Earth did, but only in a kitschy "I'm wearing a flannel shirt and toque and therefore must be ready for the apocalypse, so look at how different and awesome I am," kind of annoying

hipster way. *In an interesting twist of fate, none of those people ended up surviving* The Turning. *Most, as predicted, were consumed by their 'alternative' friends-turned-zombies while the remainder stayed holed up in their studio apartments, curled up in the fetal position, and reciting Dave Matthews Band lyrics until they died of dehydration. Kyle and Chad were among the vast majority of the population that, a) didn't see any merit in the music of Dave Matthews Band, and b) didn't see the apocalypse coming.*

This, however, didn't stop them from sitting on the couch and trying their darndest to brainstorm at least a few survival scenarios.

In terms of basic requirements, our heroes deduced that three things were needed - shelter, water, and food. The chalet provided them with shelter. It had a front door and back door, both of which could be locked. Further, as long as they didn't make any noise or turn on the lights at night, they should be quite safe from any zombies that might be milling about.

Chad and Kyle checked the water situation; the taps were still working, so water wouldn't be an issue as long as they could store enough of it to sustain them while they remained in the chalet. Our heroes decided that they would fill the bathtub, the sinks, and every available container with water. They would continue to use the taps for drinking until the water stopped working and use the tub, sinks, and containers as emergency stores.

Food, however, was the big issue. Being on a vacation, Kyle and Chad had brought only enough food for their long weekend getaway. With rationing, they estimated they could last a week or so, but eventually the food situation would need to be sorted out.

After a couple of hours of these ruminations and realizing that they were most probably safe for now in the chalet, fear decided it was high time to pay a visit.

Paralyzing, utter terror, in fact.

It's the kind of fear that you hope you never have to experience. The sudden realization that these two men and their sweet little puppies were now living in the midst of a zombie apocalypse was almost too much to bear. Safety was not a certainty by any stretch and any inclination to go outdoors had a very high probability of leading to certain death.

And then there were things that you never think you're going have to sort out in the land of the undead - where do the puppies go to do their business? It is a fact of life that all animals need to perform some variation of peeing and pooping, and Bronx and Brooklyn were, of course, no exception. As long as the water kept running, our heroes' own bathroom requirements would be taken care of, but what about when the running water stopped flowing?

These may have seemed like small and insignificant issues compared to the basic need to survive, but one must retain some modicum of a civilized approach to life, even in the midst of the zombie apocalypse; it's not like Kyle and Chad were tree people, after all.

Sleep would remain an evasive little bastard that first night after The Turning. *Kyle and Chad spent most of the time amassing water, watching videos of the carnage on the internet, and formulating possibilities for their long-term survival in this new reality. Realizing that the zombies were acutely aware of their surroundings and attracted to the slightest noise, movement, or lights, they huddled in the middle of the living room floor in complete darkness with the laptop on its dimmest setting and the sound barely audible.*

Fortunately, the night was uneventful. They did hear some faint noises outside, but nothing (or no one) made a sound loud enough to spook the puppies. The very last thing they needed was for Bronx, with his superb hearing, to begin barking and attracting a Nipsy-Russell of zombies to their abode.

By the next morning, Kyle and Chad had come up with the basics of a plan they thought might increase their chances of long-term survival. They had decided, quite obviously, that attempting to navigate their way back their home in Greater Vancouver was a bad idea.

A very, very, very bad idea.

They reasoned, quite rightly we might add Loyal Reader, that since the news reports seemed to indicate that a vast majority of people had spontaneously turned into zombies, going anywhere near a populated area was asking for trouble. Land lines and cell phones stopped working altogether not long after dark, so there was no potential for communicating with anyone in the outside world through conventional means. In a desperate attempt to find out if any of their loved ones had survived, our heroes sent off e-mails and messages throughout the night, with no responses. The internet quietly faded away by morning. This was a source of great sadness, of course, and left Kyle and Chad with the conclusion that they were going to have to ride out the apocalypse together with their puppies.

Things were just frighteningly awful, Loyal Reader, but it definitely could have been worse - much, much worse.

With populated areas out of the question, Kyle and Chad debated using the chalet as their new home and hunkering down there for an extended period of time. While this was certainly a possibility, our heroes didn't think that it was the best long-term solution. Ridgecrest Pines, though somewhat isolated, was under 10 km from Revelstoke, British Columbia.

Revelstoke, not a large city by any stretch of anyone's imagination ever, had a population of somewhere around 7,000 people on May 22nd and if the Internet was to be believed, over 5,000 of them were now zombies. With the speed that some of the undead were displaying online, Kyle and Chad surmised that the odds were pretty good that it might not been too long before hordes of those creatures would arrive at their location. Adding to the likelihood of this possibility was the fact that Ridgecrest Pines was located right off of the Trans-Canada Highway, a thoroughfare that would most likely provide a handy artery through which the zombies could flow.

Armed with this this knowledge, our heroes decided that the sooner they got themselves off of the beaten path, the better. Opting to find a more isolated location, Kyle and Chad decided that, for better or for worse, they would pack up everything they could and leave Ridgecrest Pines behind the following day.

Once inside the tree line, Bronx's trail was not that difficult to follow. Though the snow was coming down quite heavily, the trees managed to prevent a good deal of it from obscuring the path that he followed. There were some other trails branching off in different directions around the area, but given the recent nature of Bronx's travels, his were the freshest and least masked by the snowfall. By this time, Kyle and Chad estimated that it might be upwards of five minutes since Bronx sprinted off, but, in reality, it was only three minutes and six seconds. That being said, a puppy on the run can cover some serious ground in that time.

While the area surrounding the cabin had some heavily forested parts, there were also a number of clearings. In the summer months, our heroes envisioned that these areas would be perfect spots for a leisurely picnic and lazing about in the shade. On this winter day, however, when Kyle and Chad emerged into the first clearing, visibility was so restricted by what was now a full-on blizzard that they had no idea in which direction to search. Not being able to see more than a few feet in front of them was one thing, but further complicating matters was the presence of multiple tracks, all of which could have been formed by Bronx and all running in different, rather haphazard directions.

This was most certainly not a good thing.

The clearing wasn't tremendously large but was broad enough that there were several options to choose from in deciding which way to search for Bronx. Of the multiple trails that snaked their way around and across the clearing, three of them seemed to be fresher than the rest, so our heroes decided they were likely the best candidates for leading them to their handsome little man. While this was a promising turn of events, it was also very disheartening; all three paths led in different directions.

Of course, they did, Loyal Reader.

One of them did an almost a 90° turn to the tree line on the left, one ran almost perfectly straight across to the trees, while the other veered slightly to the right, ending up about 12 meters (fuck you, Imperial System) from where the center trail entered the woods.

With three trails emerging as the most probable candidates for finding Bronx, Kyle and Chad accepted the sad realization that they could only follow two of them. The unfortunate reality of this situation was that there was a 33.3% chance that Bronx had gone down the one path they weren't going to follow. Kyle chose the path to the left and Chad chose the path that ran almost straight across the clearing. They each had their walkie-talkies, so whoever found Bronx could notify the other.

As our heroes made their way down their respective paths into the tree line, they hoped and pleaded to the Universe to have let one of them picked the right path. The Universe, however, was under no such obligation to listen to anyone's pleas. Why? Because it's the fucking Universe - it has absolutely no business caring about such things, nor should it.

This was unfortunate.

If the Universe was able to give a sweet lick about any of its inhabitants, perhaps it would have somehow managed to notify Kyle and Chad that neither of them chose the correct trail.

Bronx had instead bolted across the clearing to the right.

Shit cakes!

As an aside, we are pretty sure we mentioned lately, Loyal Reader, just how much pure, blind luck factored into Kyle and Chad's survival after *The Turning*. If not, it's worth repeating again here.

The reason, you may ask. Once again it would seem that fate, fortune, luck, or whatever the sweet sultry Elton John you may choose to call it, was watching over the proceedings and managed to prevent what realistically could turn out to be a disastrous outcome of epic proportions for our heroes.

Kyle couldn't hear Bronx barking.

Chad couldn't hear Bronx barking.

However, even with the muffling effect of the blizzard around them, both Donner and Blitzen heard Bronx barking. Apparently, it was either that all reindeer have really, really good hearing or just that Santa's reindeer are equipped with a whole new level of aural sensitivity. Regardless, as Kyle and Chad were just about to enter the woods down their respective paths, both Donner and Blitzen stopped dead in their tracks.

This was most confusing to our heroes, but especially to Chad, who was nearly thrown off Blitzen when he abruptly decided he was not going to go any further. Once stopped, both reindeer, regardless of the amount of pulling on the reins and vocal protests by their riders, turned to the right and began sprinting towards the muffled barks they heard mere seconds ago.

Kyle and Chad were communicating over the walkie-talkies, both stating exactly the same thing - each of their reindeer seemed to have gone rogue and was on a serious mission.

Luckily, before our heroes had time to think that all hope of finding Bronx was lost, they both began to hear the unmistakable sound that was attracting both Donner and Blitzen - and what a wonderful and glorious sound it was.

If pressed to tell the truth, the whole truth, and nothing but the truth, both Kyle and Chad would agree that Bronx's barking was, in the past, considered grating, especially when he was adamant that someone either, a) find his fucking ball that he lost under the exact same corner of the bloody sofa for the six-hundred-thousandth spaghetti monster-damned time, b) rescue the very same fucking ball from the evil clutches of whatever it happened to roll behind (usually the broom), or c) throw the fucking ball. At this moment in time, Kyle and Chad could not think any other sound in the world that would have given them more joy.

Donner, having been led down the left-hand path by Kyle, was a fair distance behind Blitzen once they began their sprint. He managed, though, to make up this gap quite quickly and was soon caught up. And so, Loyal reader, less than a minute (53 seconds, if you're keeping track at home) after the two reindeer abruptly came to a stop and just as quickly decided to suddenly change course, they were now striding side-by side through the forest towards the barking of one seriously cute little handsome fella named Bronx.

Though it didn't seem like it at the time, our heroes had travelled a pretty good distance from the cabin. Bronx, it seemed, must have been running and bouncing through the snow pretty much at full tilt to have made it as far as he did. On a grand scale, the actual distance wasn't that far, 746 meters as it turns out, but very impressive nonetheless for a puppy on the move, and in the middle of quite a nasty blizzard, no less. Less than 10 minutes had passed since he bolted across the back yard of the cabin and disappeared into the woods, but to Kyle and Chad it felt like an eternity. The immense and complete joy our two heroes felt at the sound of his barking actually managed to pale in comparison to the elation they felt when they finally laid eyes on their little man.

Donner and Blitzen raced through the forest and brought Kyle and Chad to a second clearing; appreciably smaller than the first one, and interestingly, with a massively impressive hemlock tree smack dab in its center. It was under said massively impressive hemlock tree and sheltered from the heavily falling snow, that they found their noisy little boy.

Bronx had no idea that his daddies had found him. Instead, he was in rapt attention, cataract-filled eyes, useless as they were at this moment in time, fixed quite intently at the tree, looking up towards the upper branches, hackles on full display, and barking like his proverbial and adorable little life depended on it.

CHAPTER 10

THE WHIRLY BIRD

Just trust us, Loyal Reader, when we inform you that it is a verified statement of fact that little Bronx was a very good boy. Born on a cool morning in late February, he displayed all the characteristics that Kyle and Chad were looking for in a new family member. One of these characteristics, as it turned out, would seal the deal. A couple of weeks after he was born, our heroes had visited Kyle's mother's house (Bronx is the son of one of her doggies, Daisy) to visit the newest litter of puppies and decide which one would be joining them in a happy forever home. While observing the group of cute little beasts during their feeding time, one of them, the pudgiest of the bunch, had managed to wedge himself into the bowl of food and stood there, oblivious to his siblings around him, and ate to his heart's content.

This, concluded Kyle and Chad, as they both looked down at this amazing little man and then up at one another, *is the puppy for us.*

And so, a mere eight weeks after he was introduced to the world, our heroes took Bronx to his new home, where he would forever be coddled and cuddled and loved like there was no tomorrow.

That, of course is not entirely true Loyal Reader, as Bronx was currently occupying some prime real estate under a rather stately hemlock tree and barking away at what appeared to be absolutely nothing.

Currently a curmudgeonly old man of about 13 years, Bronx's vision was not what it used to be. As we alluded to a bit earlier Loyal Reader, Bronx suffered from juvenile cataracts that had matured into nasty little dispersive viscoelastic cataracts. As the veterinary eye specialist had communicated to his daddies, it was like having a film of wax paper over his eyes, with the effect getting worse as he got older. This, of course, was not the end of the world; Bronx still displayed enough visual fortitude to navigate his surroundings most of the time, but he did tend to run into things every now and then if he found himself in unfamiliar territory or if it was particularly bright wherever he happened to be plodding along.

The morning of December 26th was indeed very bright. Though the sun wasn't able to shine through the light cloud cover, the blanket of snow currently smothering the ground provided ample surface area for a good amount of residual albedo.

Bronx's daddies had spent the better part of that early morning dealing with something outside, which suited Bronx just fine for the most part as lazy mornings were his specialty. However, as the morning droned on, daddies had not reappeared and it was only after what seemed like an eternity, that Daddy Chad finally opened the door to let Bronx and Brooklyn out for their morning business.

At first, all seemed to progress according to plan. There were a variety of scents and smells around the yard, especially along the wooden fence where Bronx had proudly marked his territory over and over again. Business of the excretory variety was eventually conducted, after which Bronx continued to meander his way along the enclosure. Along the back portion, though, about halfway between the corner and the closed gate, Bronx picked up a scent. Though his eyes would not cooperate like they once did, his nose and ears were in fabulous shape. The odour he encountered was quite simply intoxicating; it was like nothing he had ever encountered before.

Please keep in mind, Loyal Reader, that a smell considered intoxicating to a dog need not be what a human being considers to be a good smell or even remotely pleasant for that matter. Bronx was a little dude that, on many, many occasions, would stumble across an old pile of poop and sniff the bejeezus out of it. Not the most discerning of noses, to be sure.

This particular irresistible scent on this particular morning along this particular stretch of fence just happened to have its origin at a convenient Bronx-sized hole. The smell continued through the hole and into the area beyond the yard.

Somewhere deep inside, Bronx knew that he shouldn't be venturing out of the yard; for some reason, Daddy Kyle and Daddy Chad rarely let him beyond its confines. Unfortunately, the part of Bronx's brain that knew this was currently in the process of being beaten into submission by the curiosity center of his brain. Being part of the complex reward pathway, it was instructing Bronx that the entirety of his doggy desires lay at the end of this particular olfactory rainbow.

As Bronx gingerly stepped through the hole and into the expanse of the unfenced portion of the back yard, his curiosity and resolve remained unwavering. The scent was getting stronger now and led him directly across the yard and towards the forested tree line. Bronx, of course, had no idea to where he was being led - his head was down, and he was unusually focused on keeping his nose directly on top of the snow cover. If, perhaps, he had realized where he was going, he might have paused and reflected on the path he was about to take. Then again, maybe he wouldn't - he could sometimes be a delightful little assmunch that way.

Bronx continued to move rather slowly across the yard, and had he maintained that leisurely pace, he most definitely would have been noticed by one of his daddies before making it to the woods.

All hopes of this occurring, however, were dashed when his acute hearing picked up on some strange and enticing sounds emanating from the forest. Combining these angelic sounds with the ambrosia of a scent he was following was the perfect storm of circumstance that set his brain into overdrive. Without a care in the world, and without making a sound, Bronx bolted across the remaining real estate of the back yard and into the waiting arms of the forest. So pure was his determination to find the source of this scent and noise that he didn't even register the frantic yelling of Daddy Chad calling and begging for him to return.

Given Bronx's eyesight, it was nothing short of a literal Christmas miracle that he made it all the way to the giant hemlock tree without bashing into anything. He completed the trip running at full tilt, following his insatiable curiosity for that damned smell, and the haunting call of the noises he heard. Once arriving at the tree, the noises stopped, but that ungodly beautiful scent was unmistakably coming from the branches directly above him. It was Bronx's sworn duty as a good little boy to inform everyone within earshot, including his daddies that he didn't even process had just arrived, that he had proudly discovered the source of this miraculous scent and had it trapped in the tree above him.

Immediately upon arriving in the second clearing, our heroes approached the tree, dismounted from their reindeer, and ran to their little dude. Bronx still wasn't even remotely interested in processing the fact that his daddies had arrived. Instead of turning towards them as they called his name, Bronx simply continued his unabated barking and his unwavering gaze on the branches of the tree above him. Kyle managed to pick up Bronx while Chad took out a towel to dry him off and a blanket to wrap around him and get him warm.

Bronx, of course, was having none of this. He was still completely engrossed with the tree and continued his barking. It was only once Chad wrapped him in the blanket that he seemed to snap out of his laser-like focus and registered that his daddies were talking to him. As Kyle held him on his back and both daddies spoke to him in soothing and reassuring voices, he finally calmed down. His eyes, though, continued to stare in the direction of the tree, much to his daddies' confusion and curiosity.

The hemlock tree was humongous, at least it appeared so. In actuality, it probably wasn't much bigger than your average really big hemlock tree would be, but its lone occupancy in the middle of this clearing seemed to give the illusion that it was obscenely large. The branches didn't start until about 20 or so feet off of the ground, but once they did, they were quite dense. If indeed something or someone was up in that tree, as Bronx's barking and hackles seemed to indicate, our heroes couldn't determine what it was, let alone if anything was indeed there.

Donner and Blitzen, true to form, were indifferent to the whole affair and didn't seem to find anything in the branches of the tree that interesting at all. Instead, they spent this downtime eating some lichens growing on the far side of the trunk and making noises that magical reindeer make when chomping down on available nutrition. There was no realistic way to climb up into the tree to see what all the doggy fuss was about, and our heroes were not all that eager to find out. Given the way things had progressed since yesterday morning, it was entirely possible that whatever Bronx sensed wanted nothing more than to see the lot of them dead.

With that in mind, Kyle and Chad thought it best to leave this particular Matlock Mystery unsolved and make their way back to the cabin.

Getting Bronx back to the cabin could have been a very awkward affair. Riding the reindeer out to the clearing was difficult enough without a saddle let alone whilst carrying a blanket-wrapped Bronx. The latter could realistically have proved quite impossible. Luckily, though, our heroes came prepared. The backpack that Chad brought with him was not only a handy-dandy towel and blanket carrier, it was a puppy carrier as well.

In the early days of the apocalypse, during a supply run to a pet store, Kyle and Chad had found two Pet Gear dog carriers. They would serve not only as spacious backpacks but, when required, each one comfortably allowed a little furry bundle of love to be toted along for the ride.

Chad brought Bronx's backpack with him, so Kyle quickly placed Bronx inside, and Chad helped Kyle get the backpack onto his shoulders. As if anticipating that the group was about to leave, Donner and Blitzen finished their lichen lunch, and each walked over to their respective human and knelt down in the snow. Our heroes found it refreshing that the reindeer didn't decide to take this opportunity to be complete asses. Instead, the duo was able to mount their steeds with relative ease.

Unbelievably, the blizzard appeared to be getting worse. As Kyle and Chad began to direct the reindeer back the way they came, it appeared that this was easier said than done. In the short time it had taken to get Bronx settled and packaged up for the trip home, their tracks had been completely filled in with snow. Our heroes tried making the reindeer fly again, even going as far as reciting that damn poem again, but apparently solo flights are not a common occurrence for Santa's reindeer. Not that flying would have done a bit of good anyway, visibility was essentially nil at this point and being in the air might have caused them to get even more lost than they already were.

In retrospect, Kyle and Chad would have done well to have used a compass to get their bearings during their journey so they knew at least what general direction the cabin was located. However, the emergent nature of Bronx's bolting precluded them from doing their best boy scout impressions. In fact, it hadn't even crossed their minds that sooner rather than later they would find themselves lost in the woods. Chad had no idea which way they should go, but Kyle thought he could kind of make out their tracks going off in a direction slightly left of where they were currently facing. With no other options garnering any approval, that was the path they chose.

As our heroes set off across the clearing towards the tree line, they were unaware of two things: 1) they were heading in a direction that was not ever going to take them anywhere near their cabin, and 2) a pair of glowing red eyes watching their every movement from upper branches of the hemlock tree that slowly faded into the distance behind them.

It was exactly eight minutes and fifteen seconds into their journey back to the cabin that Kyle and Chad realized things were once again going to shit. They had entered the forest from the second clearing and had continued through dense trees the entire time. In a comical twist of fate, the forest actually seemed to be getting denser and denser by the minute. If they were on the correct track back to the cabin (and they weren't), they should have definitely encountered the first clearing by now. Our heroes, realizing that something wasn't quite right, stopped for a moment to consider the situation.

- *Should they continue on in the direction they were travelling?*
- *Should they turn around, go back to the second clearing (if they could find it), and choose a new path?*
- *Should they randomly choose another direction and hope for the best?*
- *Should they do their darndest to invent a reindeer language and ask Donner and Blitzen why the fuck they can't seem to find their way back to the other six reindeer?*

So many questions!
The unfortunate reality was that the answers to each and every one of them had the distinct probability of getting them further and further away from not only the cabin and the remainder of the reindeer, but also their furry little girl Brooklyn.
One thing was certain - this was no easy decision.
After a brief discussion of the options, our heroes decided to continue on in their current direction for another five minutes and then reassess.
Kyle and Chad didn't need those five minutes and in fact, Kyle and Chad would not get the chance to further reassess their current situation. You see, Loyal Reader, three minutes and thirty-two seconds into the second leg of what they desperately hoped was their journey back to the cabin, they stumbled upon a third clearing.
Apparently, this forest was all about clearings!
At first, this seemed to be a very good sign. Both Kyle and Chad thought this to be the first clearing they had encountered. If this were the case, they correctly surmised this would mean they wouldn't be too far from the

cabin at all. However, this cute and adorable pre-emptive excitement was quickly dashed when our heroes realized this was not the first clearing at all; not by a long shot.

With the blizzard still raging around them, one might reasonably ask how Kyle and Chad could be so sure that this was not the first clearing. The answer, of course, came in the form of the discovery of a fucking helicopter sitting proudly to one side of the clearing.

The right side, if you're keeping score at home, Loyal Reader.

As much as our heroes were eager to make their way back to the cabin, the discovery of a helicopter was just far, far too cool of an opportunity to pass up. They had not been gone for very long and it was highly unlikely that Brooklyn would be facing any trouble whilst locked in the cabin. In fact, if all bets were placed, the lion's share of the money would be placed squarely on the tile that indicated she would be fast asleep and snoring like a bloody freight train.

Besides, there was a freaking helicopter just waiting to be explored!

The helicopter was quite a good size and looked very intimidating, as most helicopters are apt to do when placed rather cryptically to the side of a clearing in the middle of a forest in the aftermath of a zombie apocalypse. It was longer than our heroes expected and, based on the camouflage green colour and the word CANADA stenciled in black on the door, was of a military origin. Kyle and Chad dismounted Donner and Blitzen and approached this incredibly impressive contraption for a closer look.

There were no zombies in or around it, so that was good. Further, it didn't seem like the helicopter crash-landed here, as it was sitting atop the snow in what appeared to be perfect condition (as far as out heroes could assess, anyway). There was a good amount of snow built up around the perimeter of the helicopter, so it appeared to have been here for quite some time. The fuel door was open, so perhaps someone had encountered it and siphoned its contents.

Kyle slid open the side door, removed his Bronx-containing backpack, and set it down inside the main cabin. Bronx had been asleep and seemed content to stay in the carrier and snooze the day away - he did, after all, have quite the exciting morning.

Our heroes entered the cabin and took a look around. The five seats were intact and there were a bunch of cables and wires strewn about. Other than that, it was remarkably empty. Kyle sandwiched himself between the rather slim space between two cockpit seats and made his way to the pilot's side of the cockpit. There were no keys in the ignition of course, and nothing of note was left lying around the cabin. The instrument panel appeared to be intact, and nothing appeared to have been vandalized or pilfered. Our heroes were hoping that there might be something exciting to find within the helicopter, but not every rainbow leads to a pot of gold. This was, apparently, just your run-of-the-mill Canadian Armed Forces helicopter sitting on the edge of a forested clearing in southern British Columbia. Just another day at the office for our intrepid pair.

It was at that moment the jingling began.

CHAPTER 11

KILLER FUCKING ZOMBIE ELVES

Keen to possess the element of surprise, and just when it seemed the Universe would be a complete and utter dickwad the entire day, the blizzard began to subside. The snow was still falling, mind you, but not nearly with the frequency or ferocity of earlier that morning. Though a relief, it was unlikely to pose a significant increase in the likelihood that Kyle and Chad would have an easy time finding their way back to the cabin. Still, any reduction, no matter how subtle, in the Universe's churlish attitude was a welcome change.

Just as our heroes, Chad in the cabin and Kyle in the cockpit of the helicopter, were finalizing their scavenging with absolutely nothing to show for it, they heard Donner and Blitzen putting up a bit of a fuss in the clearing outside. Kyle had fastened the two reindeers' tethers to the branches of a tree on the edge of the clearing beside the helicopter. As our heroes emerged yet again to see what fresh Hellscape awaited them, they were surprised to see no evidence of anything untoward. Both reindeer, though, were reacting to something as they pulled at their reins quite frenetically in what appeared to be an attempt to free themselves. With each passing moment their levels of annoyance at the futility of this process seemed to grow exponentially. Kyle and Chad made their way over to the reindeer to try and calm them down and figure out what was causing them to get so irritated. It was then that our heroes finally managed to hear the faint yet distinct sound of bells (jingle bells, of course, Loyal Reader) in the distance.

    Any logically thinking human would no doubt argue that there exist a scant few scenarios where one can imagine that the seemingly innocent and angelic sound of bells jingling would be considered an alarming event.

    As it turns out, Loyal Reader, Ravina Kinnerds of Thompson, Manitoba did manage to cleverly and succinctly dictate no less than 38 of these very scenarios in a psilocybin-fueled afternoon of hallucinations on October 17th, 2011.

    Interestingly, Ravina's verbiage was the direct result of her being under the distinct impression that she was standing trial for the murder of her beloved rustic Harmony Bells wind chime set. Ravina was unreservedly convinced that her bells had earlier that morning come to life, gained sentience, and had the jumbo-sized cojones to mock her choice of fabric softener, all the while ringing those fucking bells for all to hear.

    Ravina was justifiably certain of her ability to convince a jury of licorice-flavoured pickled herring that she was well within her rights to relieve the world of this traitorous, metallic, ringing, piece of filth; her defense, of course, centered around the unquestionable threatening presence of those unwavering ringing bells.

    It is an unfortunate circumstance that no other human was present to hear Ravina's inspired account of the many, many ways that ringing bells could elicit a fight-or-flight response. Indeed, were an objective witness present, they would hardly be surprised to learn that one of those very scenarios, identical to the tiniest miniscule detail, was now playing out with sufficient drama in the backwoods of the province of British Columbia.

    Why were our heroes alarmed at the sound of bells ringing in the forest? Loyal Reader, please do consider the following:

> - *One does not normally find bells attached to things in the middle of the forest.*
> - *Bells do not normally jingle of their own accord.*

    Though unaware of Ravina and her mid-October caterwauling, the two above-mentioned conditions meant that not only was something or someone in close proximity, but they had no qualms about announcing their presence to anyone within earshot in the middle of a zombie apocalypse. Kyle and Chad quickly realized this was not a good thing and decided to leave as soon as was humanly and reindeerly (yes, Loyal Reader, that's now also a word) possible.

This, as had become commonplace of late, was easier said than done.

Chad fetched the Bronx-containing backpack from the cabin of the helicopter while Kyle began to rapidly untie the reindeer. As soon as he managed to get the reins free from the branches, Donner and Blitzen bolted towards the clearing, ripping the reins loose from Kyle's hands. Kyle called after the pair, but ultimately ended up watching helplessly as the two raced across the clearing to about the halfway point, and then rose gracefully into the air and flew away.

"Are you kidding me!?" Kyle shouted. "Fucking asshole reindeer," he muttered to himself in disbelief.

Kyle struggled to comprehend not only how Donner and Blitzen could just abandon them, but more importantly why the Hell they all of a sudden decided they could fly without the other reindeer present. Chad emerged from the cabin of the helicopter as the pair of reindeer flew off into the distance and joined Kyle amongst the ranks of the miffed.

Realizing their mode of transportation had just evaporated, and with the jingling sounds getting louder and louder, Kyle and Chad decided they could either set off on foot through the forest and hopefully escape whatever jingling threat was imminent, or they could hunker down in the cabin or cockpit of the helicopter and assess the emerging threat from relative safety.

The unknown is a bitch of a fucker of a thing.

In their current situation, for example, our heroes knew precious little about what was causing the jingling of the bells and how much of a danger said reason would turn out to be. Had Kyle and Chad been armed with this knowledge, their eventual decision on how to respond would probably have been much different.

You see, Loyal Reader, what they did not know was that the jingling sounds were coming from the tree line just across the right side of the clearing from the helicopter. The light snow that was falling and the blanket of snow all over the clearing was sufficiently muffling the jingling sounds, making it somewhat impossible for our heroes to determine from which direction they were originating. As such, Kyle and Chad had no clue as to which direction would have been safe for them to escape and instead decided to hunker down in the cabin of helicopter, hopefully being able to respond to any possible threats accordingly.

"Well this is just great," mused Chad, as he and Kyle entered the cabin. Not only were they essentially sealing themselves in a potential metal tomb, but his body decided right now was the most appropriate time to let him know that he really, really needed to pee.

As Kyle slid the helicopter's side door shut, Chad put down the backpack and took out Bronx, who had been awakened by the commotion and was now just a fair bit irritated by the thought of having to get settled in the cabin of the helicopter. Chad wrapped Bronx back in the blanket, held him nice and tight, and did his best to keep him calm and hopefully bark-free while the events began to unfold around them.

The doors of the helicopter each had two windows that occupied most of their upper half. The cockpit, of course, was encased completely by windows. Since the seats in the cockpit formed the front 'wall' of the cabin, as long as one was standing, you could easily look out the cockpit to see what was going on. Our heroes noted that this setup would provide ample opportunity for them to observe anything that moved around in virtually all directions. The only slight area that wouldn't be visible would be the behind the helicopter's tail. Since the Universe appeared to be a righteous prick this particular holiday season, Kyle and Chad assumed that exact blind spot would be where all the possibly deadly events in the next little while would occur.

Luckily, they were wrong.

It wasn't her excessively loud snoring that woke Brooklyn, but rather a noisy and abrupt bout of flatulence. Scientifically speaking, it actually would not come as a complete surprise to the average person that the sound of her snoring didn't wake her. You see, Loyal Reader, Brooklyn - daddies' little sugar-coated princess - didn't hear too well. Playing Devil's Advocate for a moment, though, this particular instance of snoring was quite loud, even by her lofty standards.

On this crisp, snowy Boxing Day morning, Brooklyn was producing a whopping 82-94 decibels (dB) with each droning snore. It wasn't her loudest snore ever produced - that particular doozie occurred in the middle of the night on March 11th, 2007 and clocked in at a whopping 108 db. For ease of reference, the average garbage disposal produces about 80 dB, a belt sander 95 dB, and your average chainsaw a whopping 105 dB.

Let us all take just a moment and marvel at the sound production of this sweet, little noise machine.

Once Daddy Chad had abruptly picked her up from the yard and plopped her down on the couch that morning, she had spent 94.6% of the time since then - 76 minutes - asleep. She was, after all, a good little girl, and good little girls need their sleep. Of the four minutes she was awake, three of those occurred in the time immediately following Daddy Chad leaving the cabin and locking the door behind him.

One of those minutes was spent getting comfortable on the couch, a ritual that involved scratching on her favourite blanket until it was a scrunched-up mess, walking in a circle around said blanket three to six times, and finally plopping herself down on some portion of said blanket, in no predictable or repeatable fashion that could be ascertained.

The second of those minutes was wondering where Bronx was. This was not out of any particular concern for him, but rather she worried that if she couldn't see him then perhaps he was off somewhere eating food that she could be eating instead. Brooklyn didn't remember Bronx coming in with Daddy Chad, so she surmised that he must still be out in the cold yard. Knowing that she was snuggling quite comfortably on a blanket at that moment gave her a swelling sense of awesomeness that lasted for the entirety of the third minute.

The last of the four awake minutes before she drifted into a peaceful, snore-filled slumber, was spent thinking about Daddy Kyle and Daddy Chad and how much she loved them.

Brooklyn didn't usually make particularly loud farts. They were almost always vile and disgusting olfactory experiences, but not habitually of the loud variety. Perhaps it was the cold temperature in the cabin, perhaps it was the flaked chicken she and Bronx had for dinner last night, or perhaps she was destined to wake up. Regardless, she let out a screamer that would most definitely have impressed an average full-grown chili-guzzling man. So then, it should come as no surprise that it was sufficient enough to jostle her awake. Having no linear concept of time, of course, she didn't realize that it hadn't been much more than an hour since her Daddies had left. She knew it had been a while, but no so long that she felt abandoned or anything heart-wrenching like that.

Snoring, however, does have the unfortunate side effect of making one parched. Brooklyn, an Olympic snorer, made her way from the couch to the kitchen and had a refreshing drink of water. Having expended more energy than initially planned, she made her way back to the couch and assumed her sleeping position once again. Sleep came much faster this time. Her eyes stayed open only for 24 seconds, just long enough to spy Betty and Veronica resting against the wall beside the back door, but not long enough and of course without the cognitive wherewithal to find it odd that Daddies had left them behind.

"Why the Hell didn't we bring Betty and Veronica?" Kyle exclaimed.
Chad, of course, knew the answer to that rhetorical question.
Chad also knew that Kyle knew the answer to that rhetorical question.
Kyle also knew that Chad knew that Kyle knew the answer to that rhetorical question.
However, in the interest of not initiating mid-apocalypse divorce proceedings, Chad kept the answer to himself and instead focused on the creatures approaching from the tree line in front of the helicopter.

In case you haven't been following these proceedings closely, Loyal Reader, earlier in the morning our heroes realized Bronx had bolted, and now time was very much of the essence.
Decisions had to be made, and they had to be made very, very quickly. The choice to pursue their little man on the backs of Donner and Blitzen, bastard cowardly reindeer they turned out to be, for example, was made so fast that it didn't even occur to Chad to grab Betty and Veronica from the cabin. Had this realization been made, it would very quickly have been further realized that these two lovely 'ladies' would have been virtually impossible to carry whilst riding on the backs of the large, galloping beasts.
Now that you're all caught up, we can rejoin Kyle and Chad as they once again found themselves at a loss as to how to comprehend what the fuck hey were witnessing.
In short, they were now watching a small horde of zombie elves advancing rather quickly upon their current position.
Exactly how did our heroes know that these were actual bona-fide zombie elves? We thought you'd never ask, Loyal Reader.

Imagine the pre-apocalyptic world, if you will.

Imagine, also, your average North American town.

In this zombie-free expanse, imagine that it is Christmas time in your average North American town.

During this average North American town's festive yuletide holiday season (with a distinct lack of the undead), imagine you are at the mall.

What mall, you may ask? Any mall. It doesn't matter. Don't get too caught up in the details, lest you ruin the fun for everyone involved, Loyal Reader.

In this particular mall, in some backwards armpit of your average zombie-lacking North American town, in whatever county of whatever state or province you have imagined, is a long line of your average townsfolk. Some of them are tall and some of them are short. Some of them are fat and some of them are skinny. You get the idea, Loyal Reader.

Imagine further that this extended line of average townsfolk is moving very slowly - at a rate seemingly slower than that of a bloody tectonic plate - but still, it's moving.

As the average townsfolk wait impatiently in this particular line for what seems like exactly three lifetimes, they finally arrive at their destination. You expect angels to be singing and villagers to be rejoicing at the very sight of such a miraculous occurrence, but none of this transpires. Malls are only very rarely the epicenter of Christian miracles. Still, the average townsfolk would have made it to their destination and that certainly has to account for something.

Not much, mind you, but something.

At the terminus of this line, in this painfully average mall, during this happy and merry holiday season, with not a zombie in sight, the holy grail is finally within sight; sitting not 15 feet away is a fat, bearded man in a red velvet suit. Let us impart upon him the name Theodore Pederson (Teddy Peddy to his friends - all seven of them), a morbidly obese alcoholic of a man. Every year in December, like clockwork, he scrapes himself off of whatever crusty object he happens to be chemically bonding with and works as a mall Santa to earn extra cash for his special yearly yuletide drinking binge.

As the average townsfolk stand proudly and squarely at the Santa's doorstep, eager to take their holiday photo with good old wheezing Teddy Peddy, one could swear that on approach, they could discern new and exciting blood vessel capillaries emerging from their hypertensive bliss and bursting on the tip of his nose.

Seated on his royal, perspiration-soaked mall throne, Santa rules with a cellulite fist. Day after December day, one can imagine him beckoning endless streams of average townsfolk - old and young alike - some believing he will orchestrate the arrival of their most cherished gift, while other dragged unwillingly to be held hostage for the cover of the family Christmas card.

Executing Santa's commands and, to be truthful, running the entire show each and every day in this imaginary Christmas scenario, would be Santa's elves. This imaginary mall doesn't have real elves, of course, just like it doesn't have the real Santa Claus - that would just be silly! Instead, in our imaginary scene the elves are played by two local high school freshmen - let's call them William (Billy) Jamieson and Daniel (Danny) Skinner - both proud and founding members of their school's Dungeons & Dragons Club (of course), both bullied mercilessly each and every week of the school year, and both with short, yet surprisingly lanky bodies. If you didn't know any better, Loyal Reader, you would have been hard pressed to not think these two were actually elves. Seriously, though, so similar were these young boys to the standard vision of an elf, that all they were lacking were the pointed ears.

Crazy, right?

Just as good old Saint Pickled Nick was dressed the part, so too were Billy and Danny. Imagine if you will, the classic elf costume; this little slice of humiliation was what each of the boys was sporting.

Adorning each of their heads was a long, tapered, curling green hat with a jingle bell at the tip, red triangles jutting out all around the bottom, and plastic prosthetic pointy eared tops protruding above the hat line. Their jackets were the same shade of green as their hats, but with the added bling of distasteful gold buttons running down the front, all the way down from the red-lined collars to the red-lined bottom hem. To add that extra bit of desperately needed flair to the ensemble, a red belt with matching gold buckle was fastened around the hips.

Had Billy and Danny any friends of social standing, this pair would have been suitably embarrassed to be seen in such outfits.

Luckily, they did not, and they were not.

As if not gaudy enough, the pants Billy and Danny were wearing is where the outfits began to race out of control. To be fair, they weren't really what one would consider to be pants at all, but rather spanx - an ungodly spandex/pants abomination that arose from the fiery pits of Atlanta, Georgia at the turn of the 21st century. Elf spanx, apparently, not only could inform interested viewers as to what possible religion Billy and Danny might subscribe, but they were also as loud as they were tight; each pair imprinted with concentric, repeating patters of horizontal stripes of alternating green, red, and white.

To add an extra protective measure against the average male elf constantly displaying a prominent bulge through his spanx, a pair of red 'outerwear underwear' was added. These looked more like thin, red diapers than anything else, but miraculously, they did somehow manage to bring the whole ensemble together in the boys' private areas.

Last, and most certainly not least, imagine both Billy and Danny wearing a pair of green fabric slippers - the ends of each one long and tapering and curling inwards. Each slipper was adorned with a lone jingle bell at the tip, one that perfectly matched the jingle bell located at the top of their respective green hats. Like the bottom hems of the hats and jackets, and the top hem of the latter, each slipper was lined with red around its most superior edges.

You might be wondering, Loyal Reader, why in the name of all that is fantabulous have we spent so much time letting our collective imaginations ruminate on the aforementioned elf-laden, yet oddly riveting scenario. The answer, as is usually the case, is as disarmingly simple as it is obvious: Billy and Danny, the unfortunate nergasmic heroes of our needlessly complex imaginings, were dressed exactly like the short and gaunt zombies that were currently zigzagging their way across the clearing and to the front of the helicopter.

As if you aren't already convinced, dear friends, their spot-on Christmas appearance is what led Kyle and Chad to believe that they were indeed bona fide zombie elves.

Killer zombie elves, as it turns out, weren't obscenely short; if hard pressed during the course of current events to hazard a guess, our heroes would have placed them somewhere in the general vicinity of 3 feet tall. They moved a bit faster than the larger 'normal' zombies did (being smaller and thinner would certainly assist in that department, one would think), something that one might argue could be the tiniest bit maddening if you were trying to flee from them, but in reality, not so much.

If still being hard pressed to answer questions about their current predicament, Kyle and Chad would somewhat shamefully admit that the two most disconcerting parts of this whole zombie elf affair were as follows:

> *- The juxtaposition of seeing what essentially resembled undead skinny kids in elf costumes ambling towards you at a good pace and making a happy jingling sound with every lurch.*
> *- Their tiny, beady, glowing red eyes (this, as they say in the business, Loyal Reader, is a not-so-cleverly-written callback).*

For our heroes this was almost too much to comprehend. The human brain wants to feel happy and jolly when it hears those bells, but then the sad realization hits that these zombie elves want nothing more than to devour your delicious, delicious flesh. It was incredibly difficult for their tiny little brains to reconcile.

As for their eyes, they were just creepy as shit.

Kyle and Chad reasoned that they would have no issues outrunning the elves and for a moment considered opening the sliding door nearest to the tree line (about 15 feet away, if you are keen to care about such things, Loyal Reader) and making a run for it. That was, of course, until Chad looked out the window on that side of the helicopter and saw what appeared to be even more zombie elves approaching from that direction. Kyle estimated there were about 25 zombie elves in the clearing (now about 30 feet from the front of the helicopter) and Chad could see at least that many now emerging through the tree line to their right. In small numbers, these pint-sized bastards probably wouldn't be too difficult to deal with, especially if our heroes had Betty and Veronica with them (see our earlier recount of the rhetorically vented statement by Kyle), but given that there appeared to be more than 50 of these creatures, bad things could and most likely would happen very quickly. Coupling all of this with the fact that there very well could be more of them - many, many more of them - in the surrounding woods, meant our heroes decided that they were going to stay put and see how this all played out.

Probably the most confusing thing about the behavior of the zombie elves was that they were displaying such directed movement. For some unknown reason, they were making their way directly to the helicopter. The average zombie one might encounter wandering around your average environment tends not to be so focused. The only instances that Kyle and Chad had ever witnessed the undead displaying such ambition and drive was when they would have been attracted by a loud noise or some kind of visually arresting stimulus. Our heroes found it unlikely that the helicopter would provide such ocular focus for the undead. It was a large machine, yes, but it wasn't moving or calling attention to itself in any way, shape, or form. Zombies would normally become attracted to things that displayed continued or periodic movement, something to grab their attention and hold on to it, otherwise, they would eventually amble away to go and find new shiny things to chase and hopefully eat.

These zombie elves, however, were on a mission. From the moment they emerged from across the clearing, they presumably only had glowing red eyes for the helicopter and our heroes that were hiding within. Likewise, the group that had just emerged from the right-hand side of the clearing seemed to have the same destination in mind.

This, my dear sweet Loyal Reader, was a real problem.

Kyle and Chad hypothesized that once the zombie elves reached the helicopter, they were likely to surround it and maintain that position until something distracted them. Further, once they reached the helicopter and started banging on the outside, as they would most certainly do any moment now, that would cause Bronx to start barking. This would cause them to become even more enthralled with what is inside the helicopter, causing them to bang some more. This would cause Bronx to bark some more, which would cause them to bang some more. And so, this positive feedback loop would likely continue until some sort of tipping point was reached and exhausted the system.

Exactly what this tipping point might be, our heroes dared not predict, but they knew in their hearts that it probably wouldn't be good.

The zombie elves were closing in on the helicopter, now no more than 5 feet away from the metal hull, with their jingling becoming more and more pronounced with every lurching step. It was at this very precarious juncture that the elven undead became distracted by a tremendously low and obnoxiously loud series of three booming sounds seeming to originate from quite some distance away and straight across the clearing.

The trio of thunderous noises was unmistakably something most everyone in the free world had heard before, the familiar calling card of none other than Santa Claus himself. As "Ho! Ho! Ho!" resonated deeply across the land, this had all the ingredients of something that threatened to make life very, very difficult for Kyle and Chad, bringing back more memories of the early days of *The Turning*.

CHAPTER 12

BACK BY POPULAR DEMAND: UNDEAD MARTIN

*L**et us begin, Loyal Reader, with the immortal and blessed words of Mazda:*
       "The new CX-9 takes the three-row, family crossover SUV into fresh territory. Crafted with an eye for the details that create a great drive, the CX-9 delivers exceptional handling and best-in-class standard torque and combined fuel economy. This is one SUV you'll love to drive."

Indeed, Kyle and Chad loved driving their CX-9. It was an exceptionally quiet and smooth experience that also, compared to their previous car, the CX-5, had a bit more pep under the hood. Given that our heroes were the only human members in their family of four, one could have argued that it did seem a tad bit excessive to buy a car that seats seven, but Kyle and Chad could remember sitting in the dealership and quite distinctly recalling a number of situations in years past where having that capability would have proven useful. 'Better to have the room for when you might need it,' was the phrase that bobbled around Chad's head as he agreed they go for the CX-9.

Little did Kyle and Chad realize that not too long after that, faced with the dawn of a zombie apocalypse and planning to pack up and head for the remotest area possible, they would be counting their lucky stars that they opted for purchasing a vehicle that had such an amazing amount of storage space.

Though it had only been a little over a day (exactly 27 hours and 12 minutes, to be precise) since their world turned upside down, inside out, and every other possible dimensional movement, Kyle and Chad felt a good measure of comfort knowing that they had made the decision to leave the chalet and travel to a more distant location. It was now the morning of May 23rd, and their situation, as they understood it, had finally begun to sink in.

The temptation to stay put in the chalet was quite strong. Our heroes had no evidence that hordes of zombies would come barreling down the highway in droves, making pit stop after pit stop in Ridgecrest Pines. There was, however, always a chance of that happening. Further, other humans were guaranteed to have survived The Turning.

Kyle and Chad were, based on the summaries and projections that they managed to glean from the internet the previous day, part of the twenty-or-so percent that were (un)lucky enough to have stayed human, footloose, and fancy free. This, of course, meant there were other people right now, possibly even somewhere in that very resort, in roughly the same boat as our heroes. Leaving the presumed safety of the chalet meant not only dealing with the flesh-craving undead, but also most likely having to cope with other people.

This was not such a good thing at all.

Let's be brutally honest, Loyal Reader - people suck. They suck big, hairy, sweaty horse balls, and that's just a fact of life. You need not look any further than a local news broadcast or website focused on the Pumpkin-In-Chief and its supporters to find daily evidence of just how frighteningly awful people can be. If one understands that this level of unpleasantness existed in the pre-zombie apocalypse world, imagine what righteous tardblogs people would become now.

The prospects are truly horrifying.

At least when you are dealing with zombies, you know what you're getting; they have a singular focus and won't backstab you as quickly as they'd look at you. A good number of the humans left alive would probably have been driven mad by the events unfolding around them and those that managed to somehow maintain their sanity would almost certainly do everything in their power to stay alive and Jennifer Aniston help anyone whom they perceived as a threat to that survival.

As with the general traits of a zombie apocalypse, post-apocalyptic television shows and movies have produced an almost endless play-by-play of just how dreadful people are envisioned to be, and let's take a moment for more brutal honesty - as a predictor, they're probably not wrong.

  As previously mentioned, our heroes felt reassured in having an action plan. Regardless as to whether or not the plan was the right thing to do, having made the decision to leave Ridgecrest Pines made Kyle and Chad feel like men of action and if nothing else, gave the illusion of some measure of control over the situation, no matter how apparent or real it may have been. This plan of action was formulated during the remainder of this second day of the apocalypse.
  Like the day before it, the second day was nerve-wracking, but for a whole new reason. While the first night after The Turning was uneventful, the next morning, just three hours and 39 minutes after deciding they were going to leave, the harsh reality of the dangers of this undead-filled new world made itself abundantly and horrifyingly clear with the unceremonious return of everyone's favourite zombie, Undead Martin.
  Traditionally, May wasn't the busiest season at Ridgecrest Pines; the major tourist rush didn't usually start until about the middle-to-end of June. As such, there weren't that many people staying at the resort the morning of The Turning. Of the three chalets on site, only one was occupied (by our heroes, no less), while only three of the twelve family suites had been rented out. Aside from these, the resort also had extensive camping grounds that covered a very respectable amount of acreage in the immediately adjacent forests.
  In total there were 156 campsites, and in the middle of summer virtually all of these would be full. This would most definitely have contributed not only to a local zombie epidemic at Ridgecrest Pines, but also the swift demise of our heroes. Luckily for Kyle and Chad, only 19 of these campsites had occupants in the wee hours of May 22nd, and of those, 15 were RV 'campers' with their resident zombies safely trapped inside their first-class camping accommodations.
  All of this contributed to a rather relatively low 'roaming zombie' count within the confines of Ridgecrest Pines. This, combined with the dense wilderness in the surrounding areas, meant our heroes were unlikely to face life threatening dangers on a frequent scale, as compared to those people who arose after The Turning in more urban and populated areas. Perhaps due to all this real estate just ripe for the wandering, the arrival of Undead

Martin - Kyle and Chad's first zombie visitor to their chalet - didn't occur until the second day.

According to the Official Record, Brooklyn and Bronx are the cutest little puppies that ever existed. The Official Record was, perhaps not that surprisingly, written by Chad - one of their two daddies. No doubt there were those people who might have found Chad's conclusions regarding historical global puppy cuteness to be a smidge biased, but, in Chad's own words, "They're all a bunch of hipster bastards!"
Touché.
Perhaps they totally are.
But what if they're not?
Regardless, the Official Record does stand (one must remain civilized, Loyal Reader, even in the face of global crisis). Unfortunately, at 11:53 am on May 23rd, the puppies' cuteness was temporarily overshadowed by sheer mortal dread.

Like any newly formed zombie, Undead Martin had been speeding around the general area of Ridgecrest Pines since first becoming acquainted with the side of our heroes' car slightly less than 24 hours ago. Still in his first fortnight of zombification, Undead Martin had, as expected, a single defining attribute to his existence - to race around his environment at top speed in search of flesh. Only when he heard a noise or detected visual changes in his environment did his movements become somewhat more directed. And may The Giant Spaghetti Monster in The Sky *help whatever/whomever managed to get his attention.*
As more luck would have it, at 11:53 am on the second day of The Turning, Undead Martin's attention was turned to our heroes' chalet.

It all happened very quickly Loyal Reader, and in poor Bronxie's defense, the events were shrouded in complete sugar-coated puppy innocence.

Undead Martin was of course doing what newly formed zombies do best - running at full tilt in whatever direction he happened to be running in - when he (for the second time in as many days) collided with Kyle and Chad's car. On your average day in **The Turning,** *this would not be cause for any real concern at all, apart from the requisite lamenting about laws of probability and such, of course.*

Undead Martin was not fazed in the least by his commendable car slam and was preparing himself to begin running off in some other direction of interest when he heard a sound. As we alluded to just a moment ago, this was the auditory contribution of a good little boy named Bronx. Not that Undead Martin knew the sound of a dog barking from any other sound in his undead environment. What he did know was that a) it was a sound, b) sounds often lead to living things, c) living things are made of flesh, and d) flesh is what he craved most in this world.

The sound of something crashing into our heroes' car was startling for them, that much we can all agree on. However, it was only startling in an 'unexpected sound suddenly appears' kind of way. The sound wasn't especially loud. However, given the comparable silence of the morning that preceded it, the sound did seem much louder than it actually was.

The sound, of course, also startled Bronx. As we alluded to already, unlike Brooklyn, Bronx's hearing was just fine, thank you very much. The sound startled him in an 'unexpected sound suddenly appears and will probably kill us all and even though my daddies can clearly hear it, I better warn them of this new source of impending doom' kind of way.

And so, with that, Bronx began to bark.

The sweet strains of Bronx's barking weren't that loud, by any stretch of the imagination, but they were audible, and in the end, that's all that mattered. Undead Martin was already making his way across the front lawn towards the next chalet in the row (having impressively and rather instantly recovered from slamming into the side of the car at breakneck speed) when he heard the muffled barking sounds. His reaction time was not only beyond extraordinary, but practically Olympic. A mere 3.16 seconds after hearing Bronx's barking, Undead Martin was at the front of the chalet, repeatedly bashing his body against the building with some serious amounts of force.

As you can imagine, Loyal Reader, Kyle and Chad were quite concerned when Bronx began to bark. However, they in no way ever thought that a zombie would be smashing into the door almost immediately after. This delightful turn of events was concerning on a couple of new and different levels.

The most obvious concern was that the violent slamming of Undead Martin into the door was now causing both puppies to bark; Brooklyn, again not to be outdone by her uncle, joined in the chorus of alerting her daddies to the outside sounds. Of course, Bronx and Brooklyn had no idea that it was none other than Undead Martin at the door making all the noise. All they knew was that something was making a noise and that daddies must be warned.

They're awesome doggies that way.

Once Kyle had grabbed Bronx and Chad had grabbed Brooklyn, our heroes made their way up to the master bedroom and secured the puppies inside. It was then that Kyle and Chad rested for a moment to regain their composure and brainstorm a way to deal with Undead Martin.

There were, realistically, a few things our heroes could do. The path of least resistance would be to see if poor Undead Martin tuckered himself out. After a couple of minutes of sitting in the bedroom and listening to the disgusting sounds coming from the door, it didn't appear like he was going to stop wanting to enter the chalet and eat them anytime soon.

Kyle and Chad mulled over the idea of quietly sneaking out the back door of the chalet and perhaps finding something to throw off in the distance to lure Undead Martin away from the chalet. This prospect seemed to have a good chance of succeeding, but if something went horribly wrong and our heroes accidentally got Undead Martin's attention, then things would almost certainly progress from bad to really fucking worse in no time at all.

It was in the middle of this upstairs bedroom discussion that Kyle noticed two words that could possibly spell the end to all of their Undead Martin-related troubles - Arctic King.

From the outside, the front of the chalet looked quite majestic. The first floor appeared very much like a really, really large and fancy version of a log cabin. The top floor housed the master bedroom and had a vaulted triangular ceiling. Two massive triangular bay windows filled the eastern wall of the bedroom. Along the bottom of each of the two windows were four smaller, rectangular windows, two of which could slide open sideways. Positioned in the smaller window on the right side was an air conditioner - the glorious Arctic King *- with 5,000 BTUs of raw, uncut, cooling power. While Kyle and Chad would normally be thankful for the cooling effect that your average air conditioner would provide, Kyle eyed this particular beast* *for an entirely different purpose - 5,000 BTUs of raw, uncut, zombie-smashing power.*

The plan was as delicious as it was a plan. The small rectangular window was just to the right of the center of the chalet, so getting the air conditioner that presently occupied this window to drop down upon Undead Martin seemed like quite the super-duper easy task. Undead Martin was currently occupying himself with the incessant banging and banging and banging and banging ... you get the idea, Loyal Reader ... roundabouts the front door, a door that was perfectly positioned in the center of the chalet's front side. Though Undead Martin's movements were erratic (to say the least) he did seem to focus his energies on one specific area of the front of the chalet.

See? A beautiful and vivacious a plan as there ever was, Loyal Reader. To summarize:

> **Step 1:** Kyle would drop the *Arctic King* onto the unsuspecting head of Undead Martin.
> **Step 2:** The aforementioned unsuspecting head of Undead Martin would be summarily gooified.
> **Step 3:** Undead Martin would then be rendered harmless to our heroes.

Unfortunately, the above simple, yet elegant plan did not work.

Had Undead Martin not been so spastic in his movements, the odds of the Arctic King *hammering him squarely in the head would actually have been quite high. Kyle had perfectly estimated the exact center of the deck in front of the door and the* Arctic King *indeed did arrive at that precise location. Unfortunately, though, Undead Martin's head was not occupying that precise location at that particular moment in time. Instead, Undead Martin's head was about a foot or so to the right of center and the* Arctic King's *46 lbs of raw, uncut, air-conditioning power resulted in an unfortunate, but otherwise quite impressive lopping off of Undead Martin's right arm at the shoulder joint.*

Icky-poo!

One might be inclined to think that this magnitude of damage to the poor zombie would result in at least some measurable difference in how he was behaving.

Unfortunately, Loyal Reader, one would be wrong.

It seems that losing a right arm did absolutely nothing to deter our dear Undead Martin from trying to get inside the chalet and eat the source of the earlier noises he had heard. Now, had the Artic King managed to mutilate one of Undead Martin's legs, then that would at least have provided a mobility issue. Losing a right arm, however, did not. In fact, whilst gazing down below at the bloody results of his efforts, Kyle was convinced that Undead Martin was instead displaying newfound vim and vigor towards his current mission.

Ugh.

Chad was watching the brachial carnage unfold from the left side window and drew a similar impressed-yet-depressed conclusion. Realizing that their options were limited, Chad volunteered to take a stab at the other plan of action they came up with - sneaking out the back door and throwing something to distract Undead Martin.

Chad had no sooner volunteered when Kyle pointed out the painfully obvious - why risk life and limb going outside to distract the zombie by throwing something when you could accomplish the very same end result from the comfort and safety of the chalet? Chad thought about this for a few seconds, still unsure what in the name of all that is good and true in the Universe Kyle meant, and then, as usual, his brain finally agreed to comply with his neural request and he understood what most everyone else on the planet would have comprehended pretty much instantaneously - our heroes should be able to find something in the chalet big enough to throw from one of the windows.

Yet another plan that displayed healthy doses of simplicity and elegance.

Again, Loyal Reader, in case you're not paying attention, let us provide yet another delicious tidbit of a summary:

Step 1: One or both of our heroes would throw something of some sufficient structural fortitude from one of the upstairs windows of the chalet.

Step 2: The something of sufficient structural fortitude that was thrown from one of the upstairs windows of the chalet would land on the ground and make a rather loudish noise.

Step 3: The rather loudish noise made by the throwing of something of sufficient structural fortitude from one of the upstairs windows of the chalet would distract Undead Martin.

Step 4: Undead Martin, now distracted by the loudish noise caused by the throwing of some of sufficient structural fortitude from one of the chalet windows, would race off in some direction away from the chalet, leaving Kyle and Chad once more Undead Martin-free.

Luckily for our heroes, the above simple, yet elegant plan eventually did work, but only tangentially and not because of anything performed by Kyle and Chad.

Of course.

Given that our heroes were in the throes of a zombie apocalypse, there really was no worry about what could or could not be thrown out the window. It's not like Kyle and Chad were going to be charged for breaking things when they 'checked out' of Ridgecrest Pines the following morning. With this in mind, Chad grabbed the alarm clock from the bedside table and launched it out towards the gravel road in front of the chalet. The clock flew through the air, did 16.5 revolutions, and came firmly to rest on the chalet's front lawn. The gravel road was difficult to reach for Chad, who - according to the laws of biomechanics - did not possess the arm length or muscular requirements to throw an alarm clock the necessary distance to reach the road.

The alarm clock did, however, make a dull thud.

This thud, however, was not loud enough to distract Undead Martin, whose own noises from bashing into the front door were loud enough, our heroes estimated, to compete with a fucking chorus of chainsaws.

97

Realizing this, Kyle decided to try tossing one of the bedside lamps out onto the road. Unlike Chad's rather miserable attempt, the lamp did travel further, but, like Chad's attempt, it did not manage to land on the road. Instead, the lamp managed to get smashed when it hit the lawn and made a considerably louder noise than the still intact alarm clock laying some distance away. Undead Martin did register this sound, which was a moral victory. He paused his incessant pounding of the front door for 0.88 seconds after the smash, looked in the general vicinity of where the sound originated from, and then promptly returned to his door bashing.

"Dammit!" Kyle mumbled.

Our heroes decided, quite rightly, that even though the sound of the lamp shattering on the lawn was enough to distract Undead Martin ever so temporarily, a sound that was perhaps sharper and louder might actually get him to abandon his current post. This, of course, as it always seems to do, led Kyle and Chad to the very sad realization that the only item outside the front of the chalet that not only possessed the necessary noise generating power and was located close enough to reach by throwing something out of the small chalet window was their car, innocently sitting in the driveway.

As you probably gleaned from the two previous failed attempts described above, Loyal Reader, the chalets at Ridgecrest Pines were set back a fair bit from the road. A soft gravel short driveway connected to said road and led to a beautiful and winding stone path that wove its way up to the front door. As such, chalet occupants had to walk a good distance to make it to the entrance. Under normal circumstances, some patrons have viewed this as a minor annoyance while most found it a quaint way of adding old timey ambiance. On this particular day, Kyle and Chad were quite thankful that their car was set back such a distance from the front of the building. If our heroes were able to hit the car with a large enough item, the sound should not only be loud and sharp enough to disturb Undead Martin, but the noise would be set far enough back to get him to run in that direction and away from the chalet, without, hopefully, realizing that the car was the source of the noise. Having Undead Martin simply shift his repeated whacking from the chalet door to the car would definitely not go down in history as one of the brightest moments from Kyle and Chad.

With the puppies safely located in the bedroom, our heroes set off on a scavenger hunt around the chalet looking for something small enough to fit through one of the windows and yet with enough oomph so as to make sufficient zombie enticing noises. Chad was assigned the kitchen while Kyle took the living room, bathroom, and hallways. After a few minutes of searching and collecting their three best candidate items each, our heroes reconvened in the bedroom for the moment of truth.

Chad had brought up a coffee pot from the Hamilton Beach 12-cup coffee maker, a Sunbeam 2-slice toaster, and a 2-liter bottle of Coke Zero. Kyle returned to the bedroom with a vintage glass ashtray from above the fireplace, a 5"x7" pewter picture frame with a mediocre photograph of some local mountain or something or other inside it, and a toilet plunger.

Kyle, as expected, was elected the thrower. The logic for this decision can be broken down into three easy-to-swallow bite-sized reasons:

- Chad sucked at throwing,
- The situation was dire, and
- The previous two reasons pretty much covered it.

Choosing which of the six items to begin with was somewhat problematic as there was a suite of considerations affecting this decision. First, and perhaps most importantly, Kyle wanted to make sure that he actually hit the car. Given there were six items to choose from, odds were that he would be successful in hitting the car for most of them, but they all were different sizes and weighed different amounts - two factors that would have a direct bearing on the likelihood of successful car hitting. Second, and not as immediately critical, but still somewhat imperative in the long run, was where on the car the item(s) should hit. Hitting the windshield or the sunroof could definitely result in cracking the glass and compromising their structural integrity. Given that our heroes' car was going to play a critical role in getting them out of Ridgecrest Pines and to greener, hopefully zombie-free pastures, an intact windshield and sunroof would go a long way to making that journey more feasible. Ideally, the thrown item would hit the metal hood of the car or, failing that, the non-sunroof portion of the car's top. Unfortunately, these were the only reliable metal targets as the car was parked almost perfectly perpendicular to the front of the chalet, making the sides not ripe for the hitting.

With all of the aforementioned factors swirling around in Kyle's mind, he decided that the vintage ashtray was the most suitable choice for his first throw. It was small enough for him to grasp with one hand and was solid enough (looked to be made of marble or some such material) that when (if) it hit the car's hood (hopefully) the sound would be loud and strong (again, hopefully).

Given the amount of time Kyle spent lining up his throw, you might be tricked into thinking that this was some hardcore training regime for the Olympics. After no less than eight practice swings, Kyle was ready for the real thing. He pulled back his arm and began throwing in an arc so beautiful and true that there was almost no question that the vintage marble ashtray would make contact dead center of the car's hood. A casual observer would be quite correct in assuming that it would take something on the order of a massive explosion to interrupt such a beautiful and true swing. Unfortunately for Kyle, a massive explosion did take place just as he was beginning his swing, and he was very much startled.

Consequently, the vintage marble ashtray flew only one quarter of the distance to the car and landed softly on the well-manicured lawn.

Coincidence, Loyal Reader?

No, of course not.

Just over thirty-three kilometers away, just seconds before Kyle was beginning his magical vintage marble ashtray throw, something caused an enormous explosion in Revelstoke, British Columbia. Of course, our heroes had no idea what caused the explosion, and actually didn't even know that it had occurred in Revelstoke. What they did know was that the sound was fucking loud and came from somewhere to the west of their present location.

Though the sound of the explosion caused the immediate effect of the vintage marble ashtray veering wildly off course, it had the secondary effect of causing Undead Martin to finally be completely absorbed by something other than the front door of the chalet.

As yet more luck would have it, the chalet faced west. As such, at the completion of the thunderous sound from the explosion, Undead Martin ran away from chalet, across the lawn and road, and into the forest.

While the mystery explosion seemed to have solved the dilemma of what to do about Undead Martin and thus seemed to have saved our heroes from having to damage their only source of transportation, it did raise a number of other questions, first among them being what in the holy crapstash had *happened? The answer to that question, of course, was completely lost on our heroes. What was not lost, however, was realizing the sheer amount of luck involved in what had just transpired. The odds of such a perfectly timed sound of that magnitude appearing just when our heroes needed it the most seemed so remote as to defy quantification. Clearly, this level of providence couldn't possibly be duplicated again in their lifetime.*

But then, as you are perhaps divining at this very moment Loyal Reader, just seven months later, it totally did.

Much like Undead Martin back in Ridgecrest Pines, the zombie elves that surrounded the helicopter were sufficiently distracted by the booming "Ho! Ho! Ho!" emanating from the nearby hills to the east. The elves immediately began walking towards the direction of the sound. As you can imagine, Kyle and Chad were once more filled with disbelief that the Universe would find the time and occasion to provide them with this level of fortune. Our heroes looked at each other, shrugged, and displayed an amazing amount of casual acceptance with how these events were unfolding.

Kyle and Chad weren't given very long to bask in their casual acceptance before another in a series of screwed up events decided to pay an afternoon visit.

The zombie elves, now shambling across the clearing at a reasonably brisk pace through the snow, no longer appeared to be a threat to our heroes, so long as Kyle and Chad gave them no reason to turn around. Waiting until the zombies were over halfway across the clearing, our heroes (and Bronx tucked away safely in his carrier) decided to follow at a cautiously safe distance. If indeed Santa himself was responsible for drawing the elves away from our heroes, then perhaps answers were not that far away.

Any potential long-term threat that the zombie elves may have represented, vanished quite swiftly and completely when five men - very, very good-looking men, as it turned out (like, really, really good-looking men) - emerged from the tree line in front of the elves. Dressed in military fatigues (which increased their level of hotness by no less than a factor of twelve, in case you were biting at the chomp to learn, Loyal Reader) and armed with sledgehammers, the five burly, bearded, insanely attractive men took exactly two minutes and twenty-six seconds to neutralize the roughly 50 or so zombie elves.

Anyone who knew Kyle and Chad knew that the sight of five beefy, bearded, military men was not a sight that our heroes were inclined to avoid. In fact, such a sight was more likely to have a blinking neon sign above it that read *This Way, Kyle and Chad!* This was, however, the zombie apocalypse, and not only had the world changed, but our heroes had to change with it. Kyle and Chad had encountered other human survivors on just three separate occasions since *The Turning*, and as we believe has been said before, Loyal Reader, they did not go well.

Consequently, no amount of raw, physical attraction was enough for Kyle and Chad to stick around and find out why these five zombie-elf killing specimens happened to appear in this particular clearing at this particular time.

Well, that's not exactly true, Loyal Reader.

There did exist some wildly outrageous tipping point that would, in fact, result in Kyle and Chad running at full speed towards these men, but common decency prohibits any exposition of those particular circumstances. Given that these specific conditions were not currently at play, our heroes promptly did a one-eighty in a commendable effort to leave the clearing without being noticed.

However, as Kyle and Chad turned around, they were rather quickly discovered. Not by the five gorgeous specimens at the far edge of the clearing mind you, but instead by the solitary insanely attractive man now standing before them in the shadow of the helicopter.

CHAPTER 13

RANGER FUCKING ROD

Most everyone knows, Loyal Reader, that beauty, they say, is in the eye of the beholder. Everyone, that is, except for the aforementioned inhabitants of Bastardstown, of course.

In our current situation, two of these beholders existed - Kyle and Chad. Our heroes, as we are apt to call them, were currently standing in front of a staggeringly beautiful man who had just emerged from a shadow cast by a helicopter that had, at some point in the past, plopped itself down on the edge of a forest-enclosed clearing. Though our heroes thought it would be rather impossible, he was, by every single ocular metric available to them, at least an order of magnitude more good looking than any of the five members of the Beefy McBearly clan (as Chad had so lovingly mentally named them) that had earlier used a clinical approach to completely dismantle the zombie elves and were now walking across the clearing towards the helicopter.

"My name is Ranger Rod," he stated in an authoritative, sexy, and downright reassuring voice.

Of course, you are, Chad thought to himself and giggled furiously.

"Are you guys okay?"

Kyle and Chad both nodded in agreement, unable to convince their brains to form anything resembling a complete sentence at this particular moment in time. Still dumbfounded by the appearance of six people in the clearing and in a schoolboy tizzy about how amazingly handsome Ranger Rod and the other men were, it is interesting to note that both Kyle and Chad would have nodded in agreement to just about absolutely anything he said. He *literally* could have told them that he was sent by a secret government organization to remove their vital internal organs, and their responses would have been no different.

By now, the five really, really good-looking men from across the clearing had arrived and stood stoically at attention in a perfect line (of course) behind the man who called himself Ranger Rod. It was remarkable just how similar the six men were to one another. Chad, true to form, surmised that it appeared to be the result of some spectacularly successful homosexual eugenics experiment gone horribly, horribly right. All of the previously mentioned ruggedly handsome features that the five subordinates displayed were ticked off in the Ranger Rod column as well, but the latter just seemed to take every single one of those characteristics to a whole new sexy level.

Enough of our prattling narrative, Loyal Reader, and on to the issue at hand.

Ranger Rod finally broke the 33-second awkward silence that followed his initial introduction.

"I suppose you're both wondering why we've come looking for you."

Again, there was only complete silence accompanied by the familiar nodding of heads from Kyle and Chad.

"It's okay to speak, you know," Ranger Rod noted before continuing.

Our heroes continued to nod.

"Actually, as it turns out, we were sent to find you by the Government," Ranger Rod continued.

"Shut the front door!" Chad said with just a bit too much exuberance than the current situation called for.

Ranger Rod looked at our heroes, turned his head slightly, and squinted his eyes. In the animal world, this is a near universal sign of concerned confusion (not to be confused with the completely different look of confused concern).

We say near universal, Loyal Reader, because of a bitch-faced asshole of an animal called the cassowary. Don't feel bad if you've never heard of this righteous cockhole of a critter as it can only be found being a complete dick in the rain forests of Indonesia, New Guinea, and Australia.

If, however, you were unfortunate enough to stumble across an unsuspecting cassowary, you'd recognize the shit stain of a bird as soon you laid eyes on it.

How? Great question! Let's have some fun Loyal Reader and do a mental exercise.

Imagine an ostrich. Got it? Excellent. Now, imagine the head of that ostrich all gussied up in the cheapest makeup available and applied by a four-year-old child with a penchant for exploding clowns. Why? Perhaps for an evening out on the town? Perhaps as the opening act for the one Australian drag queen to rule them all, Ms. Courtney Act? Perhaps just for kicks? Perhaps we'll never know, and that's ok. Regardless, being able to imagine that hideously fabulous ostrich will give you an idea of what a cassowary looks like - a bird splashed with Technicolor and possessing a terminal case of resting bitch face.

Some people may perchance argue that the cassowary gets a bad rap, but they're just wrong. Those cassowary-loving hipsters would of course note that only one person in recorded history has ever been confirmed to have been killed by one of these dick fuckers, and that was way, way back in April of 1926, and the 16-year-old in question might have been a bit … abled in a slightly more challenging way … as some might say.

That being said, though not a ruthless and efficient killer, the published list of incidents where a cassowary has attacked an otherwise innocent bystander and caused some reasonable harm turns out to be fucking huge.

Why?

The answer is obvious, Loyal Reader. Haven't you been listening? We really *do* need to work on your attention span.

Imagine someone - let's say a tourist - is walking through a well-manicured trail in a section of the southern lowland tropical rainforest of New Guinea. Our tourist, a 27-year-old male who we'll give the initials K.H., is enjoying his visit and has been snapping an impressive average of 28.2 pictures per minute since arriving. As young Mr. K.H. is innocently strolling through the walkways, he comes upon a majestic creature occupying the trail in front of him - a female majestic creature, no less, who we shall, for the purposes of our exposition, name Matilda.

K.H. correctly surmises that Matilda is a bird. The beautiful black and bushy feathers that cover her rotund body are quite the dead giveaway. However, what is not so clear and what doesn't quite compute to K.H. is how oddly enormous Matilda is - standing 6 feet tall at the apex of her gaudy, multicoloured head. Her legs are long and thick, each with three toes tipped with 5-inch dagger-like claws. Matilda's head and neck are an artist's nightmare - an abhorrent visage of neon teal, brilliant indigo, and outrageous magenta. As imposing as Matilda's height, stature, and warning coloration are, it is the death stare that disturbs poor K.H. the most.

Matilda looks seriously pissed.

Our protagonist had never seen a cassowary before and thus was not prepared for this mid-trail encounter he now found himself fully embroiled in. As such, perplexity was the order of the day.

Given the totality of these circumstances, one can't blame poor K.H. for what happened next. He did what most people do when they are confronted by a puzzling situation - he cocked his head and squinted his eyes, trying to make sense of the situation unfolding before him. Matilda, unfortunately, like most other individuals of her species, did not register his head actions as confusion. In the world of the cassowary, these exact movements are considered a display of aggression.

K.H., poor fucker that he was, had no idea that Matilda spends each waking hour of her life looking for a good old-fashioned fight.

Can you can see where we are going with this Loyal Reader? In a matter of seconds (4.3, to be exact), Matilda registered what she believed to be this pathetic animal's intent to battle her for complete and total domination over the rainforest.

As such, she attacked.

Matilda's strikes were as stylish and beautiful as they were lethal. She didn't peck at K.H. like some gutter-trash peasant bird (no offense, chickens and pigeons everywhere), but rather, she used her formidable leg strength and razor-sharp claws.

The outcome of this confrontation, we are sad to report, was never ever in doubt. Armed only with his digital camera and seven multigrain crackers (gross!) and unable to match Matilda's top running speed of 50 km/h, K.H. was left to her deadly devices. Luckily for him, though, Matilda was not completely without mercy. Realizing her opponent was no match for her ninja skills, Matilda left him broken and bleeding, but still very much alive on that fateful rainforest trail.

Kyle and Chad were confused.

Like, really, really, confused.

This confusion was mixed with a liberal dose of *'we can't believe this fucking shit is happening'* and a dash of *'this is too good to be true.'* It was, in reality, the mixture of these three competing sentiments that led to the looks that crossed their faces when this man, apparently named Ranger Rod, told them in no uncertain terms that the Government had deemed the pair of them important enough to send a team of six sexy men to find them.

Bronx was confused as well. Situated inside the pet carrier on Kyle's back, his acute hearing registered the voice as not being one of his daddies and barked accordingly.

Kyle spoke to Bronx is soft, gentle tones, doing his best to ease Bronx's anxiety. "Shh! It's okay little man. Calm down."

"The Government?" Chad asked in bewilderment, uttering his first coherent words to Ranger Rod.

"Yes," Ranger Rod replied.

"They want to find *us*?" Kyle added, sounding just as baffled as Chad did.

"The Government?" Chad asked again, seemingly oblivious to the fact that he was repeating the same words over again.

Ranger Rod's expression had now changed from slight confusion to slight irritation, mixed with a liberal dose of understanding. We're not sure there is a word for that look, Loyal Reader, and you'll be happy to know that we aren't about to bow to tradition and make one up on the fly here. "Yes, the Government. They dispatched myself and my men to find you and bring you back."

"Back to where?" Chad asked. "Are you, like, the Prime Minister or something?" As these words escaped his mouth, everyone, but especially Chad, realized how insanely idiotic that sounded.

One of the five beautiful men began to chuckle, but a quick darting look from Ranger Rod brought an immediate end to such a momentary break in protocol.

Kyle looked over to Chad, wide-eyed. "Is he the Prime Minister? Is that *really* where your brain went with that information?"

Chad, embarrassed by his verbal slip, became just a tad bit defensive and tried his best to save face in front of their apparent newfound saviors. "It's a zombie apocalypse; anything could happen."

"Sending the Prime Minister on a reconnaissance mission to retrieve the two of us? No way is that a possibility."

"Umm, yeah. It totally could. In fact-"

Ranger Rod, now visibly increasing his level of irritation, interjected. "If you two ninnies are done arguing about who might be the leader of the-"

"Ninnies?! Did he seriously just call us ninnies? Chad exclaimed in disbelief as he turned towards Kyle. "Is that a backhanded gay comment?"

"So help me if either one of you interrupts me again, I will leave the two of you and your dog here in the middle of absolutely nowhere."

Chad, doing his best impression of a scolded student, put up his hand.

"Oh, dear sweet Zombie Jesus," Ranger Rod said, as he rolled his eyes. "What is it? And you had better think long and hard about what you're going to say to me. It had better not be that you need to go potty or something."

Long and hard, Chad giggled to himself and smiled.

"We actually have two dogs, Mr. Ranger Rod. Or is it Mr. Rod? Or just Rod? Or perhaps even Ranger? Whatever. You see, the other one, her name is Brooklyn, she is just the cutest little princess that ever existed, but she doesn't hear too well and we had to leave her back at our cabin because her uncle, Bronx is his name, and he's the cutest little dude in the whole wide world, the one in the carrier on Kyle's back, bolted from our back yard after we had rescued Santa's reindeer in an attempt to find Santa himself after we heard a noise this morning, leading us here."

"Okay, you," Ranger Rod demanded as he pointed squarely at Chad. "What's your name?"

"Chad."

"Okay. Chad. You will not speak to me anymore unless I personally have pointed directly at you and have asked you, and only you, a question. If you think you want to speak and I haven't pointed at you and you haven't been asked a question, reconsider uttering a single syllable."

It took all of Kyle's will power not to laugh.

Ranger Rod's expression softened somewhat, and he continued. "Look, I know you're both confused. I get it. But, the longer we stand here arguing about who sent who and who the ninnies are, the longer it's going to take to get you two and your dog-"

Ranger Rod shot a look squarely at Chad, almost defying him to say something. "-your two dogs, to safety. Here's what's going to happen. I will tell you everything I know, and trust me, I know only the bare minimum. Everything else is classified and above my pay grade. Then, once you're both all caught up, we can go back to my transport unit and get the flying fuck out of here. How does that sound?"

"I can live with that," Kyle responded.

Ranger Rod pointed at Chad.

"Sounds good," Chad added, looking suitably admonished from their previous exchange.

"Fantastic," Ranger Rod replied and began his explanation. "I work for a group of people. Don't bother asking the name or even what it really

108

represents now. Suffice to say that it is as close as we're able to come at this point to a functioning Government. With the number of people that turned or died last year, it's amazing that any semblance of leadership still exists, but it does. What remained of the Government started to build a series of safe zones in urban areas not completely destroyed in the aftermath. Slowly, over the past seven months, survivors have been amassing in these zones. Initially, the zones consisted of people who were lucky or skilled enough to make it there on their own. However, over the past few months, as the populations have steadily grown, more and more resources have been amassed at these locations, including access to vehicles for searching the surrounding areas for other survivors."

Chad, good little ninny that he was, put up his hand.

"Am I pointing at you? Am I asking you a question right now?"

Chad looked blankly at Ranger Rod. Chad's expression tinged with the unmistakable look of shame.

"Christ on a cracker! What?" Ranger Rod yelled.

Blushing, Chad said, "I kinda really need to go pee. Ever since you mentioned going potty, it's all my kidneys have been able think about."

"Good fucking Lord, you are a righteous pain in the ass!"

"Trust me," Chad interjected, "you have no idea."

Kyle again pursed his lips as tight as he could, but still let out the slightest of laughs.

"Just go!" Ranger Rod yelled and pointed behind the helicopter.

Chad shuffled off out of sight and had what he estimated to be the third most satisfying pee of his life. While in the midst of this heavenly urination, our hero couldn't hear anyone talking, and could only assume that Kyle was trying his best not to succumb to a fit of laughter while Ranger Rod mentally counted down his ten favorite ways of killing Chad on this magical December afternoon.

Amazingly, Chad was 100% correct on both counts.

Once Chad returned to Kyle's side, Ranger Rod glared at him with sufficient dread and continued. "If there are no questions, we should be on our way."

"I have a question," Chad said.

"Of course, you do."

"No need to get snippy," Chad retorted. "This just doesn't make any sense at all to me. We have been hiding out in a cabin out here in the backwoods of Northern British Columbia for the better part of the last seven months. How the hell did you know where to find us?"

"I'm afraid that information is classified," Ranger Rod replied.

"And how did you know that we weren't zombies ourselves or even that we might be dead?" Chad added.

"That's classified as well."

Kyle added his two cents. "These are questions that deserve answers. How do we know this is all on the up and up? And what made those booming sounds?"

"There's no way you could know," Ranger Rod responded. "And just in case it didn't sink in the first three times, *IT! IS! CLASSIFIED!* Jesus! *I don't even know the answers to some of these questions!*"

"Well, you don't have to be rude about it," Chad said.

"I do have one more little question," Kyle said sheepishly.

Ranger Rod shook his head in disbelief. "You've got to be fucking kidding me."

"Actually, no. But trust me, it's a very fun question."

Contempt dripped off of Ranger Rod's reply. "Well, if it's very fun, then by all means, make my fucking day."

Chad couldn't help himself and interjected. "Are you sure your name isn't Ranger Snippy?"

Kyle quickly asked his question in an attempt to prevent Ranger Rod from disemboweling his husband.

"Remember how Chad said that we were searching for Santa? That's how all of this started in the first place. Yesterday something hit our cabin and I saw Santa being dragged away. Have you guys seen him at all or just the zombie Christmas elves?"

"That's-"

"Oh wait! Let me guess," Kyle said. "*Classified.*"

The emphasis Kyle placed on that last word was nothing short of magnificent.

Chad had never been prouder of his husband.

This time, there was laughter from one of Ranger Rod's men and even the head honcho himself managed to crack a smile, microscopic as it was.

"*Now* you're getting it," Ranger Rod said. He turned around, gestured to his men and then to Kyle and Chad. "Let's head home, boys."

110

CHAPTER 14

O-NAY UCK-TRAY ODAY-TAY

Navigating their way back to the rangers' truck turned out to not be as awful of an experience as our heroes anticipated.

The group continued across the expanse to the tree line from where the five soldiers had emerged to exterminate the zombie elves. It was, in fact, like walking through a minefield of blood, guts, and other random body parts just to reach the edge of the clearing. From what Kyle and Chad could discern, they were now travelling perpendicular to the clearing where they found Bronx and venturing possibly further and further away from the cabin and it's precious Brooklyn-based cargo.

As they entered the forest and began to make their way deeper and deeper into the woods, Bronx became restless. Walking a few meters behind Ranger Rod and his men, Kyle thought it probably wouldn't be an issue if Bronx was let out of his carrier and walked along with our heroes through the forest, just in case he needed to do his business whilst stretching his legs. *With any luck,* Kyle thought, *Ranger Rod wouldn't even notice.* Kyle understood, of course, that if they did notice, Ranger Rod's impatient and caustic military disposition meant that it most certainly would become an issue.

The past seven months had given Kyle and Chad ample opportunity to fine tune handling the puppies while on the move, and they had it down to a science. As Kyle kept walking, Chad retrieved Bronx's leash from the side pocket, opened up the zipper that stretched from one side, across the top, and to the other side, revealing their dashing little man. Bronx was very excited to escape from his comfy little prison and gave Daddy Chad lots of thank you kisses as his leash was attached and he was picked up and placed on the snow-covered ground.

The plan went off without a hitch, as Ranger Rod and his troop didn't even notice that Chad had freed Bronx from the carrier. It was a good thing that he did too, as Bronx apparently was in desperate need of the bathroom break. Events of the number 1 and number 2 variety occurred and though the inevitable stopping for Bronx to complete his business caused our heroes to lag behind a little bit, none of the soldiers seemed the wiser. That was, of course, until Ranger Rod turned around to check on the status of his two charges.

As Ranger Rod turned his head to survey the situation, he did a full stop, turned, and faced our heroes. Completely in tune with their commander, the three men flanking his left and the two men flanking his right did the same. Kyle and Chad froze, thinking that the metaphorical shit was about to metaphorically hit the metaphorical fan.

Bronx, of course, was oblivious to the rising tensions. He was blissfully unaware that six remarkably good-looking individuals were now standing less than 10 feet ahead of him. Bronx, however, did have the wherewithal to notice that he and his daddies had stopped. In fact, he was very thankful for this brief respite as the tree trunk he was now positioned bedside was just aching to be sniffed, and he was all too happy to accommodate such an urgent arboreal request.

Adventures in tree trunk sniffing were, unfortunately, cut short by daddy Chad leading Bronx cautiously forward. Ranger Rod, upon realizing that his company now included a leashed dog, didn't say a word. Of course, de didn't need to. Ranger Rod simply stared at Chad and gestured with his right hand for them to come forward. Chad began to speak; perhaps to apologize or perhaps to explain that cute little doggies everywhere sometimes need to go to the bathroom, but it was to no avail. Ranger Rod cut him off before Chad managed to vocalize a single syllable by raising his right index finger. Chad knew better than to test Ranger Rod's already magnificently frayed patience.

Just as our heroes were within two feet of Ranger Rod and his men, Bronx finally picked up the scent of these strange, new people in front of him, and he began to get very excited. In his mind, this represented the opportunity for someone to throw his ball so that he could go fetch that ball and bring it back again, providing ample opportunity for that someone to then throw the ball again. Bronx no doubt had visions of this cycle repeating itself over and over until the end of time, and this made him even more excited. Chad did his best to calm Bronx down, petting him and holding him down so that he didn't jump up on Ranger Rod's legs and spell certain doom for our heroes.

"Who's a cute widdle boy?" Ranger Rod cooed in a childishly comical voice. He crouched down and began to pet Bronx, letting the excited little boy jump up and give him big, wet kisses on his face. "You're a cute widdle boy! Yes, you are!"

Kyle looked at Chad.

Chad looked at Kyle.

The five men alternated between looking at each other and the spectacle before them.

"Well this is very unexpected," Kyle said in a bewildered tone.

Chad, unsurprisingly, was similarly dumbfounded. "I know, right?"

Ranger Rod appeared to be having the time of his life, showering Bronx with affection. "Alright men, two-minute puppy break!" he bellowed.

"Is this really happening right now?" Chad asked. No one responded.

The five men, good soldiers that they were, surrounded Bronx, petting him and playing with him in the snow. Bronx, thoroughly enjoying all the attention was in fact hoping against all hope that one of them had a ball and that they would throw said ball so that he could go fetch that ball and bring it back again, providing yet another ample opportunity for them to throw the ball again. Though no ball was produced, Bronx was a good sport and basked in the friendliness that was displayed.

"Is it just me or does this actually make them that much hotter?" Chad asked, knowing full well that it did.

"It's not you," Kyle said.

Ranger Rod's internal clock was most impressive. The impromptu puppy break lasted two minutes and fourteen seconds, at which time the men were ordered back into formation and Bronx to be placed back in his carrier. Kyle and Chad were most amenable to this as it was still the middle of winter and poor Bronx wasn't wearing any outdoor booties.

His daddies had been gifted booties for him a number of years back, but they were of the indoor passive aggressive variety and summarily sacrificed to the appropriate deity in an elaborate and needlessly complex ceremony shortly thereafter.

Back to his stern and commanding self, Ranger Rod ordered the group to keep marching onwards towards the truck, which, as Kyle and Chad would soon find out, wasn't that much further, taking only another 12 minutes of walking through the forest to reach the small road where the truck had been parked.

Unfortunately, though, 18 zombies, all of which singularly focused on this military vehicle, surrounded the poor, lonely truck.

The sight of a gaggle of zombies surrounding the rangers' truck would have actually been comical, had the sad reality of them being flesh-eating undead not gotten in the way of fully appreciating the current situation. The zombies looked like extras from a poorly cast, B-level 80s ski movie; the majority of them underlined the age-old stereotype of the hipster exploring a winter wonderland. The zombies were clad in checkered flannel with coordinated scarves, mittens, and the douchiest of thin fabric toques, the kind that an up-and-coming hipster would wear not keep their head warm, but because it completed the look.

Making the scene even more amusing, Loyal Reader, was that a number of the undead were wearing snowshoes, skis, or snowboards. One could only imagine that wherever they came from, there must be a whole population of them still attached to their skis and snowboards, and just flailing around on the ground, unable to make any meaningful headway in their environment.

Our heroes thought it miraculous that the majority of zombies wearing these items managed to find the coordination to move about and arrive at the transport truck with any real success. This conundrum, though, would have to wait. There was the pesky issue of dealing with these zombies first.

Trained for just such an occasion, Ranger Rod and his men wasted no time in taking care of the snow-loving undead.

"You two stay here and, for the love of all that is holy, please stay out of trouble," he thundered to Kyle and Chad.

"Not a problem," Chad responded. Not having Betty or Veronica with them, and not wishing to get in the way of the six sexy killing machines, the duo was ever so happy to comply.

It took no time at all for Ranger Rod and his men to vanquish their undead opponents. Though a tiny bit underwhelming from a cinematic point of view, there was the consolation of watching burly soldiers doing what they seemed to do best.

Once the maiming, head gooificationing, and overall dismembering had been completed, Ranger Rod vocalized what was on everyone's mind.

"What the fuck was that!?" he exclaimed. "There is absolutely no fucking way that these bastards made it here on their own. Someone who knew we were on this mission must have brought them here. This makes no goddamn sense!"

Subsequent inspection of the truck made the situation even more confusing. Though there was plenty of gore and spatter all around from the killing of the zombies, it wasn't enough to explain the fact that the truck itself was coated in blood and surrounded by fresh, non-zombie innards. It was clear to everyone involved that someone had deliberately made the rangers' truck a feeding magnet for the zombies.

To make matters infinitely worse, and yes, things could always get worse in a zombie apocalypse, all four tires were flat, with large, gaping slashes in them.

"I am not fucking impressed!" Ranger Rod fumed.

Perhaps sensing that Ranger Rod was one more piece of bad news away from a complete thermonuclear meltdown, one of the five men who was standing in front of the truck's hood cleared his throat to get his commander's attention.

"Ahem. Sir?" He sounded like he was going to wet his pants.

"What is it, soldier?" Ranger Rod replied.

"You need to come and have a look at this," he muttered as he began to slowly back away from the partially open hood.

Ranger Rod inspected the hood. It had all the telltale scratches and dents of having been forced open. He pulled up the hood, peered into the engine compartment, pursed his lips, and slowly put the hood back down, closing it with a calculated and gentle thud.

"Well that's just fucking delightful, now isn't it? It looks like someone went at the engine with a bloody sledgehammer." And with that his face became perfectly calm, which was, incredibly, even more alarming to everyone around him. "This truck is useless now. It's time for Plan B."

"There is that helicopter back in the clearing, but it has no gas and we couldn't find the keys," Kyle added, doing his best to be helpful.

"And that would be Plan B," Ranger Rod replied.

Chad couldn't help but interject. "Ummm ... Ranger Rod sir, there is the matter of no gas and no keys in the helicopter."

"What did I say about you speaking when not asked a question?" he retorted. "Don't you two worry your little heads about that. As I said before, my mission is to bring you two-"

"And our dogs!" Chad quickly interjected.

"You are a broken fucking record, aren't you?" Ranger Rod paused for five seconds, rubbed his temple, and continued. "My mission is to bring the both of you *and your dogs* back to the safe zone and that's just what I'm going to do."

With that, Ranger Rod pointed to two of his men. "Get in the back of the truck and retrieve the fuel."

Blaze Wildman and Damien Strongman, as Kyle and Chad would decide to name these two particular soldiers, did as their commander ordered. They hopped into the back of the covered transport and less than a minute later emerged and passed around five large canisters of fuel. The containers weren't labeled 'fuel' of course, but one could only assume that's what they were filled with, based on Ranger Rod's directive. Each of the five men carried a canister in one hand and their trusty sledgehammer in the other and awaited further instructions.

"Okay everyone," Ranger Rod said, "Back the way we came."

And with that the eight of them were on their way.

The journey was uneventful. No zombies were encountered, Bronx was blissfully calm, and no one had to stop for a potty break. The group made it back to the clearing and the helicopter in just under 15 minutes. During the expedition, the majority of the conversations between Ranger Rod and his men concerned whether or not it was possible to hotwire a helicopter. They all seemed to agree that it was indeed possible but had no idea if it would be in any way similar to hotwiring a car.

Kyle and Chad followed closely behind the leaders and were silently privy to these exchanges and expressed some grave reservations about the possibility of getting the helicopter started, let alone airborne. These, though, were less critical than the fundamental issues they had with everything that had transpired over the past day and a half.

As the six men continued to prattle on about hot-wiring helicopters and such, Kyle and Chad were quietly questioning why the helicopter was Plan B. Given that they were now traipsing through the forest in the middle of southern British Columbia, there was no way that the transport truck the soldiers arrived in was going to get them back to the safe zone in anything resembling an expedient manner. Driving along the small roads in the back country to eventually get to a highway and then all way back to an urban center seemed way too inefficient of a plan for this supposed rescue operation.

Our heroes concluded that something wasn't quite right and that the truck, rather than being the transportation source to the safe zone would simply function as a method for getting the group to an airfield or something

116

where a plane would be waiting to shuttle them to relative safety. It seemed most illogical to assume that Ranger Rod and the beefy boys had, a) driven all this way, and b) planned on driving all the way back. In a perfect world, Kyle and Chad would be able to voice these concerns and have them assuaged with a perfectly logical explanation, but so far, all signs have pointed to the odds of that happening being very, very remote. As such, our heroes decided it best to stay quiet and go along for the ride, hoping that everything would work out in the end.

Arriving at the helicopter, Blaze and Damien, along with their three counterparts - aptly named by Kyle and Chad as Scruffy McBurlyson, Burly McBearlyson, and Bearly McScruffyson - were ordered to fill the helicopter's fuel tank while Ranger Rod made his way to the pilot's cockpit door. Kyle and Chad followed Ranger Rod with Kyle most interested in seeing first-hand how the hot-wiring procedure was going to go. Kyle made his way around to the other cockpit door to get settled in the other front seat. Ranger Rod opened the pilot's door and paused. Kyle, opening the other door at almost the exact same time as Ranger Rod opened his and similarly paused.

Chad, having taken the pet carrier from Kyle, was oblivious to the dramatic pauses that were occurring in the cockpit, as he was busy getting Bronx out of the carrier, leashed, and ready to stretch his legs before the flight back to Greater Vancouver.

"What the Hell?" Ranger Rod remarked.

"Umm, Chad, you should come have a look at this," Kyle said.

Chad, now a few feet away and waiting for Bronx to finish his pee, smartly replied "Let me guess, while we were gone someone took a sledgehammer to the helicopter's controls and we're now stuck here and going to die in the wilderness."

Ranger Rod continued to be unimpressed with the whole situation. "Is this some kind of joke? Did the two of you put this here before we left for the truck?"

"I swear to you, neither of us have any idea how this got here," Kyle replied. "I'm just as confused as you are, and Chad will be too, *as soon as he gets over here!*" The last three words were said in a musical tone that softly, yet firmly suggested to Chad that he hurry on over to the cockpit of the helicopter.

"I'm coming!" Chad reassured his husband and gently pulled along his little boy in that general direction.

That's what he said, Kyle muttered to himself dryly and giggled.

Chad made his way to the left side of the helicopter and pulled open the sliding door. He lifted Bronx up into the cabin, fastened his leash to the support of one of the seats, and poked his head into the cockpit area to see what all the fuss was about. Ranger Rod's men were still busy at the back of helicopter, pouring what our heroes hoped was aviation-compatible fuel into the helicopter's tank.

Chad's first thought was that the Christmas present was impeccably wrapped.

Like, almost annoyingly so.

He was immediately impressed and supremely jealous of the wrapping skills it took to make such a beautifully presented gift. The box was medium-sized and lovingly enveloped in glossy, yet silky fire engine red wrapping paper, shimmering in the afternoon light. This breathtaking red wrapping paper was adorned with the tiniest of white dots throughout, creating a softened, professional and stylish look. An elegant, deep forest green ribbon with brilliant gold ridges had been wrapped around each side of the box and tied into the most stunning of crowning bows.

Ranger Rod and Kyle, perhaps subconsciously impressed as well, were more immediately concerned as to why there was a Christmas present sitting on the pilot's seat in the first place.

To add even more fuel to this puzzling fire, an understated gift tag of pale green parchment paper was taped to the box. On this gift tag, in tasteful, but unassumingly perfect dark red ink handwriting was the text, '*From Santa.*'

"You're telling me neither of you put this here?" Ranger Rod asked.

"Nope," Kyle replied.

"Double nope," Chad added.

"It could be a bomb," Ranger Rod mused to himself. "Granted, blowing us all to Kingdom Come would be a sweet escape from you two right about now."

"You know, we can hear you," Chad remarked.

Ranger Rod grabbed the package and tore it open, causing Chad to die a little inside at the sight of such an exquisite wrapping job being torn to shreds so viciously.

Once the wrapping had been ruthlessly torn away, a soft, white cotton-like material billowed out of the top.

This material was, in fact, cotton.

Ranger Rod removed the cotton from the box and eventually found the gift that was hiding in the center. He reached in, grabbed it, and when his hand emerged, he was holding a key.

Tied through the small hole in the handle of the key was a piece of string. Tied to the other end of the string was a note, written in the same impeccable script and on the same sophisticated paper as the gift tag. Ranger Rod read the contents of the note aloud.

"Just because you can't see something doesn't mean it doesn't exist. -Santa Claus."

"Why would he sign the gift tag Santa and the actual gift Santa Claus?" Chad wondered aloud. "Does he have a brother named Santa Smith or something that we might confuse him with? Why would Santa use a triple-negative sentence? And more importantly, why the frack didn't *I* get a gift?"

"Because you talk too much," said Ranger Rod.

"Ass," Chad murmured, hoping against all hope that Ranger Rod didn't hear him.

"This is good news," Ranger Rod continued, choosing to pretend to not register what Chad said.

Ranger Rod's men had finished filling the gas tank and were now crowded around the cockpit door.

"That is clearly the key for the ignition and now we don't have to worry about hot wiring; we can just fly out of here," Ranger Rod instructed.

"Of course, you can fly a helicopter," Chad said, rolling his eyes.

"It's all part of Plan B," Ranger Rod concluded.

Chad sat down on one of the seats in the cabin. "Okay, we are seriously going to ignore the fact that Santa himself just happened to leave a key in the helicopter after we left for the truck?" He slowly put his hand on Bronx's head and gently stroked his fur. "This makes absolutely no sense. What the fuck is happening?" he again asked no one in particular.

Fittingly, again, no one in particular responded.

"You," Ranger Rod then bellowed as he pointed to Kyle. "You're riding up front with me. Hopefully you can get us to your cabin so we can collect the magical other dog that your worse half keeps prattling on about."

"I can still hear you, you know," Chad reminded Ranger Rod from behind.

Kyle made his way back to the cabin while Ranger Rod jumped in the pilot's seat. Kyle sat beside Chad, put his arm around him and said, "Don't worry. Everything will work out." Kyle gave Chad a quick peck on the cheek, helped him with his seat belt, put Bronx back in his carrier, and made his way to the front of the helicopter, ready as he would ever be to ride shotgun for the upcoming trip.

Chad picked up the carrier and cradled it on his lap, still dumbfounded by recent revelations.

"Get in, boys!" Ranger Rod yelled. The five soldiers entered the helicopter, slid the door closed, and buckled themselves in.

Ranger Rod turned the ignition and the helicopter thundered to life. He flicked switches, turned knobs, inspected gauges, and within five minutes the helicopter was ready to take off.

The prospect of collecting their little girl and finally making it to a populated safe zone made this particular journey certainly one of the most exciting since the early days of *The Turning* and our heroes' departure from Ridgecrest Pines.

CHAPTER 15

A CONVENIENT STORE

*O*nce the explosion had scared off Undead Martin, Kyle and Chad had considered packing up the car and leaving Ridgecrest Pines later that afternoon. However, once the adrenaline rush of the blast had worn off, cooler heads prevailed. Our heroes knew that once they left the chalet, they would be heading into the unknown, and the unknown can (and most probably would) be a very, very dangerous place. As such, Kyle and Chad wanted to make sure they had as much daylight as possible so as to minimize the amount of uncertainty they would be facing on the road.

The general mechanics of the plan remained blissfully unchanged. The next morning - May 24th in case you are keeping track at home, Loyal Reader - at the crack of dawn, Kyle and Chad would grab the puppies, get in the car, and drive somewhere (hopefully) very secluded, away from as many people as possible, human or undead. Isolation, our heroes thought, was going to factor quite significantly in their continued survival.

Contrary to what you might read on bathroom stalls and the like, Loyal Reader, Kyle and Chad were not complete fucking morons when it came to being able to find a way to survive in the wild. Though it may be true that the virtues of camping and 'getting away from it all' were lost on our heroes, the basic fact that they were two very intelligent men meant that they knew what it would take to stay alive. While there wouldn't be any five-star resorts waiting for them in the foreseeable future, the basics of what was needed for the journey ahead were simple.

Once Kyle and Chad managed to get themselves into an isolated location, they would need to be as self-sufficient as possible. This meant making sure that whatever location they ended up at was well stocked with *food and within relatively easy travelling distance to a long-term source of potable fresh water.*

Finding water that won't make you sick would turn out to be one of the easier tasks in the backwoods of British Columbia. No matter where Kyle and Chad would decide to travel to, they would have no problem finding unpolluted rivers or streams from which to hydrate. All they would need to do would be to make sure they brought enough drinking water on their journey to last them until they managed to get settled.

As mentioned previously, Loyal Reader, our heroes, upon realizing that the entire world had completely gone to shit, had already filled the tub, the sinks, and every available bowl and container they could find in their chalet with drinking water. While this was a genius move that would provide them with months of drinking water once the utilities stopped functioning, there was the not-so-small problem of how they were going to transport said water in the car. Large volumes of drinking water were currently at their disposal, but an effective means of getting the water into the car and keeping it safely contained during transport was an issue.

The only volumes of water that were currently in sealed containers were those currently filling two plastic 2L Coke Zero bottles. Apart from these, the rest of it was occupying open containers that were not suitable for vehicular transport in a zombie apocalypse. Luckily, Kyle and Chad's brainstorming session about food provided a possible solution to the water conundrum.

Unlike water, there was of course no way that our heroes would expect to find a remote cabin our house or cottage that was completely stocked with non-perishable food items. Finding such a magical abode would be akin to standing in an open field in northwest China (Xingjiang Province, to be exact, very near to the Kazakhstan border) - geographically, the furthest spot on our fair planet from any sea or ocean - and being devoured by a very much living great white shark.

This is not an impossibility, Loyal Reader, as one can imagine a number of highly convoluted and needlessly complex scenarios where an evil genius trying to take over the world would be able to accomplish just such a shark-based task in what would probably end up being a futile attempt to kill some international spy-type person. The above is, however, so very unlikely a scenario that it is a practical impossibility.

Consequently, Kyle and Chad were in desperate need of figuring out a way of getting themselves some food stores to last them for the beginning of the (hopefully) long and healthy lives they intended to live in remote seclusion. A long-term solution would need to be figured out eventually, but baby steps were in order.

As our heroes were making a list of what they would need for their trip the next morning, the issue of food was one of the first conversations they had. Their current list of groceries in the chalet contained the following: a package of buttermilk crumpets, a jar of Kraft peanut butter, a jar of Kraft raspberry jam, a small container of International Delight Cinnabon coffee whitener, one-third of a bag of trail mix, and two small bags of Skittles.

As you can imagine, Loyal Reader, this is not nearly enough food for even an average morning in Kyle and Chad's world, let alone for any real length of time at the beginning of their post-apocalyptic lives. Upon taking stock of what they had, Kyle almost immediately proposed that they relieve the Ridgecrest Pines convenience store of some of its wares.

There were, of course, risks associated with such a venture. To be honest though, the new reality of the world around them meant that there would be risks associated with every single decision they would make from that point forward, so why not start with a relatively easy one?

The convenience store was located at the entrance to the Ridgecrest Pines property. The store itself was part of a large one-story building on the right-hand side as you entered the resort. The building was adorned with a big blue sign proudly decorated with imposing white text that read 'Registration.' A respectably enormous white arrow pointed in the direction of the appropriate building, outside of which could be found ample parking.

Given the amount of effort poured into making the sign, visitors often found it just a bit surprising that the building in question was only a few steps away from the parking lot. Interested approaching parties would then be offered two choices - the door on the left or the door on the right. Luckily, both of these doors were also labeled with overcompensating text, preventing any confusion as to their respective contents. The sign above the left door read 'Registration' while above the right door was a similarly decorated sign that read 'Store.'

Our heroes had been to the convenience store once already. The afternoon that they arrived (two days ago, though it seemed like an entirely different lifetime away), Kyle and Chad had gone into the store to buy some Coke Zero after checking in with the registration desk. The store itself was a single large space with all the things that a small convenience store would stock to accommodate resort visitors. The actual food items were of the potato chips and candy variety, although there was a selection of fresh fruit and basic condiments and requirements for making small breakfast and lunch-type meals. One thing that both Kyle and Chad thought they noticed while perusing the shelves was the large selection of cans of soup, taking up the vast majority of one entire shelf near the back right of the store. Perhaps this was in response to the number of campers who would be looking for meals of the quick-and-easy variety. Or perhaps the resort owners had a quasi-sexual obsession, bordering on a pathological fetish, for various soups. Who can say? In the end, the reasons were irrelevant. All that mattered was for our heroes to get all of this nutrition into the car as quickly and painlessly as possible.

By the time Kyle and Chad had managed to mentally recover from the 'Undead Martin and the Super Mega Explosion' episode and then have the wherewithal to formulate the next day's journey, it was just about 4:00 pm. There will still large plumes of black smoke on the horizon to the west and luckily no signs of activity at all in the areas around the chalet.

Kyle and Chad assumed whatever (whoever?) caused the blast sufficiently distracted Undead Martin and hopefully any other rogue zombies that were milling about the resort and had them currently running at full speed in a westward direction. There was also the possibility that any free-range zombies located east of Ridgecrest Pines could be doing exactly the same thing, which could very well put them on a collision course with our heroes' current position.

That would suck.

In this area of British Columbia, the Trans-Canada Highway follows the Illecillewaet River in a roughly southeast to northwest direction. Ridgecrest Pines, as it turns out, is located in an area of land between two bridges that cross this river, providing a bit of good fortune for Kyle and Chad. Any of the zombies that might have been attracted by the explosion in Revelstoke would find themselves running right along the river. The odds of a zombie finding and crossing the bridge east of the resort were actually pretty slim, given that your average zombie wouldn't consciously recognize a bridge any more than it would the incomparably unparalleled Catherine O'Hara. As such, fate would be firmly in control of whatever zombies managed to wind their way to our heroes' location.

Darkness would be arriving in a little under two hours and the sky was already ripe with the telltale signs of twilight. Kyle and Chad decided time was of the essence as everything (excluding them and the puppies) would need to be loaded into the car by nightfall, ready for their departure at first light. It would be too much of a risk to try and get the food in the dark as nighttime was very much their mortal enemy. It is immeasurably more difficult to protect against dangers and hazards that you can't see and given how fast these zombies could move; the more visual notice, the better.

Knowing this, Kyle and Chad wasted no time. They put on their shoes, grabbed their coats and the toaster, checked to make sure the coast was clear in front of the chalet, told the puppies they loved them, ran to the car, and less than a minute later were safe and sound in the car. Every sound and every move our heroes made was accompanied by a laser-focused scan of their surroundings to see if zombie hordes were running towards them. It was as exhilarating as it was terrifying and luckily, neither of them had shit their pants.

The journey to the store was nice and quick, taking just over two minutes. In fact, if Kyle was driving on a normal afternoon, it would have taken about 30 seconds. However, given the current circumstances, the drive was slow and measured, with Kyle taking care to not make any sounds above what was absolutely necessary to get them to the store.

Kyle and Chad, as they approached the store, reviewed their plan. Kyle would gingerly back the car into a spot directly in front of the store's door. Then, the pair would somehow force their way into the store through said door. Once access was gained, one of them would remain standing at the door while the other would run back and forth with the foodstuffs. This scenario would allow for someone to have eyes on the parking lot at all times in case something or someone made an appearance. The end result would hopefully be the glorious cramming of as much food as possible into the back of the car.

The plan, we are happy to report Loyal Reader, started off without a hitch as Kyle expertly backed the car into the parking spot directly in front of the convenience store door.

As our heroes approached the building, they noticed that the windows and door were intact - a very good sign. If other people at the resort were still alive, they had not yet figured out (or remembered, or even cared, perhaps) where the nearest food repository was located. Kyle parked the car as close to the door as he could (while still being able to raise the hatch) and then shut off the engine. Kyle and Chad looked at each other, both suffering from the anxiety of knowing that every step into the outside world was fraught with peril.

It seemed like an eternity. Both of them stared, blinked, stared some more, and didn't say a word.

Eventually it was Chad who broke the silence. "Shall we?" he asked.

"Let's do this," Kyle replied, and with that our heroes got out of the car and set about getting access to the store.

There was no danger of zombies being in the store, as the store didn't open until 8:00 am and all hell broke loose at 3:42 am. The person who was supposed to be showing up for their shift the morning of May 23rd was likely either dead, undead, or scared shitless and with much, much bigger problems to worry about than arriving at work on time.

In actuality, Loyal Reader, since we know how attentive you are to such details, you will be delighted to learn that the employee who was originally scheduled to work not only the morning of the 23rd, but also this fateful morning of the 24th, was a young woman by the name of Rhonda Tillerson. While Kyle and Chad were figuring out how to break into the store, Rhonda was indeed very much alive.

See? Some good news for a change!

Rhonda, however, was currently in her second day of being trapped in the bathroom of her fourth-floor apartment in downtown Revelstoke.

Okay, perhaps not the greatest news.

Rhonda's zombified roommate, Jenna Carvello, had been incessantly and repeatedly throwing herself at the bathroom door any time Rhonda made the slightest noise. As such, the door was now hanging on by only the slightest of threads and Rhonda was, understandably, not even thinking about the fact that she wasn't tending the convenience store, but instead was considering that her available options for survival were rapidly evaporating.

Hmm ... let's not focus on this anymore, Loyal Reader. Things did not end well for poor Rhonda.

Other people's trials and tribulations aside, Kyle and Chad peered through the front windows of the store to make sure all was quiet and (hopefully) harmless. Not seeing any overt signs of danger, Kyle grabbed the toaster and unceremoniously broke the door's window. He then reached in with his left hand, unlocked the door, and swung it open. Meanwhile, Chad was busy darting his head and eyes back and forth, making sure that the sound of the glass breaking didn't catch the attention of any possible nearby zombies.

It didn't.

This is where we are torn, Loyal Reader. We could recount for you every single item that our heroes stole. We could talk about how Kyle was the one who retrieved the food and Chad was the one that stood watch at the door. We could wax on poetically about the minutia of everything that happened during the 18 minutes that Kyle and Chad were at the convenience store.

However, we won't.

To be brutally honest, nothing out of the ordinary happened and the whole affair was rather lackluster and as uneventful as typing out the words 'watching paint dry.' Undead Martin did not return to reminisce with our heroes and Rhonda Tillerson did not arrive ready for some gripping convenience store escapades (she was, sadly, just 46 minutes away from becoming Jenna's dinner). It was all so very unbefitting of a zombie apocalypse.

Yawn

Having said that, this was, as you know, a good thing for our heroes. Kyle and Chad were positively giddy to not have to worry about dying whilst stocking up on food for their impending journey. Once they had stuffed as much as they could into the back of the car, Kyle drove to the chalet, this time making sure to park the car as close to the front steps as possible.

The rest of the afternoon and the evening were spent carefully and quietly moving all of their belongings into the car. It was a bit of a tight fit to get everything into the car with all the food and drinks that were already packed in there, but somehow it all managed to fit. By the time they were done, it was all organized and ready to go.

Once dawn managed to arrive, Kyle and Chad would grab the puppies, stuff themselves into the car, and begin the most important journey of their life. No one knew that just seven months later, another journey would prove to be just as important.

CHAPTER 16

COME FLY WITH ME

P rior to take off, Ranger Rod spoke into the microphone affixed to his helmet in a calm, remarkably reassuring voice. "Once we make our way to your cabin and collect the other dog-"

"Her name," Chad lovingly reminded him, "is Brooklyn."

"As I was saying, once we collect the *other dog,* we'll have a long trip ahead of us, so get nice and comfy."

The helicopter then slowly ascended above the snow and made its way over the treetops, affording Kyle and Chad their first aerial view of the region they had called home for the better part of the last seven months.

The scenery was breathtaking in its beauty. The blanketing of snow gave the landscape an eerie, serene, and ethereal quality that belied the dangers our heroes knew too well often lurked silently within.

Kyle and Ranger Rod spent the first few minutes engaging in a back and forth about what direction our heroes' cabin might be located and what landmarks could be used to gage its position. It wasn't long before Kyle noticed the service road that their cabin was situated along and only one minute and fifteen seconds after that the helicopter was touching down.

Given that the group had lifted off just less than five minutes ago, being able to arrive at the cabin so quickly spoke to just how close they were to making their way back there when they stumbled upon the helicopter in the second clearing. Our heroes had, in fact, travelled less than 5 km in the search for their little boy and the ensuing futile effort to find their way home.

The helicopter was deposited in the large backyard area of their cabin. Once landed, Ranger Rod and his men agreed to stand guard around the cabin to ensure any zombies attracted by the sounds of the landing would be dealt with accordingly.

Meanwhile, Kyle and Chad, while making their way to the cabin to rescue their precious little girl, noticed that the five reindeer they had left tied to the fence were now conspicuously absent.

Unlike an insanely cute Boston Terrier all alone and on the move, a missing reindeer or five was not cause for alarm; these beasts are naturally found in cold, forested areas, so our heroes reasoned they should be right at home. In fact, the greater likelihood is that they flew off to join Donner and Blitzen to do whatever it is that reindeer do when they're not transporting Santa and his cargo around the world.

How frightfully metabolic.

Good for them.

Brooklyn, as expected, was quite excited to see her daddies, and true to form, seemingly couldn't care less that Bronx had returned with them. Kyle and Chad didn't have much time to gather their things and to be honest, other than the puppies, there weren't that many things to gather. They each grabbed some clothes and bottles of water for everyone. The puppies were both let out into the fenced-in area to make their peeps and poops and inside of 10 minutes after landing it was time to say good-bye to the cabin, the only real home they had known for pretty much the entirety of the past seven months.

Kyle and Chad gently placed both puppies into their respective pet carriers, opened the back door to the cabin, stepped outside, and turned around.

Kyle was the stoic of thew two; it would take a situation on par with the emotional gravity of Tom and B'Elanna near death and floating in space for his eyes to begin to water. Chad, however, was fully engrossed in tears as he was closing the cabin door. The cabin in the woods had been good to them and good *for* them in so many ways, and for that, Chad was tremendously grateful.

Ranger Rod saw that Kyle and Chad were returning to the helicopter and instructed his men to do the same. Once everyone was belted in safe and sound, Ranger Rod once again skillfully took off and began the final leg of their trip.

The first 26 minutes of the trip were uneventful. The helicopter did what helicopters do, Bronx and Brooklyn were snoring like freight trains, and Chad kept trying not to make the whole situation awkward by not staring too much at the beautiful men that surrounded him. Instead, Chad tried to distract himself.

"Do we have enough fuel for the trip to the nearest safe zone or are we going to have to stop and refuel somewhere?" Chad asked over the intercom.

"This thing beast has a range of about 600 klicks on a full tank," Ranger Rod replied.

"So that would be a yes?"

"We have more than enough fuel to get us to where we need to go," Ranger Rod replied matter-of-factly.

"That was an unnecessarily cryptic response," Chad noted.

"Wasn't it, though?" Kyle added. He smiled wryly as he looked over at Ranger Rod's expression of contempt.

Chad giggled slightly as he spoke. "How long until we reach the safe zone?"

"It's a while yet," Ranger Rod replied. "We'll be making a slight course correction up ahead," Ranger Rod said. "The terrain becomes quite mountainous. If we divert to the south, we'll have an easier time of it."

"Roger that!" Kyle replied, proudly sounding all military-like.

Kyle had just managed to get that last reply out of his mouth when he suddenly jolted in his seat and began pointing at something in the distance directly ahead of them. "Look over there!" he exclaimed to Ranger Rod.

Kyle was aiming his trusty pointing finger at a house, but not just any house. This house had a very large, snow-covered front yard with the unmistakable message 'SOS' neatly printed on it in what appeared to be large rocks and pieces of wood and easily readable from their low-flying altitude. While the distress message was noteworthy and certainly got Kyle's attention, the house also had another, more ominous quality - it was surrounded by a quite a few zombies. Kyle estimated there could be as many as fifty zombies, all of them appearing to want inside the house to share in the delicious humanoid meal that probably awaited them within. "We need to help the people inside that house."

"That's not going to happen," Ranger Rod replied with his usual terse verbiage. "We will not deviate from our current course."

"Who do we need to help?" Chad asked. He couldn't see the house or the distress signal from his admittedly wonderful vantage point, sandwiched amongst the five burly soldiers in the back.

Kyle was quick to make his case. "We're about to fly over a house just up ahead. 'SOS' is printed on the lawn in big letters and zombies are surrounding the house. We have to help whoever is inside that house." As Kyle spoke, the helicopter was now less than 200 meters away from the house and he hoped against all hope that Ranger Rod would be reasonable about his request.

Kyle was wrong.

"We are not to diverge from the mission parameters. Do I make myself clear?"

"But your men can easily kill those zombies and we totally have more than enough room in the helicopter for-" Ranger Rod cut him off before Kyle could finish his justification.

"This is your last warning. We're not stopping. End of story."

"Fine."

"Actually, while I have your attention, I'd like to propose a course correction."

"We're diverting south to avoid the mountains; you told us that already."

"I'm afraid it's somewhat more involved than that," Ranger Rod explained, reaching into his jacket and taking out a small, rectangular device. It was about the size of a mobile phone, but thicker by at least an inch. A square black screen occupied the upper half of the front of the device with the only other noticeable feature being the word 'HOME' in thick, white, reassuring text along the bottom. Ranger Rod held the device in his hand, flicked a switch on the right-hand side, and the device began to hum.

"What is that?" Kyle asked.

The device took about 15 seconds to decide what it was going to do before the screen began to display a single, vibrant, blinking red arrowhead that occupied the entirety of the screen. The blinking arrow pointed left.

"This is a classified piece of technology," Ranger Rod replied. He set the device down on a flat portion of the cockpit's console in front of them. "I simply turn the helicopter until the arrow is pointing straight ahead."

"So it's a glorified compass," Chad interjected. "How sophistical!"

"You are exhausting," Ranger Rod sighed as he turned to glare at Chad.

Focusing his attention back to Kyle, he continued, "We just follow the arrow and we will eventually arrive at our destination."

"And which safe zone are we travelling to?"

"That's classified."

"Of course, it is." Kyle's words dripped to the floor in contempt.

132

The rest of the flight was blissfully uneventful. Chad fell asleep very soon after they left the cabin and he remained unconscious for the remainder of the flight. The helicopter appeared to be keeping them on a roughly southward course, leading Kyle to conclude that they would eventually be entering what used to be the United States.

The device fascinated Kyle. It was definitely more than just a compass-type device; it seemed to be doing more than just pointing to a distant location, altering its display based on the terrain the helicopter was flying through. The device kept them flying south over lowland areas with the mountains positioned to the east. The arrow would alter its position anytime the helicopter began to approach foothills, diverting them over the immediately adjacent lower elevation plains.

Ninety-six minutes after making the initial course correction, Kyle spied what he believed to be their destination. It had become dark over an hour ago and as they flew, everything was pitch black as far as they could see. It was tremendously unsettling. The fact that the helicopter was now flying directly towards lights on the horizon was clearly no coincidence - this was the terminus.

"Look! Lights!" Kyle exclaimed as he pointed directly ahead.

Chad awoke from his slumber, not registering what Kyle had said, but attempting to look like he knew what was going on.

"I take it that's where we are going?" Kyle asked of Ranger Rod.

"Is that where the arrow is pointing?" Ranger Rod replied smartly.

"Ass."

It took less than 10 minutes to reach the lights, which, as they got closer and closer, Kyle noticed had the distinctive illumination pattern of an airport. There were two runways, both quite long and looked capable of handling pretty much any sized aircraft. Accompanying the two runways were two buildings, one small and the other incredibly massive. A mountain rose up quite quickly behind the buildings, and the colossal one seemed to be built right into the foothill.

To Kyle, the smaller building looked like a standard administrative and air traffic control building that any airport would have. It was three stories high, with the top one serving as a classic control tower, although the use of the word tower might be contentious.

The other building - the mammoth one - was clearly a hangar, with two massive doors and a row of windows, the latter being positioned above the doors and emitting an eerie, orange glow.

"I'll set us down in front of the hangar over there," Ranger Rod said as he pointed in front of the left side of the hangar.

The landing was textbook and soon the entire group was out on the asphalt and stretching their legs, including Brooklyn and Bronx, who were busy finding the exact right place to pee. For Bronx, this was on the front of the right skid while Brooklyn, as usual, was less discerning and decided to urinate on an area that had no particular quality that could be discerned by the human eye.

Ranger Rod and his men quickly gathered their things from the cabin of the helicopter. "Alright everyone," he said. "Let's go inside," he continued and pointed towards the doors of the hangar as they began to open.

CHAPTER 17

THE ARRIVAL

Quite simply, family is everything, Loyal Reader. It didn't take a zombie apocalypse for Kyle and Chad to figure this out. However, finding oneself thrown into the midst of a global cataclysm certainly does have many effects on the psyche and one of those effects is to appreciate and cherish the memories of those we have loved.

Kyle and Chad, as if in the midst of some very demented Olympic sport, had gasped in perfect harmony as the hangar doors opened.

A perfect 10 from the judges! said no one.

There they were, standing on the tarmac of a small airport in the middle of nowhere, in front of a gargantuan hangar, and surrounded by six of the most beautiful men that the apocalypse could scare up.

The past two days had been eventful, to say the least.

And yet, with all that they had been through, nothing could have prepared them for what happened next.

The hangar door slid open slowly; positively glacial one might say. It was as if our heroes were on a game show and had just chosen what was behind hangar door #1 instead of taking the $10,000 jackpot. The studio audience would be on pins and needles, wondering if the prize was fabulous or simply another dud.

The prize behind this door, Loyal Reader, was no dud, and Kyle and Chad could not believe their eyes, hence the aforementioned gasps. Standing there, in the middle of the hangar entrance was none other than one of our heroes' closest friends - Suzie Matheson.

Seeing her standing there was so very unexpected, that Kyle and Chad couldn't even process what they were seeing at first.

"Suzie!?" Chad yelled.

"What? How?" was all Kyle could manage to say before Suzie ran over to them for a colossal hugging session.

Brooklyn and Bronx were also very excited to see Suzie. Bronx assumed that she had brought a super awesome ball with her and that she was going to throw the ball so that Bronx could go find the ball and bring it back to her again to be thrown once more. Meanwhile, Brooklyn assumed that Suzie had brought super awesome treats just for her. Though neither of these eventualities came into existence, the puppies were still glad to see her after all this time.

Hugs and teary-eyed hellos lasted for quite some time. Ranger Rod and his men, not involved in such shenanigans (though Kyle and Chad would not have protested should they have wanted to join in on the hugging action), continued walking into the hangar and disappeared out of sight.

"I'm so glad to see you guys!" Suzie exclaimed.

"I know, right?" Chad replied. "How crazy is this?"

"We have so many questions," Kyle added.

"I'll answer as many as I can," Suzie answered. "Although, to be honest, it's all very cloak-and-dagger here; they don't tell us a whole lot."

"Who are they?" Kyle asked.

"Good question, and we'll get to that. First, let's go inside and get you cleaned up and then get you some food. You must be starving."

"You have food here?" Kyle inquired in disbelief.

"Yay!" Chad responded.

Suzie smiled as she led Kyle and Chad into the hangar.

From the outside, the hangar was massively large. Though Kyle and Chad didn't know it, the portion of the hangar visible from the outside occupied well over 600,000 sq. ft. What did our heroes know? It was really freakin' big! Even more impressive, Loyal Reader, was that no self-respecting hangar expert in the world (*The Turning*, unfortunately, saw fit to only have two of them still left alive - Hildenbrandt Wächtler of Mannheim, Germany and Kenneth Davidson of Little Rock, Arkansas) could have anticipated just how ridiculously big it was on the inside. The portion of the hangar that was visible from the tarmac (the portion that our heroes entered through) was as mammoth and impressive as predicted. However, once inside, the back of the hangar extended well beyond any reasonable expectation. In fact, Kyle and Chad were hard pressed to comprehend just how extensive it was from their vantage point.

"My God, this place is fucking huge," Chad said, stating the obvious, and virtually flabbergasted by the whole experience.

"I know, right?" Suzie replied as the trio made their way through the spacious entry area of the hangar. "This building is just the entryway to a much, much larger complex that is built into the side of the mountain."

"Cool," Kyle said.

The hangar doors began to close, making a sound that was loud, but surprisingly not startling, given their gigantic size. Even Bronx barely registered the presence of the sound, and he was usually quite the dependable barometer of sensitivity for such low-register noises.

Suzie was leading Kyle and Chad down the middle of the entryway. There were a number of vehicles, all trucks of various sizes and clearly military in origin, parked in this initial portion of the hangar. They were lined up in perfectly organized rows to the left and right, dripping with military OCD. Kyle and Chad found it peculiar that there were no planes or helicopters in the hangar. In fact, the only air vehicle that our heroes observed so far was the one they landed in.

"Where are the planes and helicopters?" Kyle asked, as if on cue.

"They never store any in here," Suzie replied. "Every now and then one will arrive and bring supplies or survivors, but they never stay long."

"How odd," Chad said.

"How curious," Kyle added.

The parked trucks took up about a third of the forward space in the hangar entryway. The remainder appeared to be used for storage. A variety of boxes, crates, and shipping containers were stacked to create a labyrinth of walkways, all emanating from a central path that Kyle, Chad, and Suzie were now taking towards the back of the preliminary portion of the hangar - the entrance to the expansive underground section.

Whereas the hangar proper was what you would expect - extremely wide and extremely tall - the section that was built into the mountainside began with an atrium that dwarfed the hangar in all dimensions. Chad's brain could find no real-world example of something of similar size to compare it to, so he instead likened it to the ginormosity (yes, that is also a word; stop being such a bitch face, Loyal Reader!) of the hangars in the *Death Star*. The atrium was encased by glass and provided a view of what Kyle counted to be upwards of 20 floors that extended well into the mountainside.

Apart from being really, really tall, the atrium was also considerably wider than the hangar. Six sets of glass elevators were set against the back wall, providing access to the floors above and whatever subterranean network might have existed as well; three of them each to the right and left of a large first floor entrance bay. Unlike the hangar that was pretty much devoid of people, other than a few military-garbed men milling about, the atrium was much busier - people were walking back and forth across the atrium floor and the elevators were consistently shuttling people up and down.

Suzie led Kyle and Chad across the atrium and into the entrance bay.

"They seem to be a bit lax with security here," Chad pointed out. "We've managed to waltz in from the apocalypse and not a single person has given us a second look." It seemed to be more than that. Kyle and Chad both noticed that everyone walking in the atrium had a singular focus on their destination; they looked straight ahead, their vision never seeming to stray.

It was most unsettling.

"Yeah, the staff and soldiers here are very-," Suzie struggled with her words, "driven. They don't have much time for anything except their work. And you didn't just waltz in here. Ranger Rod and his men were your ticket inside, and I've been assigned to show you around the public, civilian areas of the complex."

Suzie stopped at a door on the left side of the main floor entrance. A large black sign hung above the door. *Civilian Quarters,* it read in stark yellow letters. A keypad was positioned waist-height beside the door. Suzie entered her four-digit code, a small red light turned green, and the door unlocked with a loud, clunking noise. Suzie opened the door and led Kyle and Chad inside to a large, rectangular, well-lit foyer.

The foyer, though well-lit, was as Spartan as the rest of the complex, completely devoid of any furniture. Five grey doors lined the longer wall opposite them, each one labeled with a single white stenciled letter - *A, B, C, D,* and *E.*

"These doors lead to the civilian sleeping quarters," Suzie noted. "They're essentially hallway after hallway of dormitories. Not much more than beds and sinks in most of the rooms with communal washrooms and showers."

"Showers?" Chad asked in disbelief.

"Yup!" Suzie quipped. "Most of the rooms have single beds. Not much need for family-style living in an apocalypse, I guess. My room is down in *Section C.* Luckily, some rooms have double beds, so they've put you two up in one of those. Head through the door labeled *Section E* and it will be Room

10. Here's the key." Suzie produced a single key from her jacket pocket and handed it to Kyle.

"Room 10. Got it!" Kyle responded.

"The larger rooms have their own showers and toilets, so why don't you guys go and get settled? I'll come by your room in an hour or so and we'll go get some food."

"That sounds fantastic!" Chad said and gave Suzie a tremendous hug "You really are a sight for sore eyes."

Kyle hugged Suzie for good measure. "See you in a bit."

Suzie exited through the door that led to the civilian accommodations and walked across the atrium. She was relieved that Kyle and Chad had finally arrived and were now safely tucked away in their room. She made it about halfway across the atrium, abruptly stopped, and reached into her front left pants pocket to remove a buzzing cellphone. She rolled her eyes and pressed a large green button that glowed at the bottom of the screen.

Lifting the phone to her right ear, she took a deep breath.

"Suzie," she stated, listened intently for a few seconds, then took a sharp breath and replied, "Yes. They're here and in their room."

Her brow furrowed, as she seemingly struggled to understand what she was now hearing on the other end.

"No, they don't know anything yet. I'm taking them to the mess hall in a bit and I'll make sure they don't-"

The voice on the other end had clearly cut her off, causing Suzie's expression to turn to one of exasperated annoyance.

"Understood," she stated dryly. "It's in their room, don't worry. They don't suspect a thing."

There was more silence on Suzie's end, this time briefer than before. *"I said,* they don't suspect a *thing."* The last word being uttered with three-and-a-half assloads of pure, unadulterated contempt.

Suzie hung up the phone, placed it back in her pocket, and briskly walked to one of the elevators, pressing the button with three times more force than was necessary or required, for that matter.

"Idiots," she mumbled to herself as she waited for the doors to open.

Eight seconds later, they did just that.

Suzie got in, pressed a button, again with considerable force, and as the elevator's doors closed in front of her, she murmured once more, "All of them. Fucking idiots."

CHAPTER 18

NOM, NOM, NOM

Relishing the thought of a hot shower, our heroes hurriedly opened the door to Section E as Suzie left the foyer. The passage was narrow, surprisingly long, and clearly in the running for the *World's Most Boring Hallway*. This quality was remarkably consistent with everything else Kyle and Chad had encountered in the facility thus far. The sheer number of doors, however, was very impressive; Chad estimated there must have been 50 or more on each side. This, of course, led directly to Chad mentally noting how much it would suck to be assigned a room at the end of the hall.

"This is insane!" Chad remarked. "How many people are they planning to rescue?"

Thankfully, their room was the fifth door on the right. Kyle opened it with the key, and they went inside.

The single, oval overhead light hesitated ever so briefly, flickering for a few seconds before deciding the appropriate plan of action was to reveal to Kyle and Chad their new abode. The accommodations were definitely not palatial, at least not by pre-apocalypse standards, causing momentary regret on behalf of the overhead light. It flickered once more in sympathy before deciding it was best to just shut up and do its fucking job.

For our heroes on this late December evening, though, the room may as well have been the Ritz Carlton on Fifth Avenue. Not that either of our heroes had experienced said hotel but talk 'round the water cooler had insinuated it was suitably chalk full of the requisite pomp and circumstance.

The interior décor was *Nouveau Prison Chic,* and perfectly in line with our heroes' expectations. The walls were concrete and coated in suicide grey. The floor was covered with a tough, indoor/outdoor carpet in a darker shade of almost suicide grey. The room itself was just wide enough to fit the double bed pressed against the right wall, a small bedside table containing a lamp and a digital clock, and next to that, a single door leading to the bathroom. The sheets on the bed were muted light brown, practically Technicolor compared to the walls and carpet. For their lounging comfort there was a couch that could comfortably seat two small children, with a colour scheme lifted from the communal area of a psychiatric ward. This fabric, of course, was one of the 639 shades of grey chosen by Satan to adorn the complex. Beside the couch was a four-drawer light brown dresser, and to no one's surprise, expertly matching the bed sheets.

"This is ... homey," Chad said, as he relieved Brooklyn and Bronx of their leashes and harnesses. Both puppies immediately began exploring the relative merits of the carpet as a backscratcher.

Kyle and Chad left the dogs to their own devices, writhing in ecstasy on the floor, and took a moment to reflect.

"I can hardly believe all this is real," Kyle remarked.

"I know, right?" Chad added. "It's funny, though; after everything we've been through these past two days, the secret military base in the side of a mountain is the part we're now having trouble believing is real."

"And don't forget Suzie suddenly appearing. Crazy, right?"

"Totes!"

Chad, being the nosy type, walked over to the dresser and opened the drawers.

"The dresser is filled with clothes!" Chad exclaimed. "Look! Socks, underwear, shirts, jeans, cargo pants, and sweatpants," he continued as he opened and closed each drawer in succession, leafing through the contents. "And there are two pairs of sneakers under the dresser in our sizes!"

Kyle hurried over and joined Chad in the clothing inspection, looking to see what sizes were represented. "The sizes seem good," Kyle said as he lifted up a blue t-shirt and pressed it against the front of his chest. Chad did the same with a few t-shirts. As Kyle picked up a pair of cargo pants and unfolded them, something fell to the floor with a thud.

"What was that?" Chad asked.

Kyle looked down at the floor and saw what, at first glance, appeared to be a cellphone laying in front of the dresser. "What the-?"

"What is it?" Chad interrupted, looking at Kyle, who was picking up the device.

It certainly looked like an older, sturdier version of the classic iPhone with a button-like depression on one end of the shiny, glass-like side, but lacking any other buttons or ports on the surface.

"Looks like a phone or something," Kyle remarked, as he inspected the item thoroughly. He flipped the device over in his hands to reveal a small yellow paper note stuck to the metallic side. The note contained a message in painfully neat hand-written black text.

*This will come in handy when the time is right.
Mum's the word!*

"How ominous," Chad commented.

"I know, right?" Kyle said as he pressed down on the button.

Nothing happened.

"Try holding it down for 10 seconds," Chad suggested.

Kyle complied, but still nothing happened. "Doesn't seem to want to turn on."

"Weird," Chad noted. "The note did say it'll come in handy, so I guess we wait until someone asks to borrow a phone to call their aunt's cousin's daughter's former roommate or something like that."

"Or something like that," Kyle replied with a smile. "But first," he added as he placed the device in the pocket of the pants he was going to change into, "it's shower time!"

With that, our heroes set about basking in the bliss that was running hot water. This was the first experience Kyle and Chad had with a working hot shower in a long time and it was, as expected, completely euphoric.

The washroom was equipped with all the necessities: face cloths, hand towels, bath towels, generic face and bath soaps, and shampoo. Everything lacked any visible branding and was probably manufactured in bulk specifically for the military. This, though, didn't matter to Kyle and Chad, as the deliriously hot water made everything seem okay.

Our heroes showered separately, but with a few minutes of overlap, as was their pre-apocalypse routine every single morning. Kyle jumped in the shower first, while Chad cuddled on the bed with Brooklyn and Bronx, joining Kyle in the shower after a few minutes. It was borderline obscene how wonderful it felt to be doing something that seemed so very normal.

"I could get used to this again," Kyle whispered as the pair soaked up the moment.

"And I could stay in here all night," Chad admitted, and that was no exaggeration.

Kyle got out and dried off, still in a blissful state of rapture. Chad was finished a few minutes later, dried himself off, and entered the bedroom to find Kyle lying on the bed, dressed in the best outfit that the military complex fashionistas had to offer - blue t-shirt and jeans - and sound asleep with the puppies. Chad sauntered over to the dresser, put on a red t-shirt and black sweatpants, then joined his family on the bed. Kyle awoke for just a few seconds, barely registering that Chad had joined them, and put his arms around his husband.

Sixteen seconds later they were both dead asleep.

The third round of banging on Kyle and Chad's door finally prompted a response. Suzie was waiting patiently, a pre-emptive smile plastered upon her face. She had knocked normally the first time, three solid bangs on the door, before coming to the realization that the odds of her two friends and their dogs being conscious were less than zero.

Suzie was correct.

After pausing for a few seconds, she knocked a second time, three louder bangs than the first. A few seconds passed, and still no signs of life. Suzie patted her right front pants pocket, confirming that she had a copy of Kyle and Chad's room key in her possession. *Shouldn't be necessary,* she thought to herself, as she hammered loudly three times, for the third time, on the door.

As expected, it was Bronx that registered the banging first. He awoke from his stupor, barked loudly at the invisible threat on the other side of the door, jumped off the bed, bolted to the source of the noise, and promptly ran head-first into the door.

Kyle awoke a few milliseconds after Bronx woofed his warnings and hollered "Hold on!" as he sluggishly got out of bed. This was enough to wake up Chad and Brooklyn, both too groggy to fully comprehend what was happening.

"It's dinner time," Suzie sang gleefully from the other side of the door.

Kyle took longer than anyone expected to stumble to the door. Like Chad and the puppies, he was dead asleep just seconds ago and his brain was not yet firing on all cylinders.

At least he was vertical.

Chad and Brooklyn were still attempting to approach a state that in some way resembled consciousness.

"C'mon in," Kyle said as he opened the door, revealing Suzie's smiling face.

"Sorry to wake you guys," she said with a sincere and apologetic tone as she gave Bronx ample attention, "but it's best you get some food into you before getting a good night's sleep."

"Agreed," Kyle said as he put his shoes on.

"How were your showers? And your nap?"

By now, Chad was managing to extract himself from the bed while Brooklyn realized Suzie was here and went over for some attention.

"Just awesome, on both counts!" Chad answered.

"Can we take the dogs with us or should we just bring them back some food?" Kyle inquired.

"They can come and eat too," Suzie answered. "As long as you keep them leashed and out of the kitchen proper, it shouldn't be a problem at all."

"Yay!" Chad said, putting Bronx and Brooklyn back into their harnesses and attaching their leashes.

"How long were we asleep? Has it been an hour already?" Kyle asked.

Suzie looked at her watch. "It's been a little over an hour and a half since I dropped you off here. I thought you could use a few extra minutes of nap time."

"Thanks for that," Chad said. "It was just heavenly. What time is it now?"

"About 8:30 pm. Okay, let's go get some food!" Suzie said as she opened the door and led our heroes back out and into the atrium.

Immediately after exiting the accommodations sector, Kyle and Chad followed Suzie to the right of the atrium and into an area that appeared to be directly behind the elevators and underneath the multitude of floors that comprised the complex. There were considerably fewer people walking about the atrium now and the majority of the upper floors were dark. A large number of hallways branched off to the right, but instead Suzie led them through a single door on the left side labeled *MESS HALL*.

For Kyle and Chad, the mess hall brought back memories of a high school cafeteria. The room was spacious and rectangular. The vast majority of the floor space was filled with row after row of tables, easily able to feed a hundred people at a time. The right side of the room had the standard rolling metal racks for storing meal trays while the left side was where the food was served. No one was operating the serving area now, of course, but one could imagine a stereotypically rugged and ellipsoid, yet acerbically lovable woman named Gladys dolling out ladle after ladle of food that would, on a good day, almost convincingly resemble such gold standards as Salisbury steak, creamed corn, mashed potatoes, and gravy.

"We'll need to go back into the kitchen," Suzie said as she led them along the wall and through a swinging door to the left of the serving area. "They don't have people operating the kitchen and serving area outside of mealtimes. You'll need to tie Brooklyn and Bronx to one of the table legs while we go in; no animals allowed in the food preparation area."

Kyle and Chad each fastened a doggy to a table and entered the industrial-sized kitchen with Suzie. Everything was, as expected, grey.

"How many people are there here?" Kyle asked.

"I'm not sure," Suzie replied. "They are pretty strict about keeping the rescued civilians separate from the military personnel and staff. We even have our own separate times when we come to eat. Since you guys are new arrivals, we have permission to come in here tonight and get some food." Suzie pointed out two walk-in freezers, two walk-in refrigerators, and three walk-in pantries. "Help yourselves to whatever you like, just don't waste anything."

"Oh, there is absolutely no risk of that, I assure you," Chad said.

"I'll go wait in the eating area and watch the pups while you guys get some food together," Suzie suggested.

"Sounds good," Kyle said, as he and Chad began to walk through the closest pantry like two proverbial kids in a candy store.

How cliché.

It had been far too long since our heroes had what could be considered a good meal. In fact, Kyle and Chad would be hard pressed to remember exactly when the last time was that they ate good quality food without having to think about rationing portions.

We won't bore you, Loyal Reader, with the details of what foodstuffs were available and how many tears of joy Kyle and Chad shed at the sight of such a nutritious splendor. Suffice to say that our heroes were overwhelmed with having to choose what to eat and soldiered through like the good little apocalypse survivors they were.

Suzie and the puppies didn't have to wait that long for Kyle and Chad to return. In fact, she was quite impressed that they were out of the kitchen with their plates of food in less than five minutes.

"Look at you two!" Suzie remarked. 'Got some good stuff did ya?"

"Oh yes," Chad replied. He was carrying his plate as well as a good-sized bowl of chicken and rice for Brooklyn. Kyle was carrying a similar one for Bronx. Suzie took the puppies' bowls and gave them their dinner while Kyle and Chad sat down at the table and began to feast.

Kyle and Chad had both opted for sandwiches (sliced chicken, lettuce, and tomato on white bread with mayo and mustard), a garden salad with ranch dressing, and a slice of chocolate cake for dessert. Our heroes were in gustatory ecstasy, practically moaning in delight with every single mouthful. Brooklyn and Bronx were similarly enthralled with their dinners.

For the briefest of moments, all seemed right with the world.

"So, I imagine you've got some questions," Suzie said as Kyle and Chad were finishing their respective plates.

"Ummm, yeah," Kyle replied. "Just a few," he added.

"Why don't I take you on a walk around one of the civilian areas of the complex, and we'll talk as we go? Then we can sit down in your room and chat for as long as you like."

"Or as long as we can stay awake," Chad added with a smile.

"Did one or both of you get a present from Santa Claus?" Suzie inquired as she led them out the mess hall door and into the recessed portion of the atrium's ground floor.

"I did," Kyle responded.

"Let me guess. It had a note attached to it that said, *'Just because you can't see something, doesn't mean it doesn't exist?'*"

Kyle and Chad looked baffled. "Did you get one too?" Kyle asked.

"All the civilians that were rescued and brought here did; it's apparently the one thing we all have in common," Suzie said.

"That's crazy," Chad added.

"Yup."

They had stopped in front of the hallways that branched off opposite the mess hall.

Suzie pointed to the hallways. "These lead to a gymnasium and fitness complex and some other rooms that are off limits to civilians."

"So how long have you been here?" Chad inquired.

"I've only been here a little over three weeks," Suzie replied. From what the other rescued people here have said, no one's been here for more than a month."

"How did you know we were coming? It can't possibly have been a coincidence that you were the one waiting for us when we arrived at the hangar." Chad asked.

"It's protocol here for the names of the arrivals to be shared with the staff and civilians in case friends and/or family are here too. Since I've been here I don't think anyone has recognized a name, but then tonight one of the Rangers - Ranger Rick, I think - said you guys would be arriving and it seemed too good to be true; I wasn't convinced it was actually going to be you guys until the hangar doors opened."

"Ranger Rick?" Kyle asked. "Really?"

"I know, right?" Suzie said, leading them back out into the atrium. As they passed by the door to the civilian accommodations, Kyle and Chad could both feel the siren call of their bed but continued to resist its temptation for at least a little while longer. There were, after all, Scooby-Doo mysteries that desperately needed solving.

Suzie steered our heroes to the other side of the atrium, passing the elevators once again.

"How many people have been rescued?" Kyle asked.

"I've counted only 13 of us civilians in the complex so far - 15 now with you guys."

Kyle and Chad looked concerned.

"That's not a lot of people," Kyle said.

"I know, right?" Suzie replied. "I'm not sure why they aren't finding more survivors."

The group had now made their way to the other side of the atrium. They stopped in front of a single door labeled *LOUNGE*.

"There are usually a few people in here. Other than sitting in our rooms, this place and the fitness center are really the only other places to go."

"Where exactly are we, geographically speaking?" Chad asked.

"We're just outside of a town in Washington called Hunters; northwest of Spokane," Suzie said.

Suzie led Kyle and Chad into the lounge. Unsurprisingly, grey continued to suffocate the walls and furniture. Our heroes were amazed at how big the room was. It looked like it could comfortably hold at least 150 people. There were four pool tables and two air hockey tables in one end of the lounge with a huge flat screen TV on the other end. In between were sections of tables and chairs interspersed with sofas of various sizes. Bookshelves lined the far wall of the lounge, with a wide selection of board games to play, books to read, and DVDs to watch.

Five people were in the lounge, every one of them looking very curious to find out who the new faces were.

A middle-aged man and a woman who looked to be in her thirties were playing pool. "That's Ed and Vera," Suzie said, as she waved at them. They waved back, prompting Kyle and Chad to do the same.

Suzie pointed to a young woman sitting at a table doing a puzzle. "That's Wendy. She doesn't speak."

Down at the far end of the lounge were two young men watching a movie. Kyle and Chad recognized the movie immediately - *Harold & Kumar Go To White Castle* - and approved of the selection.

"Let's have a seat on a sofa," Suzie said as she motioned towards that area. Kyle and Chad sat down together on a large, moderately comfortable sofa while Bronx and Brooklyn jumped up and almost immediately fell asleep.

"So, back to what we were talking about before," Kyle said. "Is there even a-"

Kyle's question was cut short by none other than Ranger Rod bursting into the lounge.

In case you were wondering, Loyal Reader, four out of five entitled teenage hooligans named Bryce agree that Ranger Rod's arrival in the lounge received full marks for dramatic effect, with him being out of breath and covered in blood and all.

CHAPTER 19

OF JOURNEY BEGINNINGS AND DOORS THAT LEAD TO PLACES

*S*ometime in the early hours of the morning Kyle and Chad had gone through the motions of going to bed, knowing full well that sleep would be particularly elusive that night. As it did every day, the sun begrudgingly prepared to rise, signaling the arrival of May 24th.

Though neither of them discussed it, each of them spent the four hours and twenty-six minutes lying in bed awake, thinking about their family and friends. They had no way of knowing how many of them had survived. What's worse, it was essentially impossible to find out.

There was obviously a close to zero chance that our heroes could make their way back to Greater Vancouver as the sheer number of zombies inhabiting the area would be way too much to handle; it would almost certainly be a suicidal move on their part. Getting to Vancouver Island where Kyle's family was located would be an even harder task. Chad's family members were on the opposite side of the country in Nova Scotia, and the odds of our heroes being successful in managing to travel that distance was zero; not effectively zero, not almost zero, not hovering in the general vicinity of zero, but actual zero.

And so, as 6:00 am finally arrived and daylight began to snake its way through the blinds, Kyle and Chad, like many other "lucky" survivors on the planet, suffered from the effects of a textbook case of Schrödinger's

Apocalypse - *their family and friends currently existed in a quantum state of being both simultaneously alive and dead/undead.*

Metaphysics and philosophy aside, our heroes had spent a considerable amount of the time the night before mentally preparing for the morning; everything was talked over and mulled over what seemed like a billion times.

Once daylight began its show, they got out of bed, got cleaned up and dressed, went downstairs, got the puppies and themselves breakfast, took a few deep, deep breaths, and left the chalet for the last time.

Please don't worry, Loyal Reader. By now you are painfully aware that our heroes made it safely to the car, pausing ever so briefly to let their precious little puppies do their business, and survived not only that day's trip, but eight more months of trials and tribulations. Armed with this knowledge as you are, is a pretty nice position to be in.

Our heroes, however, on that fateful morning, had no idea if they were going to survive the day, let alone until Christmas. As such, everything was done with the utmost of care and rather understandably elevated blood pressure.

Truth be told, the morning went remarkably drama-free. Granted, Providence would see to it that an unfortunate set of circumstances unfolded exactly 46 minutes after our heroes left the chalet, so perhaps celebrating less than an hour of relatively smooth sailing was somewhat premature. Who can say?

Instead, let's focus on what did go well.

- Getting out of the chalet and into the car? Effortless!
- Driving out of Ridgecrest Pines and reaching the highway? Went off without a hitch!

Being two-for-two led Kyle and Chad to wonder what manner of beast might launch out of the bushes at the exit of the resort, but nothing materialized. Undead Martin, wherever he may have been, seemed to have decided to choose the better part of valor and skip the official send off.

His loss.

Once at the Trans Canada, there were blissfully only two options - head west or head east; there literally was nothing else our heroes could do. Kyle and Chad would most certainly look back someday and wonder at the simplicity of this decision-making moment; life was about to get rather complex rather quickly for our heroes. Fortunately, one of the items Kyle freed from the evil clutches of the convenience store was a handy dandy road atlas of British Columbia. Given that our heroes' cell phones were now nothing more than sleek, sexy paperweights, such paper-based maps were about to make the mother of all comebacks.

Kyle and Chad spent a good deal of the previous night pouring over pages and pages of the atlas, assessing the relative virtues of every available geographic option.

The first decision our heroes made was to head west. Heading east would bring them to the middle of the Rocky Mountains. While Kyle and Chad had nothing against hills, knolls, mountainous peaks, and the like, the deciding factor as to where they would go was not based on the picturesque nature of the terrain, but rather on the presence of the one thing that nature could reliably and continuously provide - a source of fresh water.

Water, in case you weren't paying attention in school Loyal Reader, is one of those irritating little necessities of life.

The standard rule that everyone hears about is that you can't survive more than three days without water. While this is generally considered to be more or less true by most people, there is of course a tremendous amount of variation when you begin to apply this to real life scenarios.

Someone who is expending a lot of energy in the middle of a summer afternoon in the Australian Outback will be in a shitload of trouble in less than two hours if water stores are not replenished. This steamy scenario that everyone and their pet wombat hears about is based on the scientific fact that an adult human can produce upwards of 1.5 L of sweat an hour during such arid and thermal conditions.

Alternatively, consider someone who stays relatively immobile in a cool, humid environment. They could last as long as a week without drinking any water.

So, what is the take-home message, Loyal Reader? It's all relative.

Having said that, three water-free days is probably a good estimate for the average person.

Our point, and we do have one, is that the night before their departure, Kyle and Chad opened up the atlas, took a look at where they were, and decided the best plan was to get away from major cities and towns (zombie hubs) *as quickly as possible, while still doing two things: a) maintaining access to a major road or highway that was likely to be in good condition, and b) following a reliable source of fresh water.*

Once these elements were taken into consideration, the choice was actually quite easy. Highway 23 was just a few kilometers to the west, passingly directly through Revelstoke and running north-south parallel to the Columbia River, splitting into 23N and 23S. From the looks of things, following the highway south was not as preferable as taking the road north.

The American border was less than 200 km south of Revelstoke, and although the majority of the areas would be rural, the number of other highways and roads that peppered the land were considerably more numerous than the northern route would afford. In fact, once our heroes managed to get onto the northern section of 23, no other major roads appeared, and only one small town called Mica Creek was even labeled on the map, and that was almost 150 km north of Revelstoke.

Given the apparent relative isolation of the area and the presence of some serious mountains directly east of the Columbia River, the area seemed like an adequate spot to offer our heroes some degree of respite from the zombie apocalypse.

Time marched forward and before our heroes knew it, the next morning had arrived. Packed to the gills and carrying all that had meaning to them, the car approached the Trans Canada.

Kyle paused. This decision, to leave the present relative safety and security behind for a destination practically unknown, weighed heavily on his shoulders. Kyle looked over at Chad with weary eyes.

"It's gonna be okay," Chad said reassuringly. "This is definitely our best option."

Kyle put on the left blinker (purely out of habit of course) and pulled onto the highway. Smoke still rose into the air on the horizon to the west, a chilling reminder of yesterday's explosion. It also served, Kyle mused, as one hell of an effective neon sign. Maybe they wouldn't be the only ones travelling to Revelstoke today.

That would just be their luck, *Kyle thought,* as they drove away from the rising sun.

Everyone was startled and confused. You know, there definitely should be a word for that, Loyal Reader, but bless our pudgy little heart if we can't think of what it might be right now. It must be all the stress of telling such a gripping and timeless tale.

Yes … that's it.

Perhaps we should go with starfused? Or maybe confartled?

Oh yes, Loyal Reader, we definitely like that second one.

The group of civilians in the lounge was indeed terribly confartled by Ranger Rod's explosive appearance through the door. Bronx and Brooklyn had begun to bark at the sudden commotion, adding an air of tension to the whole affair. Once everyone had turned around and looked at Ranger Rod, that's when the real confusion set in. He was covered in blood. Not metaphorically, not ironically, but *literally* covered in blood.

Wes Craven, cinematic and literary genius that he was, would have projectile-vomited his approval.

"Everyone out! Now!" he screamed.

Less than two seconds later, sirens added to the terrifying effect. Chad thought they clearly indicated that things had gone awry, but they didn't seem to convey the urgency of something that might kill you, which is what Ranger Rod seemed very preoccupied with doing. Rather, Chad thought, it was more of an alarm that the British might use in case of a fire.

"Jolly ho and all that! Could we bother you to amble your way to the nearest fire escape? The water lorry is on its way and tea and crumpets await your arrival on the front lawn. Have a spectacular day."

Chad giggled to himself at the hilarity of such an alarm. He thought better, though, of sharing this with the group. No one seemed in the mood for a good laugh, what with all the apparent impending doom and such.

"Fuck!" Kyle exclaimed. "What's going on?"

"C'mon people! *Move!*" Ranger Rod yelled.

In situations such as these, Loyal Reader, one doesn't stop to weigh the pros and cons of listening to authority figures, especially when they're dripping thick red (presumably) bodily fluids all over the floor and loud alarms all around you are preparing you for the worst.

Once everyone from the lounge had made it to the atrium, Ranger Rod, accompanied now by Blaze Wildman and the newly appointed Scruffy McBurlyson, summarized the situation. "We have a situation here, people," he stated matter-of-factly. "The base is under attack. We have multiple reports of enemy combatants in the complex and a fucking horde of zombies approaching the airfield."

"This is not a drill," Ranger Rod added. "Get to the hangar now. We are rolling out of here ASAP!"

As Ranger Rod finished his last directive, a booming sound came from the upper floors of the complex, impressing upon everyone in the room that time was of the essence.

"Can we grab our things from our rooms?" the man that had been playing pool asked. Chad thought his name was Ted or Ned or something suitably depressing like that.

"Negative!" Ranger Rod replied. "To the hangar. NOW!" he bellowed and pointed directly ahead.

"What about the rest of the civilians?" one of the men that had been watching the movie inquired. Chad was certain Suzie didn't say their names.

"Ranger Rick is on it. Now go!"

Ranger Rod and his men led the eight of them to the hangar. Kyle and Chad assumed they would all pile into the back of one of the transport trucks and drive out of the hangar into the relative safety of the night. Fate, however, had more nefarious plans.

As the group made it to the hangar door, Ranger Rod directed them to an adjacent transport truck. "Once the hangar doors open, we'll be going like a bat out of hell, so hold on tight and keep your heads down," he instructed.

Just as Scruffy and Blaze had assisted Vera and Wendy into the back of the truck, yet another commotion unfolded. An explosion sounded outside the hangar as another of Ranger Rod's men, Bearly McScruffyson this time, surged through a door on the right-hand side.

"Sir," Bearly yelled as he ran towards the truck. "Negative on the trucks. Enemies are on site and inbound."

'Fuck, fuck, fuck, fuck, FUCK!" Ranger Rod roared. "Out of the truck!" he said as the two soldiers helped Vera and Wendy back out.

"Sir," Bearly said, with a slight but noticeable quiver in his voice, "there is only one other option."

"You think I don't fucking know that, soldier?"

"No, sir!" Bearly yelled and stood at attention. "I mean, yes sir!"

Scruffy and Blaze looked concerned.

Everyone else was beyond confartled; they were terrified beyond words.

"Okay everyone, follow my men," Ranger Rod instructed.

Bearly, Scruffy, and Blaze led the group to the hangar's back left corner. Another explosion rocked outside, and voices could be heard from the atrium. The three soldiers stopped at a steel door. The door was unremarkable, with nothing to indicate it did anything other than lead outside to the base of the mountain. Much like the door to the civilian quarters, a keypad was positioned to its right.

"We are not going through that door," the guy who might have been named Ted or Ned said.

Ranger Rod's response from the back of the group was as swift as it was caustic, "You either go through that door or you die in this hangar. Your choice."

Ranger Rod then made his way past the group to the door and entered a code into the keypad.

The door's edges began to emit a bright blue light, like someone on the other side was holding the mother of all halogen bulbs.

Perhaps someone was, Chad pondered.

A second blast thundered, this time causing the left hangar door to buckle.

The blue light subsided, and as the door opened inwards Ranger Rod and his men ushered the eight civilians through to the darkness to the other side.

Suzie was the last of the group to go through. "What about the others?" she asked.

"There's no time, ma'am," Bearly replied as he, Ranger Rod and the other two soldiers followed Suzie into the black, rectangular void.

As Ranger Rod shut the door behind them, a flash of light scampered around the door's edges and accompanied the deafening sound of what appeared to be the hangar doors disintegrating. Once shut, the door again glowed blue from around its periphery, but this time only faintly and for a much briefer period of time.

There should be snow, Chad thought.

"Where are we?" Kyle's voice meekly dissolved into the darkness.

"Shouldn't the door have led outside?" Chad whispered to his husband.

Indeed, for all intents and purposes, the group should now be knee-deep in snow, at the base of the mountain, and just outside the back of the hangar.

However, they clearly were not.

In fact, the group seemed to be in a narrow hallway. Kyle and Chad were both noticing that the group now crammed just beyond the mysterious hangar door barely had room to stand two across without hitting into the sides of the smooth passageway.

It was unnervingly silent.

"Where are we?" Kyle asked again.

Again, no one answered.

Again, no one seemed to be surprised by this.

"Move aside," Ranger Rod commanded, and the civilians immediately obeyed, sandwiching themselves to either side of the corridor. He and his three men swiftly moved to the front of the line.

"Follow us, nice and slow," he continued as all four of them took out military grade glow sticks and shook them to life. An eerie green glow filled the hallway, confirming its smooth, metallic nature.

The group walked for much longer than anyone thought possible. It's an interesting phenomenon, when you think of it, Loyal Reader. Why should there have been any expectation at all of how long it would take them to get to whatever their destination was going to turn out to be?

Perhaps it was the general nature of hallways everywhere. As a rule, such architectural structures aren't often excessively long. They serve as a means to connect rooms and other passageways to one another; their connective function commonly restricting their length. Regardless of all that, the walking the group did through the glowing, green metallic channel seemed, to everyone involved, to take forever and a day.

Forever and a day, as it turned out, lasted for exactly three minutes and six seconds, at which time Ranger Rod reached another door, this one seemingly much less dramatic than the last. There was no keypad and no glowing blue light.

How frightfully commonplace, Chad thought.

That was, however, until Ranger Rod had moved his big, giant head out of the way, revealing the bold fire-engine red text that shouted rather menacingly from the green-lit door:

NO ENTRY!
EVER!

Why even add the EVER! At the end? Kyle mused to himself. *Complete overkill.*

158

What font is that? Chad wondered as he quickly reconsidered his earlier appraisal of the unfolding situation; it seemed to have all the makings of a circumstance that could escalate rather quickly.

For a door that explicitly tells one not to go through, the safeguards put in place were remarkably lackluster; Ranger Rod simply turned the round handle and pushed the door open.

As the group made their way through the door, Kyle was convinced that someone somewhere should have been fired for this.

Kyle would certainly be disappointed to learn that no one was.

Silence (of the uneasy variety, Loyal Reader) abounded as the group began to proceed through the door. This, however, was broken by two innocent little audible syllables.

"Uh-oh."

Most everyone in the group had made it through the door and they promptly rotated 180 degrees at a sound never before heard - Wendy's voice.

Yes, Loyal Reader, Wendy. She was the second-to-last person through the door, with Bearly right behind her.

The door quietly closed shut behind them.

"Wendy?" Suzie asked as she walked to the back of the group, "Are you okay? What's wrong?" These were the first words Suzie had heard Wendy say since she arrived at the complex and the timing added 642 new and exciting layers of tension to the whole affair.

"Smelly, smelly, toast and jelly," was Wendy's only reply, sung in high-pitched childish musical tones.

"What?" Kyle asked.

True to her previous form, Wendy had one again gone silent. Suzie and our heroes tried to get her to say something - anything - to explain what she meant, but to no avail.

"Well, that wasn't disturbing at all," Chad quipped as the group turned their attention to the mystery of what lay beyond the obnoxious door.

Given the marvels our heroes had witnessed these past two days, one might arguably think it would be a safe conclusion that there wasn't much more that could possibly surprise them. One, as it turned out, would be dead wrong.

Realistically, speaking, Loyal Reader, at some point in this adventure, it's worth asking: how much more fucked up could things possibly get? Though the group didn't know it yet, the Universe was in the process of cracking its knuckles, putting down it's beer, and getting the party started.

As Ranger Rod led the group away from the door, Kyle and Chad became quite confused. Each holding a puppy, they looked at each other, then looked at the scene before them, and stood in slack-jawed marvel.

Suzie, Ted/Ned/Something, Vera, and the two young men were similarly awestruck.

Wendy simply looked down at her shoes, seemingly content to one again be completely oblivious to the landscape around her.

Ranger Rod continued to look like he was in the process of cataloguing the various ways that he hated everything and everyone around him.

Ensuring that at least one part of this fucked up situation was still predictable, Bearly, Scruffy, and Blaze continued to be really, really good looking.

Like, *really* good looking.

Not to be outdone, Bronx stared at a random spot of nothingness above him.

Brooklyn registered her stamp of approval for the situation with a long, high-pitched fart.

"What is this?" Kyle asked.

"I'm confused," Chad added.

Bronx's ears perked up at the sound of his daddies, but he nonetheless continued his staring contest with the ceiling as Brooklyn passed wind once more for a comforting slice of good measure.

Once everyone had made their way through the unremarkable door, it became rapidly clear they had not traveled to outside the mountain or hangar.

While everyone clearly thought that the initial unremarkable door they went through when leaving the hangar should have led to just outside the mountain (but beside the hangar, which it most certainly did not), expectations were less optimistic this second time around.

As the group made their way through the narrow hallway to the second door, both Kyle and Chad were convinced that it led in a straight line away from the hangar. There were no perceptible changes in direction during the time they walked through the hallway; it just seemed like some really, really long and narrow pathway that led to who knows what.

However, looks, as we are sure you are intimately aware of by now Loyal Reader, can certainly be deceiving.

In retrospect, our heroes must have been mistaken. The narrow, seemingly straight hallway must have had an ever-so-slight right turn. It couldn't have continued straight away from the hangar and into the open tundra that surrounded the base of the mountain. The reason, Loyal Reader, and there most certainly is one, is that this last door did not open up to the outside world, not by a long shot.

"Wow! That's a fuckload of toys!" Chad exclaimed.

Surprisingly, he wasn't completely wrong.

CHAPTER 20

BUTT TON TO FUCKTON AND EVERYTHING IN BETWEEN

The history of the planet Earth, as incomprehensibly long as it may be for the primitive human mind to comprehend, has managed to defecate a good number of people who have had far, far too much time on their hands to spend far, far too much of this precious time pondering such things like:

- *Working out the lineage of Sith Lords in the Star Wars universe.*
- *How to say, "How am I still a fucking virgin?!" in Klingon.*
- *And, last, but certainly not least, figuring out exactly how much of something there would be in a fuckload.*

The prize for winning the latter contest must go to a Reddit user by the name of bill-merrly. While there is no guarantee that this is indeed his name (Facebook, for example, a safe haven for people of such standing, has never listed even a single person with the name Bill Merrly), we shall extend the warm, sweaty hand of politeness and cordiality and refer to him simply as Bill. It's as good a name as any, we guess.

As it turns out, and quite likely completely by chance, Bill managed to stumble upon the perfect definition for the sizing relationships that would eventually lead to the common use of fuckload as a unit of measurement.

Bill's Reddit profile listed no personal information of note, so one can only imagine the sad, friendless void that surrounded him in his daily life. Given statistical probabilities that govern the daily lives of the über nerd (uncovered 268,934 years ago by what can only be loosely described as a mathematician inhabiting the fifth planet of a cute little star system in the Fornax Cluster), one can then employ a heuristic algorithm to provide a reasonable facsimile of the kind of localized niche created and inhabited by Bill (within, of course, a statistical hypothesized deviation of no more or less than ~ 3.7%).

Below are the results of this analysis.

Subject's Name: *William Emery Holden Merrly.*
Date of Birth: *August 11th, 1985, 1:24 am, Anchorage, Alaska, USA.*
Family Members: *Mother - Verleen Tabitha Merrly - Soldotna, Alaska; cohabitant.*
Additional (Relevant?) Details:
- *Billykins, as his mother affectionately bleats at him, pays no rent.*
- *Billykins' father, Edwin Reginald Merrly, was a janitor at the local civic center who, when Billykins was just eight years old, died in a freak accident involving industrial grade floor wax, a set of high school cheer leader pom-poms, and a traffic cone.*
- *The financial settlement with the city of Soldotna and the state of Alaska left Verleen and her precious little Billykins enough money to live happily for the rest of their lives at 2164 Anthurium Street.*
- *By the time he was a rotund and pasty-faced 10-year-old, Billykins, as is the destiny of all über nerds, had developed an unnatural fondness for all things Star Trek and Star Wars.*

- *At 16, Billykins wanted to bang Lieutenant Uhura, marry Princess Leia, and kill Dr. Pulaski, the latter being an understandably common sentiment among not only Trekkies, but the greater public as well.*
- *Not that this was the only mitigating circumstance but given his uncanny morphological similarity to Jabba The Hutt, Billykins' banging and marrying escapades would forever remain the stuff of his sordid fantasies.*
- *It wasn't too long into his life that Billykins began spending more and more time watching his favourite TV shows and movies, surfing the internet, playing video games, and eating Cheetos™ rather than frolicking outdoors with his peers or feeling the warm embrace of the midday sun.*
- *It should now come as no surprise that at his prime, Billykins was a 29-year-old man spending, on average, 92.6% of his time in his childhood bedroom. (Not an Editor's Note: somewhere right now a Raw Fitness trainer is shedding a single tear.)*
- *While Billykins slowly killed himself in his bedroom, Verleen chain-smoked the days away on the couch, visiting with her best friends in the whole world, Pat Sajak and Alex Trebek. Not Drew Carey, though; it would be a cold, cold day in Hell before anyone would replace Verleen's beloved Bob Barker.*

Intergalactic algorithms and analyses aside, the Universe can be thankful for the depressing life and times of Billykins. If it weren't for his unhealthy love of all things stupid and inane, we wouldn't be here today wondering about the virtues of the word 'fuckload.'

Historical records indicate that Tuesday, November 25th, 2014, was a cold and bitter day in Soldotna, Alaska. The sun, as it had every day since the

Earth was formed some 4.5 billion years ago, rose to reveal a stiff, November gale raging outside, signaling that all remnants of fall were but a delicate and forlorn memory. Billykins was, as you have probably guessed by now, seated in his big, comfy chair, staring intently at a computer monitor, and blissfully oblivious to the world beyond his bedroom's walls. It was 11:24 am and he had just finished watching Nicki Minaj's music video *Anaconda* for the 86th time.

All judgement aside, *Anaconda* is a pretty catchy tune. Adding just a titch of judgement, Loyal Reader, we can safely conclude that it's catchiness is directly proportional to its liberal sampling of *Baby Got Back,* and nothing more. It's a sad commentary on the state of the world that this is pretty much the only positive spin we can provide at this time, Loyal Reader.

His momentary fill of Nicki complete, Billykins waded aimlessly around the internet, in a desperate attempt to fill the 36 minutes until *Star Trek: Voyager* was to air on Syfy. Billykins was looking forward to this episode - "The Raven" - as Seven of Nine was to be heavily featured.

As luck (fate?) would have it, Billykins popped by Reddit and spotted a posting by a user called TheNewUltimateJesus (Gag!) that caught his eye. The exact text of the posting read as follows:

"How many shitloads are there in a fuckton?"

As Billykins continued reading, he became far, far too excited. The question had been posted for almost a week and by this time 37 people had already chimed in. Billykins, true to form, scoffed at their responses, and rightly so; they were virtually all pedestrian attempts at toilet humour, shallow and pedantic beyond belief.

No one had taken a serious look at the issue.

Billykins, however, knew that he was clearly the man for the job.

It's not that Billykins didn't laugh at stupid and raunchy Reddit posts sometimes; he was, after all, only human (his mom had him tested). That being said, even though the question may have been a humourous attempt to see what spectrum of responses could be garnered, he found there to be no logical reason to use only a single neuron to compose a response. Instead, Billykins surmised, one should be intelligent and thoughtful with responses, ensuring that any embedded humour seeps organically from the text, readily soaked up by the reader.

Billykins cracked his knuckles and thought back to the hours and hours of conversations he and his online friends had about some of these very issues. Of particular usefulness were texts between he and a fellow with the douchey online nom de plume of DrAgOnBlAdE69.

Just typing that text, Loyal Reader, made us want to quietly drown in a sea of Mountain Dew: Code Red.

One can summarize that the 'need-to-know' message from these virtual exchanges as such:

> 1. *Shit, fuck, butt, and ass are all vivid prefixes that one can use to augment how much of something you have.*
> 2. *Butt and ass are synonyms, with butt being a more colloquial term and therefore of lesser position.*
> 3. *As shit is produced by the butt/ass, it should have a higher position.*
> 4. *Fuck is the king of all swears and rightly occupies the highest position.*
> 5. *A load can be considered less than a ton because of the same colloquial argument employed in point 2.*

Armed with the above knowledge and mentally prepared to liberally drip his wisdom all over the interwebs, Billykins began to type. His response, extracted and presented below, is as elegant as it is concise. Fetch Kleenex once again, Loyal Reader, as you may very well once more be overcome with emotion.

> *"I have had extensive debate on this. Its (sic) a logarithmic scale.*
> > *1 buttload x 10 = 1 butt ton*
> > *1 butt ton x 10 = 1 assload*
> > *1 assload x 10 = 1 asston*
> > *1 asston x 10 = 1 shitload*
> > *1 shitload x 10 = 1 shitton*
> > *1 shitton x 10 = 1 fuckload*
> > *1 fuckload x 10 = 1 fuckton*
>
> *So, to answer your initial question, 1 fuckton = 10^3 shitloads."*

167

As Billykins finished typing his response, he could feel the sweet tingle of endorphins running through his arteries and veins, and the rivulets of sweat dancing down his brow, indicative of another job well done.

"Genius," he muttered to himself as the telltale strains of *Voyager's* first seconds ambled their way across the humid, fermenting room.

"Pure fucking genius."

Of course, Billykins' explanation, as inspired as it turned out to be at providing comparative context to the issue, did not provide, unfortunately, anything at all in the way of an accurate and precise meaning to either the term shitload, fuckton, or whatsoever may lie in between or around. That, Loyal Reader, is where the rest of the internet's desolate inhabitants come into play.

True to form for the human race, it should come as no surprise to even the most casual of net surfers that countless people excel at spending their time on the little, rather meaningless things in life, perhaps under the global collective illusion that they are either being extra super witty or that all other sentient life forms will, in some way, benefit from their collective jocularity.

Billykins, as we learned mere moments ago, fell victim to this very same foul temptress. As his logarithmic scale began with a single buttload, it would be prudent to call on the collective wisdom of the internet to quantify, with some tangible amount, how this translates to known real-world weights and such.

Luckily for us, Loyal Reader, a veritable asston of online users have tackled this particular question over the years (and soon you will know exactly how much that is). And let us tell you that wading through this particular swill was, as you may have surmised, irritatingly enlightening at best and, at worst, akin to performing a self-inflicted lobotomy with a rusty ice pick. The sheer number of people who have spouted off on this issue of international importance is as impressive as it is downright frightening.

For no other reason than because it was the first result that Google spits out, we have chosen the *Right Honourable* Mr. Andrew Allingham (initially hailing from Fredericksburg, Virginia, but, in a magnificently appropriate twist of fate, now stealing valuable oxygen from the population of Greater Seattle, Washington) to answer our all-important question:

"How much of something is in a buttload?"

Unfortunately, we have it on very good authority that Andrew is a 100% Grade-A douche. We challenge you, Loyal Reader, to have a gander at his 'biographical short' and tell us with any nanoscopic degree of sincerity that he isn't likely to be someone that sports what he mentally refers to as 'outdoorsy scruff' on his face, wears flannel absolutely everywhere he goes, and cultivates an oval, parasitic, keratin-based life form on the back of his rugged (yet perfectly coiffed) head of hair. Oh, sweet Zombie Jesus save us all ...

> *"Andrew Allingham has a BA in English from the University of Mary Washington in Fredericksburg, Virginia. He has been a professional wall painter, college radio station music director, and a nuts and bolts salesman. He is currently inventory and shipping manager at a small, hip, merchandising company tasked with aggressively rebranding the Commonwealth of Kentucky. He likes his coffee black, beer strong, bourbon straight and food spicy."*

Ugh! We wish we had made that up, Loyal Reader. We really do.

It actually physically pains us to think that he wrote that paragraph about himself.

How can you not feel the undeniable need to wash out your eyes with battery acid after reading that? In fact, we feel like heading to a microbrewery right now and blowing our fucking brains out in protest.

But we digress ...

So, with Andrew's epic douchiness taken care of, we can now apply our laser-like focus to the issue that carries far more gravitas - what exactly did he conclude about the term buttload? In between sips of straight bourbon and scallops *El Diablo* of course.

The answer to the above question entered the world as a vomitus bouncing, baby blog post on June 23rd, 2011. Sadly, Andrew's blog, cleverly titled Andrew Allingham, would find its eventual virtual demise almost exactly three years later; his last post gracing the internet on June 22nd, 2014. Fittingly, Andrew's swan song to the internet was none other than a feebly constructed comic strip addressing the genetics of poor vision and a dystopian cyborg future.

Painful, Loyal Reader, just painful.

Like, really fucking painful.

Coming as absolutely no surprise whatsoever, all of Andrew's comics were a nauseating combination of visual and comic atrocities. If one concentrated hard enough and suspended neural activities in the logic and reason centers of the brain, they appeared to be making something in the remote vicinity of a comment on society, giving them the most miniscule measure of saving grace.

We know exactly what you're thinking, Loyal Reader. You're thinking that you're about to have to wade through a whole paragraph describing one of the more painful Andrew Allingham comic strips. Please do give us some credit, we're not that completely predictable. At least, we aren't now. Given how bitchy you've become about these sorts of things, we guess we'll just have to switch it up a little bit and take a different approach.

Happy now?

So, Loyal Reader, take your attitude, shove it in some waiting orifice, and have a gander at a very unfunny and perfectly representative example of the visual diarrhea that dripped out of Andrew Allingham's brain on September 16th, 2012.

See Loyal Reader? We weren't joking.

Utterly.
Fucking.
Dreadful.

Luckily, though, some of his non-cartoon-based abortions were actually bordering on tolerable. Andrew's post of relevance to our current predicament, and one of the most unobjectionable ones, Loyal Reader, is entitled "The difference between a buttload, a boatload, and a shitload."

In this missive, Andrew playfully draws from the other 8,426 people online that have presented one possible origin of using the term 'butt' as a unit of measurement. His views on shitload, however, are completely his own and of course turned out to be pedestrian beyond belief.

Please do take a moment and have a gander at what he bestowed upon us:

> *"A 'butt' is a traditional unit of volume used for wines and other alcoholic beverages. A butt is generally defined to be two hogsheads, but the size of hogsheads varies according to the contents. In the United States a hogshead is typically 63 gallons and a butt is 126 gallons."*

So, there you have it, Loyal Reader, we will follow the American trend and consider one buttload of something to be equal to 126 gallons. This, unfortunately, opens up another can of worms, but one that is much easier to wrap our collective brains around - the completely and thoroughly assbackwards imperial system of measurement.

To save time and brain cells, we won't bore you with the 435 things are wrong with the Imperial system, but rather we will skip to the inevitable summary conclusion that every country but three reached: namely, that the *International System of Units (Metric System)* is not only a more intuitive system of measurement, but loads more accessible to the average person. And what countries still use only the imperial system? None other than Myanmar (Burma), Liberia, and the United States of America.

Read into that what you will.

Having said that, it is actually a relatively pedestrian task to take imperial gallons and convert them to metric liters. We are happy to report that

1 gallon = 4.54609 liters, leading us directly to the conclusion that a single buttload would them be equal to 574.6734 liters.

Now, because the metric system is so fucking awesome, we know that one liter of water weighs one kilogram, affording us the possibility of at least being able to convert one buttload of something into an actual weight measurement, which would be 574.6734 kilograms.

How exciting!

Let us now meander our way back to the ramblings of Bill Merrly, who gave us the key to converting our buttloads to fuckloads, and boy is it a doozy! It turns out that one buttload is one-millionth of a fuckload.

Ouch.

This means, of course, that since one buttload is equal to 574.6734 kilograms, one fuckload becomes 574,673,400 or so kilograms.

Wow.

As you can see, without the hard work and dedication of social outcasts like Billykins, a statement as inherently vague and ambiguous as "Wow! That's a fuckload of toys!" can now be squarely put into a somewhat less of a muddied perspective.

Considering the knowledge that a fuckload of toys would actually be 574,673,400 kilograms of said toys, it is almost beyond belief how incredibly close Chad actually came with his off-handed estimation.

Knowing us too well by now, Loyal Reader, you know that we would be remiss if we didn't point out this discrepancy.

What Chad initially concluded was one fuckload of toys was, in actuality, 94.36812% of a fuckload of toys - 542,308,484 kilograms. Had Chad been armed with the knowledge of just how close he was to being correct, he would have probably achieved the single largest nerdgasm in the history of life on Earth.

And that's saying something.

Up until they ran over another zombie (for the second time in two days, no less) the drive to Revelstoke was uncannily humdrum. Our heroes had made their way about 16 kilometers or so down the highway and were just approaching a small road whose accompanying sign signaled that Mount Cartier was nearby when out of nowhere, a zombie appeared on the side of the road. Kyle's reaction time, impressive as it was, was still not enough for him to be able to completely avoid the undead jaywalker. There was no time to slow down the car and very little opportunity to swerve out of the way, given that the creature, upon realizing a noisemaker was barreling towards it, decided the proper course of action would be to fling itself violently towards said hurtling noisy projectile.

The resulting mess was disgusting beyond belief. Two factors, however, contributed to a much better result than one would have anticipated.

1. Kyle did actually manage to swerve a little bit, which, in retrospect, probably saved the windshield (and perhaps even Chad).
2. The zombie didn't seem all that concerned with the fine details of proper walking, running, and lunging protocols, so it pretty much fell in front of the front right-hand side of the speeding car.

Given the inherent dangers present in the external environment outside of the car, Kyle and Chad, though suitably alarmed by the hitting of the poor, undead bastard, did not stop to get out and inspect the car for damage or trailing body parts. The car kept on trucking down the road and that was enough.

Should the worst-case scenario rear its obnoxious head and the car break down, our heroes would just have to deal with such eventualities like that as they occurred.

That really is the right attitude to have in the zombie apocalypse, isn't it, Loyal Reader? When you sit back, stretch, scratch that nagging itch, and really think about it, how much control does one have over their lives at the best of times, let alone when surrounded by a world rife with the hangry undead?

The answer is, of course, not very much.

Why, Loyal Reader? We think you know the answer. Look deep down inside that fabulous little consciousness of yours and you'll realize that the lion's share of our lives has always been prescribed for us. We robotically perform the same basic tasks each and every day with a glimmer of hope that some measure of escape from the rat race will occur for a couple of weeks during the year.

So now, instead of meetings, deadlines, and that annoying bitchtard Lynda from accounting making your life a living hell every day with her mutant ability to fuck up even the most basic of life's mechanics, this buffet of incompetence has been lovingly exchanged with the ever-constant distress of knowing that at any moment you could become a zombie's mid-morning snack.

It was these sorts of thoughts that swirled through our heroes' heads as they recovered from the hit-and-run and continued to make their way towards the billowing cloud of smoke.

CHAPTER 21

VOGEL ... MIKE VOGEL

Understandably, Kyle gasped in amazement as he joined Chad and the others among the ranks of the completely dumfounded.

The group, realizing immediately they had not emerged into the cold, unforgiving terrain outside of the hangar, were instead met with a rather warm, albeit slightly musty-smelling environment. Literally everyone was looking literally everywhere in a failed attempt to process what they were seeing; it was just too fantastic.

The door had opened into a huge underground cavern. And huge, Loyal Reader, does not do it justice. It was mammoth.

No ... it was gargantuan to a size beyond anyone's wildest expectations.

Admittedly, this is a bit of a cheat as no one in the group had any realistic expectations as to a) whether or not the door would lead to an insanely colossal cavern, or b) how incomprehensibly massive said cavern might be. Even Ranger Rod seemed momentarily taken aback by the situation, a slightly puzzled look flashing across hinting at a suppressed vulnerability in his face that somehow made him even hotter.

For a cavern of such vast size, Kyle noticed that it was remarkably well lit.

"It's remarkably well lit," Kyle noticed.

Both Kyle and Chad, unbeknownst to each other, had come to same comparative conclusion concerning just how to reconcile the size and shape of the cavern with their primitive human brains - it resembled a cross between *Under the Dome* and *Warehouse 13*.

If you are not familiar with either of these pop culture references, Loyal Reader, then promptly put down this book and re-evaluate the events of your entire bleak, grey, and dismal existence.

As Kyle had just remarked, the cavern was surprisingly well lit for its size. The light wasn't bright by any stretch of their collective imaginations, but it was certainly bright enough to make out the vastness of the underground space. Further, the light seemed to originate from everywhere all at once, which seemed to be both impossible and obvious, given that there were absolutely no apparent sources of said light.

The walls of the cavern were jagged rock and they rose sharply from where the unsuspecting door had delivered them. The walls didn't go straight up though; there was a very, very slight vertical inwards curve. Following suit, where the walls met the floor seemed to have a very, very slight horizontal arc as they slipped into the distance. This, of course, is what led Kyle and Chad to equate the similarity of their current predicament with the basic premise of Stephen King's novel *Under the Dome*.

Arriving late to the party and verbalizing what we already know, Chad added his two cents. "This place is fucking huge," he said a bit too excitedly. "It's totally like *Under the Dome*."

"I know, right?" Kyle added. "I was just thinking that!"

Under the Dome was Stephen King's 48th novel, and as the ultimate source of all knowledge in the known Universe - *Wikipedia* - so eloquently noted,

> *"Tells an intricate, multi-character and point-of-view story of how the town's inhabitants contend with the calamity of being suddenly cut off from the outside world by an impassable, invisible barrier that drops out of the sky, transforming the community into a doomed city."*

Harsh, right? The book, which Kyle and Chad both found equal parts entertaining and disturbing read, was also made into a gripping television show that lasted a respectable, but ultimately unfulfilling three seasons.

The show itself was very well done, but a declining viewership and lack of compelling plot twists/story development signaled its early demise.

Kyle and Chad were proud, card-carrying members of those *Under the Dome* fans who thoroughly enjoyed the show not only because of the cool and unsettling storyline, but also (and perhaps, dare we say, perhaps even a tad bit more importantly?) the strikingly beautiful lead actor. His name, Loyal Reader, is Mike Vogel and he is, without any measure of hyperbole in our discerning minds, insanely attractive.

Don't take our word for it, Loyal Reader, when you can have the mother of all ganders for yourself. We submit, for your approval, the following pic so deliciously used by the man himself as his Twitter photo.

Now, on the so very unlikely off-chance you don't find him to be attractive, all is not lost. You don't necessarily lack a soul, but the jury is most definitely still out on that. Even if you're a straight male reading this manifesto, you should still be comfortable enough with the tattered remains of your heterosexuality in today's society to be able to admit to yourself, if not the world around you, that Mike Vogel is one helluva good-looking guy.

If, again, by some insane trick of the Universe or your dwindling eyesight, you still can't admit what is, by now, so painfully obvious, your last chance to see the light lies on the next miraculous page - an official *Under the Dome* promotional shot of Mr. Vogel.

There you have it. If, by now, you still aren't realizing just how much more physically attractive Mike is that any other man you know, or ever will know, you are obviously blind and therefore have absolutely no business whatsoever reading this book.

None whatsoever.

Put the book down, go find a cane to assist you with your daily drudge and go about your business.

The world is your oyster.

Now that we've taken care of the riff-raff, we can return to the mysterious cavern and it's undissimilarity (again, it's totally a word, so stop having a crap-attack) not only to the relative size and shape of Stephen King's literary construct, but also, as we mentioned just a few paragraphs ago, Loyal Reader, to the most righteous and excellent television program called *Warehouse 13*.

We could go on and on and on about the merits of this show and the life-changing effects it has had on countless unsuspecting hominids, but we shall, just this once, spare you the details.

Enjoy this, Loyal Reader, as it shan't happen again.

The similarities with *Warehouse 13* though, include not only the ginormous size of the cavern, but also its contents - the aforementioned 0.9436812 fuckload of toys Chad referenced upon his unceremonious arrival.

Stacks and stacks and stacks of toys.

The toys, thankfully, were largely confined to boxes. Otherwise, this cavern would have all the makings of a very hot mess. Perhaps in some apparent attempt to illustrate the diversity of toys and the relative contents of the boxes, a generous peppering of escapees littered about, so that a good number of the boxes had sample items sitting in front of them. Sort of like a really big, foreboding, and disorganized Costco.

Once the group had entered the cavern, a generously sized foyer greeted them. It was devoid of boxes and toys, affording everyone the chance to soak up their surroundings.

Group members diffused from the door as each person ambled slowly around the foyer, most of them utterly gob-smacked and mumbling corresponding sentiments to themselves and whomever happened to be nearby.

The boxes and loose toys were located on shelving units - very, very thick and sturdy ones, of course - that climbed all the way to where the encroaching dome of the cavern intervened. The shelves began at the edges of the foyer in a massive semicircle, forming 18 rows with rather claustrophobic walkways in between.

Kyle and Chad let the puppies walk about on leash for a bit while our heroes marveled at the sheer number of boxes lining every conceivable square inch of shelf space in the facility. As expected, Bronx peed on the edges of the closest stack, but no one seemed to notice or care. Brooklyn wasn't nearly so fussy, depositing a warm puddle of considerable size just to the right of the door that had led them into the cavern.

Though the contents of the shelves disappeared into the distance as one peered down the walkways, even a cursory inspection of the box diversity at the edges of the rows underlined the incredible assortment of toys contained in the cavern. There seemed to be boxes of every conceivable type of traditional Christmas toy, each one conveniently labeled with large, bold pictures of the toys they presumptively contained. The smattering of loose toys interspersed on the shelves also gave hints as to what the boxes had inside of them.

The vast majority of the boxes that lined the edges of the shelves at the foyer contained cute little Christmas-themed teddy bears. The pictures on the boxes and the bears that sat on the shelves were light brown and dressed in either a Santa suit or an elf costume.

"Oh my God!" Chad cackled in excitement as he looked at the boxes and then picked up one of the elf bears, "These totally look like the bears that Stan made in that episode of *American Dad!*"

"They totally do!" Kyle shrieked.

What Kyle and Chad could not recall at that particular point in time, Loyal Reader, was that the episode of *American Dad* in question - *American*

Dream Factory - was the 11th episode of the 3rd season and had originally aired way back on January 28th, 2007.

While it was a very strong episode of *American Dad,* it sadly doesn't even make the Top 10 of the show's crowning achievements. To truly understand the brilliance of this comedic gem, one must watch these episodes, commit them to memory, be able to relate them to multiple occurrences in everyday life, and do this on a daily basis.

The aforementioned genius-level episodes are, in order of their level of increasing fantabulous awesomeness:

>*10. Stannie Get Your Gun*
>*9. Tearjerker*
>*8. Moon Over Isla Island*
>*7. Camp Refoogee*
>*6. For Whom the Sleigh Bell Tolls*
>*5. Dope and Faith*
>*4. Bar Mitzvah Hustle*
>*3. Lincoln Lover*
>*2. The Scarlet Getter*
>*1. Shallow Vows*

Don't bother arguing with us, Loyal Reader; the above list is pure, uncut, 100% verified scientific fact.

Ranger Rod and his men were quick to capitalize on the presence of said teddy bear-containing boxes, stacking a number of them up against the door, creating a sort of *bearricade,* as it were.

Yes, Loyal Reader, your instincts are correct - we are far, far too proud of ourselves for coming up with that one.

Once the teddy bear fortification was complete, Ranger Rod corralled everyone into the center of the foyer.

"As you can probably guess, there's no going back the way we came. None of us have been here before and none of us knows why the Hell this place even exists, let alone what exactly it is."

Ted/Ned/Something shot his hand up, eager to ask a question.

"No," Ranger Rod replied dryly as he shook his head back-and-forth. Ted's/Ned's/Something's hand skulked back down. "Our job is to get out of here alive and that means sticking together, doing exactly what I say, and remaining calm. Can you all do that for me?" The group members nodded, fear and trepidation evident in their expressions.

"Good," Ranger Rod said. "Once we've-"

A sharp, audible noise originated from some distance to the interior of the cavern, sounding like some unholy cross between a whale in heat and a hippo in the throes of giving birth to a dump truck.

"What the Hell was that?" Ted/Ned/Something cried out and looked at Vera in terror.

"I think that guy and Vera are totally banging," Chad whispered quietly to Kyle.

"Agreed," Kyle whispered back.

"Everyone needs to try and remain calm," Ranger Rod instructed. "There is no need to panic. Anything could have made that noise, so let's not jump to any conclusions."

"Given how the past few days have been going," Chad said to Kyle, "It's probably something that will want to kill us."

"I know, right?" Kyle responded in commiserate resignation.

The noise pierced the air again, causing considerable agitation amongst the group.

"Here's what we're going to do," said Ranger Rod in a tone that was far too reassuring given the current state of affairs. "We're trained for situations like this," he noted while pointing at himself, Bearly, Scruffy, and Blaze in succession. "The walkways all lead away from this area, but the two here furthest from the walls look to lead in the general direction of that sound." Ranger Rod motioned to the two narrow walkways directly behind him and continued with his instructions.

"We'll take four of you down this path," he said and pointed to Blaze and then the walkway to his left. "The remainder will go with them down this one," he ordered while gesturing at Bearly and Scruffy.

Already huddled together, our heroes and Suzie were assigned to the Bearly-Scruffy team along with Wendy. True to form, Wendy had continued to remain completely silent. Ted/Ned/Something, Vera, and the two guys from the lounge joined Ranger Rod and Blaze in front of the other walkway.

"Okay," Ranger Rod commanded, "Each group will continue down their hallway. If anyone encounters anything suspicious, let the other group know on the radio. Keep walking along the path; do not turn. Understood?"

Some group members nodded while others mumbled affirmative sounds. Bearly and Scruffy, though, were their sexy soldier best and replied in unison, "Roger that!"

Ranger Rod lifted his right hand, flattened out his fingers in line with his palm, and motioned towards his walkway. Bearly and Scruffy responded by doing the same to the path before them.

With that, the two groups began to inch their way into the heart of the cavern.

CHAPTER 22

AMMUNITION AND SPINACH, TOGETHER AT LAST!

Very slowly and cautiously, Kyle and Chad moved forward behind Scruffy and Bearly along the stretching, narrow pathway.

The puppies had been sequestered back into their respective carriers on their daddies' backs and were content to take this time to relax and quietly contemplate their own blueprints for world domination and copious amounts of treat acquisition.

Wendy could very well have stayed in the foyer and not joined the group, and no one would have noticed. She was, though, making her way down the narrow path, not far behind Suzie.

The other group, presumably, was making similar headway.

The noises ahead of them continued sporadically, now becoming more background annoyance rather than signaling certain impending doom.

"It's not as dark as I thought it would be," Chad whispered to Kyle and Suzie.

"Right?" Kyle responded quietly. "How is the light even able to penetrate down here?" he added, noticing that the stacks that bordered the walkway were perilously high.

"And how do they get the boxes off of the higher shelves?" Chad asked, not expecting an answer from anyone in particular.

"You know what's weird?"

"Umm, just about absolutely everything right about now."

"Look at the boxes. They all have these big, cartoony pictures on them, probably what's inside, but that's it. There doesn't seem to be any other text or identifying markings of any kind."

Kyle moved closer to one of the boxes, this one with a picture of a child's sled on the side. As he inspected the surface of the box, he noticed the bottom corner of the side adjacent to the next box had a small barcode on it. "Look!" he said quietly to Chad and Suzie, "A barcode!"

Chad and Suzie came over and examined the barcode on the box. Suzie walked across the narrow aisle and examined a box with a teddy bear picture on it. "This one has one too!" she added.

As if to magnify the tension around them, Kyle's pocket decided it was the perfect time to emit a very short, but audible beep.

Everyone but Bearly and Scruffy jumped.

Wendy actually managed to make a low, muffled noise that zoologists later would characterize as akin to a llama choking on its own spit.

"What the fuck was that?" Scruffy barked as he and Bearly whipped around. A bit of distance now separated them from our heroes. The soldiers did not appear to be amused.

Kyle instinctively put his hands up in the air and tried to explain. "That was me. I have this device in my pocket that I found in our room and it apparently decided to turn on."

"Show us," Bearly ordered.

Kyle gingerly reached into his pocket and pulled out the rectangular device, now lit up with a single word across the front in bolded, deep red, somewhat threatening text:

SCAN

Bearly held out his hand and Kyle handed him the device, which apparently, we can now safely call a scanner. Bearly and Scruffy surveyed it for a few seconds and handed the scanner back to Kyle, who appeared somewhat confused.

"Don't you guys want to use it to scan one of the boxes?" Kyle asked.

"It's your device," Bearly responded. "Go ahead."

Kyle proudly took the scanner and approached the box with the picture of the sled on it. He pointed the front of the device at the barcode, and a bright red, shimmering line of light shot out from behind the glass cover and scanned the barcode. The front of the scanner lit up much brighter now as it displayed a very different message.

"What the-?" Kyle said. "This doesn't make any sense."

"What does it say?" Bearly asked.

Kyle looked up at the group, held up the scanner, and showed everyone what was now being displayed on the scanner.

Bearly and Scruffy looked mildly confused, and still quite sexy.

Chad and Suzie sported looks of utter confusion and alarm.

Wendy was looking down at her feet and therefore only barely aware of the situation transpiring before her.

Lucky Wendy.

The display on the scanner indicated that Kyle had scanned box 'WQ-17298' and that the contents were '50 Colt AR-15.'

For any of you naive and unsuspecting Loyal Readers at home playing Apocalypse Ammunition Bingo at home, the box appeared to contain semi-automatic rifles.

Nasty!

Bearly used his radio and informed Ranger Rod of the situation. As Ranger Rod's group had just passed a lateral pathway, he advised Bearly to wait until he arrived before proceeding further.

It took a mere 1 minute and 14 seconds for Ranger Rod and his group to arrive, assess the situation, and decide on an action plan.

"Okay," Ranger Rod began.

"Here's what we're going to do," Chad whispered to Kyle, doing his best Ranger Rod impersonation.

"What was that?" Ranger Rod asked, glaring at Chad.

"Nothing," Chad replied sheepishly, looking suitably embarrassed.

"As I was saying ... here's what we're going to do," Ranger Rod continued as Kyle and Chad giggled to themselves. "Your group will continue down this aisle towards the source of the noise. My group will stay here while I figure out if all these boxes contain weapons," Ranger Rod ordered as he relieved Kyle of the scanner.

"Why don't you open up a box so we can see what's inside?" Chad asked. "If there are weapons, they may come in handy."

Ranger Rod, as predicted, was not very amused. "On what fucking planet would I distribute guns to the likes of you? We might as well just kill each other right here and now. No. My group will remain here with me while I examine the boxes. End of discussion."

Bearly and Scruffy led the way down the pathway once more, this time more focused on working their way as quietly and quickly down the aisle as they could.

Minutes went by, but no one was counting. The noises were growing louder as the group progressed, indicating that perhaps soon things would be coming to head.

Our heroes noticed that whilst the noises were increasing in volume, the relative brightness was also increasing. Kyle and Chad would periodically peer around Bearly and Scruffy, to try and gauge if there was a proverbial (and perhaps literal, in this case) light at the end of the tunnel. Sure enough, a few minutes into their journey, the end of the pathway appeared on the horizon culminating in a deep, warm, amber glow. No other details were visible this far away, but it seemed warm, cozy and, as far as anything could be as of late, somewhat rather inviting.

As fate would have it, only one of those things would be true.

Eventually, as the group drew closer and closer to the end of the aisle, the width of the pathway began to increase dramatically. There were still no details visible of what awaited them at the end, but the noises were getting much louder and the light much brighter, such that everyone had an unearthly orangey glow about them. Bearly periodically updated Ranger Rod on the radio about their progress and it sounded like Ranger Rod's group wasn't too far behind them.

If questioned about how long it took for the group to get to the end of the walkway, Kyle and Chad would probably have estimated about 45 minutes. As it turns out, Loyal Reader, it actually took slightly more than twice that long - 93 minutes.

The end of the walkway terminated in a wall. A very short wall. The wall was so short, in fact, that even Chad, if he tried, would be able to see over the top. The wall's presence, all 1.2192 meters high of it (*Fuck You!* Imperial System), fortuitously provided an excellent method to keep hidden whilst observing what might be going on to create the noises, which were now, in case you were wondering, crystal clear. The sounds were of the *quite loud banging and thudding* variety, the kind of sound you might hear if someone were dropping something really, really big onto a very hard surface.

Bearly and Scruffy made silent motions to get everyone lined up behind the wall. Once everyone was safely out of sight, he crept to the point where the shelves met the wall and cautiously peered over the edge, his face bathed by a shade of orange that somehow made him 26% more attractive.

Bearly grimaced slightly as he processed what he saw.

It seemed like an eternity before he finally bent back down to report his findings to the group.

It was, however, only 26.32 seconds.

186

"Well?" Kyle asked. "What did you see?"

"It's a loading zone," Bearly reported. "A large area with several flatbed trucks. From what I could see, I counted at least 25 heavily armed men; they're sporting the same kinds of semi-automatic weapons supposedly in those boxes. They seem to be loading these boxes onto the trucks, getting ready to ship them out."

"That's not good," Chad said.

"Understatement of the fucking century," Scruffy added.

He wasn't wrong.

"We'll wait here until Ranger Rod and his group catch up to us," Bearly said. "Under no circumstances does anyone break cover. Understood?"

Kyle, Chad, Suzie, and Wendy (yes, she was still with the group) nodded in nervous agreement.

Bearly pointed at Scruffy. "Head over to the corner and keep an eye on their activity. Signal me if they do anything suspicious."

Scruffy obliged and took up his post peering over the ledge and watching the soldiers and their activities like a hawk.

A really, really sexy hawk.

The group sat down and waited for Ranger Rod to arrive, which he and his group did just 18 minutes later. Bearly got his commander caught up as to what he witnessed, leading Ranger Rod to wonder just how much shit they were going to have to wade through to survive this pickle of a quandary.

Though he didn't realize it, the answer was 2.64 fucktons.

Ranger Rod made his was over to the vantage point and relieved Scruffy of his post. He watched the men, their movements and habits, trying to find some weakness that could be exploited.

Just as Ranger Rod was convinced that there might be hope in getting out alive, Bronx woke up and decided it would be just wonderful to announce his newly conscious state with a series of loud and shrill barks.

The soldiers in the loading area froze and turned towards the sound.

Ranger Rod tensed.

"Fuck," he hissed to himself. "This is not good."

Vegetables, dogs, and Germans, Loyal Reader. That's where we find ourselves at the moment. You see, historically speaking, we can recall only one verifiable recorded instance where a dog's bark has had a traceable, noticeable, global consequence.

Our story begins in 1870, a year that saw the United States Democratic Party represented in a political cartoon by a donkey for the first time, Thomas Mundy Peterson becoming the first black man to vote in a United States election, Christmas being declared a national holiday in the United States, the end of the Red River Rebellion in Canada, infanticide being legally banned in India (about fucking time), and a German chemist with the name of Erich von Wolf making, in retrospect, a simple canine-induced error.

Erich loved four things in life. They are, unfortunately, in order of increasing levels of unbridled affection:

- *His angelic wife Dietlinde.*
- *His loyal doggie Albrecht.*
- *Understanding the chemical forces that govern the Universe.*
- *A leafy green asstard of a vegetable called spinach.*

So pure and true was his fascination and complete devotion to spinach that he considered suggesting to Dietlinde that their first born be named in its honour. Fortunately, this did not come to fruition. Dietlinde was many things, but frail, delicate, and understanding did not even enter her planetary orbit. Dietlinde was a statuesque woman who, as Erich luckily surmised, would have effortlessly tossed him through the next wall had he suggested naming one of their children after his fucking precious green demon weed. Dietlinde often thought it was bad enough that he spent the vast majority of his days in his bleak and depressing basement laboratory (a standard design motif for any hip and modern chemist's environment), extracting, purifying, and categorizing who-knows-what from the volumes of spinach he had squirrelled away down there.

Erich's lab was his happy place; a subterranean utopia where he passed his time using the powerful tools of chemistry to unlock the marvels of spinach. Entry to his fortress of science was limited to only himself and his noble dachshund Albrecht, who spent each day in the lab dutifully sitting at rapt attention, ready to pounce and protect his master, should nefarious anti-spinach forces dare to intrude. Not even Dietlinde would disturb her husband's self-professed ground-breaking work as distractions were to be kept to a minimum.

Albrecht was a good doggie. He was a loving, affectionate, and well-behaved companion. He wasn't a fussy eater and he had never shown any signs of aggression towards other animals or even the most annoying of younglings. His only flaw, if you could call it that, was a propensity to bark when startled.

Though Albrecht possessed a tremendous amount of cute behaviours, all of which entrenched him deeply in the hearts of those who met him, he was by far his cutest self was when he was sleeping. You see, Loyal Reader, as a breed, the dachshund was artificially selected to excel at seeking out and destroying badgers and other burrow-dwelling animals. Albrecht, though a dachshund, was never required to perform this task and consequently, was never famous for being proficient at this particular attribute. Rather, Albrecht was famous for something quite a bit different - startling himself awake whenever he would fart in his sleep. One moment he would be dozing peacefully with visions of puppy treats dancing through his head, and the next moment he would make the cutest little "phhhhht" fart, waking himself up and letting out a single bark. Very few people could witness this occurrence and not crack a smile. Clearly, these people would be simple husks of flesh, even more so than the zombies that now roam the land.

Picture it, Loyal Reader, a warm and sunny afternoon - 2:46 pm on June 23rd, 1870. Erich von Wolf was busy working feverishly away in his lab, in the final stages of quantifying, for the first time ever, the amount of iron in spinach. His wife Dietlinde sat reclined in her chaise lounge, silently pondering the world around her and silently resenting the fact that she married a spinach-obsessed chemist. Albrecht was sleeping peacefully against the basement wall on a pillow behind his master. If you listened closely enough, you could just barely hear the air entering and exiting his nostrils. Erich, as expected, was in full rapt attention, staring at the laboratory bench in front of him. He had, just that morning, completed the last of the purification steps needed to obtain his results.

Many days ago, he had started with a mere 100 grams of spinach and, through a series of laborious and complex chemical reactions (black magic), managed to reduce it down to the small amount of dark grey powder that lay on the balance in front of him.

Fate, as we have learned over and over again since we first became acquainted some time ago, Loyal Reader, is a rancid little bitch of a fucker. You see, the very instant that Erich looked at his balance to record the amount of iron present, Albrecht lovingly passed a personal record-breaking amount of wind, woke himself up, and let out quite the startling bark. The momentary surprise at hearing this sound, combined with the excitement of the culmination of these spinach-related findings, caused Erich to make the most innocent and miniscule of mistakes.

Compared to the amounts of other chemicals and compounds in spinach like carbohydrates or potassium, there really isn't all that much iron. In fact, the number that Erich had briefly viewed on his balance (just as Albrecht scared the bejesus out of him, causing Erich to bump the scale in surprise, spilling the precious powder practically everywhere), was a paltry 3.5 milligrams. Albrecht's barking, however, caused a bout of momentary bewilderment, and Erich's muddled little brain had him record the amount instead as a tenfold increase - 35 milligrams.

The scary part of this story, Loyal Reader, is that Erich's Albrecht-induced mistake managed to be published, leading the scientific community to believe that spinach was as good a source of iron as, say, eating a steak. And believe this published fact everyone did. In a horrid commentary on the tendency for people to believe what they read and propagate the results, the blunder wasn't even fully recognized until 67 years later.

Salacious!

We hear you, Loyal Reader. "So, what?" you say. "It's only spinach, and it's good for you."

While this is certainly true, the implications of Erich von Wolf's gaffe have been quite far-reaching. For example, the nutritional value of spinach became legendary after the publication of his misleading data.

How many unsuspecting children have had to choke down that vile emerald ruffage of a shrub because of this?

Won't someone think of the children!?!?

In fact, American consumption of spinach increased by 30% in the 1930s, due directly to the influence of a beloved cartoon - Popeye The Sailor. It seems that studio executives, duped into thinking that spinach was a super food, were adamant that Popeye eat cans of the plant to get his strength. It's not uncommon for doctors today - 147 years later - to recommend that their anemic patients eat considerable amounts of spinach.

The moral of our story, Loyal Reader, is actually twofold. First, and possibly foremost, is that one must not believe everything one reads (except for all information found in this book, of course). People are people, and people make mistakes (expect for us, Loyal Reader; we remain as perfect as the day the Universe sharted us out in an orgasm of rainbows and Ultrasuede). What is sometimes taken as dogma can be the result of your pet dog farting, barking, and mucking the whole thing up. Secondly, and though possibly less important on a cosmic consequence scale, relates directly to our heroes' present dog-related happenstance, even something as innocuous as a simple bark can have far-reaching implications.

Take, for example, Loyal Reader, the case of Bronx. Though no one knew it at the time, this adorable little man's ill-timed bark, one that had made an appearance at very inopportune times over the years, could very well have initiated a sequence of events that, according to all possible scenarios published by the *Probability Coalition of the Centaurus Star Cluster,* could very well have led to the complete and utter annihilation of the human race.

CHAPTER 23

WIDDLE PUPPY PEE-PEE PIE

Waiting to see what would transpire, Ranger Rod continued to tense. The soldiers, fully facing towards the wall behind which the group was hiding, began to walk in their general direction. However, instead of walking to the wall and shooting the interlopers where they stood, the soldiers stopped at a series of boxes roughly equidistant between the wall and the trucks. This puzzled Ranger Rod, and with good reason.

Just in case anyone from the group was getting antsy about what was transpiring on the other side of the wall, Ranger Rod made the universal symbol for *shut the fuck up* as he observed the activities of the soldiers.

A direct consequence of his vantage point, Ranger Rod was unaware that the soldiers were actually staring intently at the big, cartoony diagrams that were expertly drawn on the fronts of the boxes they were facing. All of the boxes displayed the same picture - a non-descript, black-spotted, white dog with the hugest smile on its face (one can only conclude this was a crude, yet cutesy attempt at drawing a Dalmatian) lifting its right leg and letting go a vibrant yellow stream of urine onto a cute, dog-friendly-sized fire hydrant. A white speech bubble was positioned above the dog with big, rounded green letters spelling the word 'RUFF!' The drawing, obvious to even the most pedestrian of minds, was meant to indicate the specific toy that would be found inside the box, assuming they weren't unceremoniously replaced by weapons of small-to-medium-scale destruction.

The soldiers, though, did not check. Instead, they stood in front of said boxes and continued to stare intently. One of them took the tip of his gun and poked at one of the boxes with enough vim and vigor that it turned around, almost enough to reveal the cartoon to Ranger Rod.

No sound emerged from the box.

Another soldier did the same, with the same response.

Though it seemed impossible at the time, Ranger Rod managed to reach a new and as yet undescribed level of confusion.

"What the fuck?" he said to himself every so softly.

Ranger Rod's confusion was, of course, completely founded. Without seeing the doggy drawing on the boxes, he had no context and therefore could not possibly comprehend why the soldiers weren't marching to the wall, intent on finding the source of the barking and killing it dead.

We would argue, Loyal Reader, that even if Ranger Rod had seen the front of the boxes, he would still be suffering from dangerously high levels of perplexity.

But, why? you might ponder.

As always, we are so very, very glad you asked, Loyal Reader and we are more than happy to oblige.

Let us begin the following diatribe by outlining the four most probable questions that would have leapt into Ranger Rod's mind, leading to his current baffled state:

> *1. Were the soldiers just so fucking stupid that they would think that the barking actually originated from a box of children's toys?*
>
> *2. Were the soldiers also so fucking stupid that they would honestly believe that the boxes actually contained the toys that are pictured on their fronts?*
>
> *3. If #2 was indeed true, and the soldiers were that fucking stupid, then is it not a remote possibility that the soldiers aren't really that fucking stupid at all, but rather that some of the boxes might actually not have any weapons in them, and instead contain children's' toys?*
>
> *4. What child in her or his right mind would want a toy that mimics the immediate and soaking effects of the canine urinary system?*

The answers to the above questions, Loyal Reader, in case you are clinically obsessed with keeping track at home, are:

1. Yes
2. Yes
3. Yes
4. Future politicians, Loyal Reader, that's who.

What the box did not indicate, which has more than a little bearing on the current conversation on children and their eventual piss-poor life choices (pun very much intended), is that everything about the toy itself is annoying as fuck.

Take the name of the toy as a prime example - *Widdle Puppy Pee-Pee Pie*. It's just stupidly awful. Once you get past the deliriously idiotic name, trying to get the box open is a fittingly frustrating introduction to the toy that awaits inside. Packaged and shipped out of who-knows-where, they apparently use a space-age polymer that chemically binds every single fiber of the box's edges to one another. Most people end up clawing at the box like a rabid animal trying to escape a death trap.

Once inside, however, you'll be pleased to note that the dog and fire hydrant are shrink-wrapped in an incredibly hard plastic shell to such an obscene degree that you will need, and we are not kidding, nothing less than an X-acto knife to gain access to the pain and suffering that awaits you inside. Be warned, though, the plastic is so rigid and so slippery that the probability of cutting yourself with the blade are, in fact, greater than the odds of shitting your pants on any given Thursday afternoon.

Having liberated the annoyingly happy dog and its fire hydrant from the plastic tomb, you will eventually come to realize exactly five extraordinarily disappointing factoids.

> *1. The dog is permanently positioned with his right leg lifted in the air, so don't go hoping that you can forego the whole urination thing and have a cute puppy sitting by a fire hydrant. No. Rather, you are now locked into giving little Harlequin or Accordion or Manhattan or whatever the shit your kid's atrocious, ludicrous, and depressing name is, nothing more than a bestiality piss fetish toy.*

2. *Nowhere on the box does it say, "Batteries Not Included," so you better have six AA batteries kicking around. Otherwise, not only will there will be no barking, there most certainly will be no pee-pee.*
3. *Widdle Puppy Pee-Pee Pie needs to be fed his urine; he doesn't make it from scratch (now that would be a revolutionary toy!). This is not a joke. Little Acheeya (pronounced Asia, for the love of all that is soul crushing) will have to take some water and mix in a dash of the provided yellow dye, and then pour the newly mixed urine into Widdle Puppy Pee-Pee Pie's mouth. Gross!*
4. *Assuming you do have six of the above-mentioned batteries in your junk drawer or your favorite "massager," you'll need to be very careful with the amount of water that little Andromeda puts into the dog. As 2,134 customers found out in the winter of 1984, the tray included at the bottom of the fire hydrant that collects the liquid that Widdle Puppy Pee-Pee Pie excretes, holds exactly one and a half cups. Interesting fact: Widdle Puppy Pee-Pee Pie's mouth can swallow a load of two cups of piss. At this point, everyone at home should now have completed the math.*
5. *This leads directly from #3. In what can only be assumed to have been considered a stroke of genius in a marketing meeting, Widdle Puppy Pee-Pee Pie manages to pee out a yellow liquid so that kids will think their plastic puppy is actually peeing. Groan. Little Lesasha or Peninsula had to physically feed the poor little bastard dog its own piss to start the whole process, so if they are amazed that yellow comes out its business end, then there is something very wrong with the state of children in today's society. And this isn't even the issue, Loyal Reader, that's the hilarious part. What drew even more ire from the droves of 1980s customers was that the yellow dye in question (a*

cheap knock-off of the oft-used standard yellow food-colouring dye tartrazine) called Super Honor Safe Yellow Fortune Good Time Lucky Captain #1 Rocket Ship Dye, stains anything it touches, and does so permanently.

So ... the bottom line can only be ... good luck with that. Disappointment would be inevitable as families were tasked with trusting their kids with a toy that can spout a volume of permanent yellow dye greater than the reservoir provided to contain it.

Well-played, Jacko Toys Trading Company, Limited, well-played.

The soldiers examined and prodded the boxes for a few moments before going back about their business of loading the flat-bed trucks. Though he was feeling incredibly puzzled by the actions of the soldiers, Ranger Rod was convinced of one thing - if they didn't take action soon, something terrible was going to happen.

Hiding behind this wall was a precarious position, and in Ranger Rod's vast experience, people rarely survived these types of situations. Returning to the group, he relayed his thoughts on the matter and outlined his plan: the group would use the boxes scattered around the area as cover, and stealthily sneak up behind the soldiers.

"That's suicide!" Ted/Ned/Something proclaimed.

"There are no other options," Scruffy reminded the group. "We can't stay hiding here forever and we can't spend the next three months walking around the cavern like mice in a maze."

Scruffy's simile was appropriate, if not well-crafted, and we are certainly not in a position to judge.

No one in the group, though, seemed to care. He was good-looking enough that he didn't need to be especially creative.

"Those men are loading up trucks. That means there's an exit out of here," Bearly added.

"And that's going to be our objective," Ranger Rod concluded.

"But we have no guns," Vera said, the terror in her voice causing the last syllable to tremble ever so slightly.

"Why don't you guys have guns?" one of the guys who had been watching *Harold & Kumar Go to White Castle* back in the lounge questioned.

We'll get to Ranger Rod's fitting and profanity-laced response in just one moment, Loyal Reader. First, however, we should cover what was running through Kyle's head as this tiny little heated exchange was taking place. The same thought process was not running through Chad's head at that particular moment in time, but it was an ever-present source of frustration.

Chad, unsurprisingly, was busy wondering when in the name of all that is good and true in the world were Bearly, Scruffy, and Blaze going to participate in the mother of all make-out sessions.

Probably not anytime soon, Chad concluded.

While Chad's adolescent brain was exploring the seventh-grade saliva-sharing possibilities of the three sexy soldiers, Kyle's was preoccupied with the fact that they had not yet been told the names of these two movie-watching guys. Of course, Kyle's brain would concede, current circumstances saw to it that there weren't very many opportunities to learn their names.

I wonder if it would be inappropriate ask their names now. Kyle thought to himself. Given the tensions that were forming, it seemed like it most certainly would have been.

Kyle thought better of this impulse and instead went back to the frustration of the duo remaining nameless. This persisted for a few microseconds, but in Kyle's brain it felt like a veritable eternity. In the end, he decided it was best for everyone involved if he just left them as nameless *Red Shirts* for now. Perhaps if they all somehow managed to survive this mega cluster-fuck, they would all learn each other's names at the after-party.

Do you think there'll be an after-party? Kyle asked to himself as his brain began to meander down the next rabbit hole.

"What the fuck did you just say to me?" Ranger Rod seethed at the nameless young man.

"Nothing," he replied, his inquisitive nature following his testicles in their hasty retreat.

Kyle leaned over to the other anonymous guy, the one not currently being eye-slaughtered by Ranger Rod. "Sorry, what's your name again?" he whispered.

"Really?" he replied.

198

Damn, I thought that might work, Kyle thought.

"You are correct Fucktard, we have no guns," Ranger Rod fumed, looking squarely at … hmmm … what should we call him Loyal Reader? Let's go with the most derivative of names - Harold. "But that doesn't mean we're going to cower here and wait for them to discover us. We know nothing about the security in the other parts of the cavern and what other activities might be going on. We have an opportunity here, and we should grab it."

"What's the plan?" asked Blaze.

"Simple; we manage to sneak out there behind the closest line of boxes and make our way to the two men stationed behind the trucks. We subdue them, grab their guns, take out the rest, grab a truck, and get the fuck out of Dodge."

"Roger that!" Blaze replied.

Bearly and Scruffy nodded in agreement.

"I am *not* going out there," Ted/Ned/Something stated.

"Me neither," Vera added. "What can we really do? We're ever so outmanned and outgunned," she gasped while sporting what she hoped would be described as the world's worst rendition of a sad clown face.

In reality, she looked constipated.

Like, really constipated.

"Ever so? Really?" Chad whispered to Kyle in scathing judgement.

"Ed! That's the guy's name," Kyle added suddenly.

"Oh yeah! Totally!" Chad replied.

"I'm not going to ask any of you to join us in taking down the soldiers," Ranger Rod replied. "The four of us are trained for that. However, you are all going with us out there and will remain hidden behind the crates while we do our job."

"No fucking way!" exclaimed the other anonymous guy that we are aptly naming Kumar. He, of course, did not resemble Kal Penn at all, but that's just going to have to be okay. Deal with it, Loyal Reader.

"Fine," Ranger Rod stated matter-of-factly. "Do whatever the fuck you want. Whoever wants to stay here can do so. We're going to have our hands full out there, I can't possibly predict how it's all going to play out, so I will not be responsible for having to defend two groups of civilians. Those that come with us will get our protection, the rest of you can fend for yourselves."

With that, Ranger Rod made a motion to his men and posed an all-important question to the group. "Who's in?"

Kyle looked at Chad, tilted his head, and raised an eyebrow. "What do you think?" Kyle asked his husband.

"I would literally follow these men to the ends of the Earth," Chad replied in complete and utter honesty.

"Classy," Kyle stated dryly.

"You love it," Chad retorted with a smile and then turned to Ranger Rod. "We're in."

"Me too," Suzie said.

Ranger Rod waited a few seconds for the others to make up their minds. Ed and Vera were holding hands and looking down at the floor; neither saying a word. Harold and Kumar continued to stare defiantly at Ranger Rod, shaking their heads back and forth. Wendy, predictably, didn't say a word, but moved to beside Suzie and gave Ranger Rod a thumbs-up accompanied by a wide-eyed grin.

"Okay," Ranger Rod commanded. "Let's move out."

Reaching, and then hiding behind the stacks of *Widdle Puppy Pee-Pee Pie* boxes was astonishingly uneventful. Ranger Rod led the group over the wall and across the open space without any of the soldiers noticing. It really was that simple. While perhaps we wish we could describe to you some tense moments when perhaps someone dropped something and made a noise that caused everyone to tighten their anal sphincters in terror, nothing of the sort materialized. In fact, within a minute of leaving the presumed safety and security of the area behind the wall, the eight of them found themselves safely sequestered behind the stacked boxes.

It was at that exact moment that every last one of the anal sphincters in the cavern did tighten just a little bit more, not because anyone made a sound and gave away their position to the soldiers. No, Loyal Reader, that would have been way too predictable and obvious.

The Universe, it seems, had something far more bizarre in store for the group.

Just as Ranger Rod finished explaining to his men a scenario that he thought had at least something of a snowball's chance in Hell of working, a whirling vortex of clouds and an insanely bright blue light appeared above and behind them.

The magical, suddenly appearing whirling vortex had four direct eventualities that manifested in the following order:

> 1. *Ed pissed his pants.*
> 2. *Vera emitted a blood-curdling scream.*
> 3. *Ed, Vera, Harold, and Kumar were consummately sucked into the vortex and disappeared forever.*
> 4. *Riding his signature baby blue Moped of Justice, famed Japanese crime fighter Ishitori Katsubi and his Hentai Girls descended effortlessly and elegantly from the vortex.*

No, Loyal Reader, we are most certainly not joking.
We really wish we were.

CHAPTER 24

WTF?

Xanadau is not only an ageless musical masterpiece production starring the fabulous Olivia Newton-John, but interestingly is also the closest that the inhabitants of Earth had ever come to witnessing the technicolour spectacle of a vortex until one of them just happened to appear in an eerily-lit subterranean cavern on December 26th.

We love a good origin story, Loyal Reader, and this one is as old as time itself.

A household name in his local prefecture of Shizuoka, Ishitori Katsubi patrols the streets on his mighty baby blue Moped of Justice. Armed with his two legendary samurai swords, Kasumi and Tokiwa, Ishitori has been single-handedly credited with making the streets of Hamamatsu once again safe.

Born Tadashi Nakamura, the only child of a shopkeeper and his seamstress wife, Tadashi spent his childhood as a sickly, gaunt boy who was teased relentlessly by his classmates. Allergic to practically everything, when he wasn't hating every moment of his life in school, he would work long hours in his father's shop.

Tadashi's meager and dismal life changed one fateful early March morning during his 17th year on Earth. Whilst walking to school, an activity that was usually a boring and predictable affair, Tadashi heard a strange and compelling noise seeping from a nearby darkened alley.

Not known to be the sharpest knife in the drawer, Tadashi thought nothing of venturing down said dark alley in search of the source of this most interesting sound. His blatant lack of self-preservation instincts aside, fortune was with Tadashi that day; as he continued to walk down the alleyway (which was much, much longer than it needed or appeared to be), the source of the noise always seemed to be just out of reach.

Finally making his way to the end of the alley, Tadashi emerged into a beautiful forested glen; a shimmering green field lined on either side by cherry trees in full bloom. At the end of the meadow, sitting comfortably cross-legged on the grass and wrapped in an iridescent royal blue cloak, an old woman beckoned him closer. Tadashi tentatively approached and sat opposite her. The woman reached behind her and produced a small cup of tea, which she offered to him.

Again, and we can't stress this enough, Loyal Reader, Tadashi seemed to lack any basic evolutionary relics of a survival instinct. He gladly accepted the tea from this stranger and drank it in a single gulp.

Eighteen seconds later he was unconscious.

Tadashi awoke some time later in a darkened space. The walls were stone and the only sources of light were several candles positioned around the perimeter of the room. Once his eyes grew accustomed to the dim environment, Tadashi sat up.

He had been placed on a stone table.

How odd, he thought to himself.

In addition to waking up in a strange place on a strange stone table, he was no longer wearing his usual clothes.

How curious, he continued.

Tadashi stood and inspected his new ensemble. It appeared to be a cloth samurai outfit of the same color and fabric as the old woman's cloak. Besides the table and candles, the only other items in the room were two swords, each resting within an open wooden display case on the wall.

Tadashi instinctively picked up each sword. He swung and fastened them over each shoulder, unsheathed them, and held them in his hands.

At that moment, what seemed like a lifetime of memories flooded into his brain, memories that were clearly not his. Though ostensibly seeming an impossibility, Tadashi knew deep within his soul that he was now a samurai master; each of the two swords no longer novelty weapons, but an extension of his mind and body.

The old woman appeared in the doorway to the chamber.

"You are now Ishitori Katsubi," she stated, her voice raspy and deep, "Defender of the Innocent."

Tadashi, confused beyond belief, and yet deep inside knowing that what she said was true, could not summon the words to reply.

The old woman turned and walked away. Tadashi followed her through the doorway, emerging into a much larger room. The old woman, however, was nowhere to be found. The room did, however, contain six attractive young women.

The girls formed a perfect line and were dressed in identical skin-tight and very, very revealing leather outfits - royal blue, of course. As Tadashi emerged from the doorway, they moved aside to reveal a single item behind them - a baby blue motorized Vespa moped.

"You are Ishitori Katsubi, Protector of Truth," said one of the girls. "This is your Moped of Justice and we are your ninja schoolgirl squad, the Hentai Girls."

"Oooooooookay," Tadashi responded. "I thought I was the Defender of the Innocent?" He really should have been more confused.

"You are all things to all people!" one of the Hentai Girls shouted, startling Ishitori and abruptly ending that particular avenue of inquiry.

Behind the Hentai Girls and at the opposite end of the room was a large opening that led to a gently upward-sloping hallway. Tadashi followed the passage, finally emerging through a large, arching doorway into a meadow; the very one where he had encountered the old woman that morning. He half-expected to see her sitting cross-legged on the grass once more, but she was not.

Tadashi never saw her again, but he would take the mantle given to him and forever protect the world from the forces of evil.

He was Ishitori Katsubi, Samurai Master!

Ishitori and his Hentai Girls provided a very well-timed, if not completely unexpected, commotion. Ranger Rod and his men had no idea what to make of the situation.

Our heroes were similarly baffled.

Ed, Vera, Harold, and Kumar were probably also perplexed, wherever they were, but no doubt for very different reasons.

Wendy, however, was clapping her hands vigorously and yelling "Ishitori!" over and over and over again. She sounded like a fourteen-year-old girl at a/an [insert culturally appropriate and vacuous teenybopper boy band reference here] concert.

We are so current, Loyal Reader!

The Moped of Justice screeched to halt beside the group. To everyone's surprise, Ishitori spoke perfect English.

"I am Ishitori Katsubi, Defender of the Innocent and Protector of the Truth!" he bellowed, "and these are my Hentai Girls." With that, each of the six young women, though brandishing an impressive variety of weapons, giggled and curtseyed.

"What the fuck is happening right now?" Kyle asked no one in particular.

"I haven't a goddamned clue," Chad replied. "I thought I was going insane."

"The soldiers will not be preoccupied for long," Ishitori said. "We need a distraction; one that will afford us the possibility of gaining the upper hand."

Loyal Reader, history books are divided on what happened next. There are purists who argue it was simply an impossibility. Their opinions, though as valid as the next idiot's, are countered by the throngs of people who fundamentally believe that the Universe unfolded exactly as planned, and that within its chaotic and entropic forces, all things are possible. The truth, of course, and as it always does, lies somewhere in between. All we can do, Loyal Reader, is relay to you what we know to have occurred that fateful evening and let you be the judge.

No one was prepared for what transpired next, least of all the person who actually perpetrated it.

Ishitori's comments must have struck a chord deep within Chad, for he immediately began rifling through the huge boxes the group was hiding behind. Chad knew, as much as he had ever known anything in this life, that this was what he was meant to do.

"What are you looking for?" Suzie asked.

"I actually have no idea," Chad replied as he searched through box after box with impressive speed. "I'll know it when I find it, though."

As it turned out, it was exactly 58 seconds later when Chad, opening a massive box, gazed awestruck into its contents. A wide-eyed smile crossed his face as he jumped into the humungous box.

Precisely 43 seconds later, Chad reappeared; this time, however, he was 6.64 times more fabulous than before, despite wearing a drab-colored dress, a short blonde wig, and a large sunhat.

Chad ran over to Ishitori and jumped on the back of his Moped of Justice. Ishitori wasted no time in racing Chad over to the back of the largest of the flatbed trucks. Chad, utterly amazed that he hadn't yet been shot multiple times by the soldiers, climbed to the top of the stacked boxes, straightened his wig, hat, and frock, and began to sing.

> *"Let's start at the very beginning,*
> *a very good place to start.*
> *When you read you begin with A-B-C.*
> *When you sing you begin with Do-Re-Mi.*
> *The first three notes just happen to be Do-Re-Mi."*

The look of shock on the faces of the group members was so complete and absolute that it would have been hilarious had it not been for the gravity of the situation. The aforementioned shock can be divided into three equal parts:

> - *Shock that Chad would dare to pull such a stunt in the middle of what was promising to be a blood bath rivalling that of biblical proportions.*
> - *Shock that of all the distraction techniques to try, this is what Chad managed to come up with.*
> - *And lastly, shock that what was currently taking place actually seemed to be working.*

The soldiers were transfixed. With what, Loyal Reader, we can't be 100% sure, but they certainly were downright mesmerized by Chad's rendition of Maria Von Trapp. So much so, in fact, that every single one of them seemed to forget about the cavern's intruders and began to sing along with Chad, who was now leading them in the mother of all life-or-death musical numbers.

> *"Doe - a deer, a female deer.*
> *Ray - a drop of golden sun.*
> *Me - a name I call myself.*
> *Far - a long, long way to run.*

207

*Sew - a needle pulling thread.
La - a note to follow so.
Tea - a drink with jam and bread.
That will bring us back to Do."*

"That is brilliant!" shouted Ranger Rod as Chad and the soldiers kept singing. "That little bastard's a fucking genius. Now let's come up with a plan."

Let us rewind a few moments, Loyal Reader. While we agree that the performance Chad was donating to the soldiers was a Kyle Award winning spectacle, even stranger things were manifesting with his husband. You see, Loyal Reader, just as Chad had begun searching through the boxes, Kyle's mind instantly and inexplicably became otherwise preoccupied. To everyone around him, he appeared to enter into a trancelike state. Unaware of what was happening, Kyle's mind began to incessantly swirl, eventually turning in on itself.

"For Christ's sake! Am I the only one who's observant here?" he yelled at no one in particular. "How can you stand it?"

"What the fuck is he going on about?" Ranger Rod asked Suzie.

"I honestly have no idea," she replied.

Kyle clenched his fists in rage and cried to the heavens, "Take me now!"

The Universe, luckily, did not.

No, Loyal Reader, the Universe had bigger plans for our hero. These plans, as it turned out, involved his little princess-pie, Brooklyn, as she came to him in a glorious and exceedingly unsettling vision.

Kyle's eyes closed as his other senses began to take heightened form. Brooklyn appeared to him, the epitome of serenity, with glowing light emanating from all around her. Time seemed to stop, and Kyle swore he could hear the sweet strains of a distant sitar and the heavenly tones of a choir of angels. Brooklyn was, remarkably, sitting in the lotus position.

It was from this magnificent visage that she spoke:

> *"You see me as an anxious little dog.*
> *However, one does not see the world as it is, but we see it as we ourselves are.*
> *You are now seeing my true form.*
> *Reach inside yourself and find the serenity within.*
> *Your personality is simply a reflection of the chaos that you choose to see amongst the world.*
> *Peace cannot be found in a mandala, for these are simply a waste of time; dusty and dirty things.*
> *Peace can only be found in the compulsive acquisition of electronics, vehicles, and drones.*
> *Only these will bring you true happiness, affording you the true path to focus your mental energy."*

"I understand," said Kyle, and in what was, in reality, only a microsecond, he saw the glow within the cavern for what it was.

"The light is like a fire," Kyle continued, his eyes still closed. "The truck symbolizes the parapet. We are all but prisoners in the cave and I cannot trust my senses. Knowledge can only be gained through philosophical reasoning."

With that, Brooklyn offered a simple, poignant reply.

"Exactly."

As she spoke, the shimmering spectral image slowly nodded, her eyes closed.

"I finally understand," Kyle said calmly. "It all makes perfect sense."

For a moment, Kyle completely understood the Entanglement Theory, and knew that he could use it for good; that his thoughts could influence reality, a reality of his own making in the sixth realm of existence.

Kyle gave his head a shake. "Fuck this!" he bellowed. "I don't have time for this shit." Kyle realized that, although, in essence, the sixth realm was all about him, what was currently transpiring in the cavern beyond his visions was not. This led to him becoming very bored and angry, snapping him out his trance and popping him unceremoniously back into the razor-sharp claws of reality.

Kyle wasn't sure how long he had been out of it. When he finally opened his eyes, he half-expected to see everything covered in blood and body parts strewn everywhere. The last thing he remembered was the arrival of the Japanese dude and his schoolgirls.

As luck would have it, the bloodbath had yet to occur. Kyle was in his trance for a grand total of two minutes and thirteen seconds, just long enough for Chad to make his way about halfway through his production.

While the majority of the group were fixated on Chad's performance (Scruffy, bless his heart, was actively singing along with the soldiers), Suzie was staring directly at Kyle and looking quite concerned.

"What was that?" she asked.

"What was what?" Kyle replied.

"You. Blanking out. Not responding to me hollering at you and shaking you."

"Oh that. No biggie. It's all good."

"Really?" Suzie said dryly in disbelief.

"Totally. But more importantly what is Chad doing?"

"Having a blast, by the looks of it.

"At least it's working."

"You're not wrong."

> *"When you know the notes to sing,*
> *You can sing most anything!*
> *Together!"*

Though Chad was having the time of his life, his distraction was beginning to wear thin. The soldiers had begun to suspect that Chad was not, in fact, Julie Andrews. Crucial to their suspicions was the discovery by one of the men of a discrepancy between Chad's size 8E New Balance runners and Julie Andrews famed women's size 6 pumps. It wasn't too much longer before a few of the soldiers began to sing with less and less vigor. Chad, noticing that some of the men were beginning to wane, added 21% more fabulousness to his rendition to try and buy the group a bit more time.

Luckily, Ranger Rod, his men, and Ishitori had just finalized their plan to battle the soldiers and were preparing to act. The plan was simple, elegant, and completely predictable - Ishitori and the Hentai girls would set about slaughtering the soldiers while Ranger Rod and his men secured the truck.

Just as they were about to strike, Kyle grabbed Ranger Rod and Ishitori by the hand.

"Wait!" he screamed. "I know what we have to do."

For some reason, Loyal Reader, Ranger Rod did not immediately dismiss our hero. Nor did he snap Kyle's arm in two. Rather, he and Ishitori were so overcome by the confidence and passion in Kyle's voice that they were powerless to do nothing except follow Kyle's lead.

Kyle set about ripping open one of the boxes. The box had a cartoon of a small, yellow, plastic ducky, the kind you might find floating in a child's bath.

Disemboweling the box revealed no rubber duckies nor did it reveal any semi-automatic weapons. Instead, Kyle found, when he reached into the box, an assortment of Tickle Me Elmos and dildo tipped Sawzall reciprocating saws.

"This is absolutely perfect!" he cried and threw the array of items to the members of his group.

Chad, for one, was particularly thankful for the influx of weapons as most of the soldiers were now beginning to feign indifference to the wiles of his riveting and ground-breaking performance of *The Sound of Music*.

"Bastard heathens!" he wailed, as he caught an Elmo Kyle had tossed and then launched himself through the air at the soldiers below.

CHAPTER 25

TIMMY, HIS MARSHMALLOWS, AND HIS DING-DONG

You know, though we end up saying this quite a bit of late, Loyal Reader, it doesn't change the fact that what happened next defies description. Safe to say that everyone, even Wendy, joined in the battle with the soldiers. It was a grizzly scene of blood, sinew, salve, wigs, entrails, and false nails. The air was filled with screaming, yelling, and giggling as the armed soldiers were tickled, pleasured, and sliced to their untimely deaths.

The battle, a term that only approximates what the average person might call it, was quite possibly the most uncoordinated spectacle that most of the group had ever laid eyes on, with the exception of Chad, who experienced something far, far more spectacular many moons ago.

Back in the early 1990s, when Chad was a spry, morbidly obese university student, he found himself one early March afternoon strolling innocently through the Student Union Building cafeteria. Tray in hand, he made his way to an empty section of the large seating area.

This particular day resembled pretty much every other day that Chad spent getting his lunch at the cafeteria. He would be eating one of his three

Olympic-training meals: western omelet and fries, clubhouse and fries, or chicken strips and fries. Chad was never (and, in a remarkable 50-ish year streak of consistency that some might actually find commendable, but most people simply label stubborn, still wasn't) known for his tendency to shake up any given particular routine that he has convinced himself to be working just fine, thank you very much.

Regardless of Chad's propensity to enjoy repeating the same behaviours over and over and over and over and over again, this little trip down Memory Lane isn't about the recurrence of any given event in Chad's life, it's about a very ... interesting ... boy who we'll simply call Timmy. Chad didn't know Timmy's name, and in fact, hadn't even set eyes on Timmy until that fateful day.

Chad sat on the end of one his favourite tables, got comfy, and began to eat. A few minutes into his meal Chad noticed Timmy in his wheelchair sitting on the end of a table about 10 rows away. A woman who Chad assumed was Timmy's mother sat to his left, seemingly oblivious to her son and the world around her. Instead, she was neck-deep in books and papers, suggesting she was getting homework done or studying or some other such drudgery.

Timmy's mother was a hefty woman, with thick glasses and a long ponytail that sported a tidy racing stripe of grey. Chad imagined she was named Beula and she was long separated from her deadbeat husband who left her for a twenty-something whore when he realized his son wasn't going to ever play university football. Chad winced a bit as his mind raced in that particular direction, but this momentary melancholy was tempered by the yumminess of that day's lunch and also the observation that Timmy was talking away to himself and appearing to be having the time of his life.

Upon first glance, not understanding what he was doing or what he was saying to himself, Chad was unsure exactly why Timmy was having such a great time. As Chad's interest piqued, however, the situation, in all its hilariousness, unfolded rather quickly.

Timmy's wheelchair had a tray positioned overtop his lap, and upon this tray was a bag of mini marshmallows. This alone could very well have been sufficient enough to make Timmy's day; marshmallows are, after all, a soft, sweet, delicious treat. Indeed, Timmy, of course, was eating the marshmallows that his mother had supplied him with all the vim and vigour that was expected of such an occasion.

As Chad watched, Timmy picked up one of the marshmallows (this took some time, as you can imagine), and as he lifted it towards his mouth, he said, "One for me!" and promptly consumed it. What Chad witnessed happening next was quite surprising, as he expected the previous sequence of events to simply repeat itself until, a) Timmy's mom decided it was time to pack up and leave, or b) Timmy finished the bag of mini marshmallows.

Timmy though, was full of surprises. He picked up the next squishy victim, but instead of bringing it up to his mouth, he promptly lowered his arm and stuck his hand into his lap saying, "And one for my ding-dong!"

Yes, Loyal Reader, Timmy's ding-dong apparently loved mini marshmallows too.

Chad was suitably amused but managed to keep his laughter internalized.

It wasn't that Timmy was performing these actions and simply muttering to himself the two phrases in question that led to such amusement on Chad's behalf, oh no. If only that were the case, Loyal Reader. Timmy was, in fact, yelling these words in a euphoric state of glee. It was, as seemingly awful and inappropriate as this may sound, one of the cutest things Chad had ever seen in his life, and to this day, Loyal Reader, it remains safely in the Top 5.

Of particular note for Chad was the disjunction that emerged from his mother studiously sitting right beside Timmy, seemingly oblivious to the penis feeding frenzy transpiring to her right.

Timmy's mom was either, a) so engrossed in her academics that she had completely tuned out everything that was happening around her, or b) quite aware that her son was shoving his treats into his pants, but that it didn't really warrant her attention or intervention.

Both of those possibilities were equally disturbing, Loyal Reader, but for vastly different reasons. Chad wondered that if it was the former, what his mother would think when she got home with Timmy and discovered a treasure trove of marshmallows in his pants?

By the time Chad finished giggling his way through lunch and made his way out of the cafeteria to go do whatever it was that Chad did on your average March afternoon, Timmy continued to soldier on and fight the good, uncoordinated fight.

While there are numerous jaw-dropping scenes that unfolded during the ensuing carnage in the massive underground cavern, none were quite so spectacular as that which occurred near the end of the battle between Chad and an unfortunate soldier named Kenneth.

For the record, Kenneth is not a name befitting of a soldier.
Kenneth is the name that a hipster douchebag ironically bestows to his vintage bicycle or German Shepherd.
Kenneth is what little asshole kids name their turtles.
That is all.

All the other members of the group were busy trouncing their own combatants, so no one actually witnessed what happened to poor, poor Kenneth. Instead, everyone was left awestruck and in total disbelief when it was all over.

Chad, to bring us back to the situation at hand, was laying on top of poor Kenneth, punching him repeatedly with a left fist full of Elmo and a right fist full of dildo.

Kenneth, to his credit, tried his damnedest to figure out what was happening, but was failing miserably in that regard. In his defense, though, Kenneth was drifting in and out of consciousness and mere seconds away from expiring.

As if the above scene weren't enough to make the average person question everything in the world around them, Chad then shot laser beams from his eyes.

Yes, you did hear us correctly, Loyal Reader.
Laser beams.
From his eyes.
Sigh.
Again, Loyal Reader, we are not joking.
And yes, we most certainly still wish we were.

You see, Loyal Reader, in this Universe, apparently not only are there zombies, Santa Claus, zombie elves, and reindeer, but also humans with superpowers. It is also worth pointing out that Chad's particular superpower involved the ability to plagiarize *Cyclops* from *The X-Men*.

Just sayin'.

Regardless, the above ludicrous scenario we just described did indeed unfold (we swear on the life of the now undead James Marsden), and a certain young man from Wichita, Kansas, by the name of Kenneth Jamieson was not amused; he was too busy being disintegrated, his ashes falling like delicate snowflakes.

Before anyone in the group had the chance to wrestle with what had just transpired, Kyle eyes widened, and he looked up in the air. He pointed with a hand that shook uncontrollably, and as he did, a brand-spanking new vortex opened up, baby blue, and directly behind the group.

As debris began to fly everywhere, Ishitori, now riding his baby blue Moped Of Justice, and his Hentai Girls were instantaneously sucked into the swirling void, which closed immediately thereafter.

That's two vortexes now, Kyle thought. *What are the odds of that?*

We could calculate those odds, Loyal Reader, but the ensuing intergalactic calculus would *literally* bore you to death. As such, we will, for once, do the right thing and uncharacteristically keep our beautiful mouths shut.

Kyle had only 6 seconds to ponder the answer to that question before a loud bang pierced the air.

"You've got to be fucking kidding me!" Ranger Rod cried.

There were a few seconds of silence followed by Chad vocalizing what everyone else was thinking.

"What fresh Hell is this?" he asked earnestly.

CHAPTER 26

THE SPECTACULAR DEMISE OF A HIPSTER NAMED SIMON

Zeitgeisted up the wazoo is the winner, Loyal Reader! We recently took an informal poll of what can only be described as four hominids loosely associated by the gossamer strings of time, space, and Rogers Video. They were tasked with crafting an opening to this chapter and boy, did one of them deliver. But we digress ...

You see, Loyal Reader, interstellar, interdimensional, and interplanetary vortexes have been the stuff of science fiction media since the first historical nerds took quill to parchment oh so many years ago. Of course, no actual examples of any of these scientific phenomena have ever been observed, categorized, and/or published in any reputable (or non-reputable, for that matter) scientific journal. As such, they seemed destined to forever be relegated to the annals of popular culture. This was, perhaps, especially likely given that the Earth had, just eight short months ago, gone to Hell in a handbasket, what with the zombie hordes doing what they do best and all.

Not so fast, Loyal Reader.

The attentive amongst us know a little secret - up until the above-mentioned occurrences of the three vortexes that appeared in the large cavern just outside of Hunters, Washington, there did exist a single, observable,

219

occurrence in 2005 of an *Interstellar Vortex,* and it was equal parts magnificent and dreadful.

This particular vortex, though, didn't transport unsuspecting individuals from one place to another in the galaxy - oh no, it did something far, far more nefarious than that.

You see, *Interstellar Vortex* can only loosely be described as a song.

A terrible song.

A horrendously awful auditory catastrophe of a song.

Four minutes and forty-two seconds of aural agony, in fact.

Just how ghastly was this song, you might ask? Most excellent question, Loyal Reader. Though no official historical records of the track's deadly impact actually exist, we can confirm, with no measure of hyperbole, that *Interstellar Vortex* was the singular root cause for a sequence of events that led to the deaths of five people in Australia one balmy spring morning.

October 15th, 2005 began innocuously enough. A bipedal primate named Simon Anderson, at this point in his life a 28-year-old hipster bartender living in Brisbane, woke to face what would turn out to be his last day on Earth.

The term hipster had only just begun to be thrown about to describe not only the fashion vomit that people like Simon sported, but also the bubble-gum metaphysical approach that he and his brood generously spunked on all matters of everyday life.

It was, as you can imagine, quite painful to watch.

This shouldn't surprise you, Loyal Reader. We know you can see the forest for the man bun, and that's one of the 723 reasons why we love you.

Simon, to his credit, was a visionary. He practically invented what it was like to be a hipster in eastern Australia. For him, it was effortless.

Simon lived alone in a brick-walled loft above a local record store. For reference, a 'record' is a disc, a hard, primarily polyvinyl black disc, that acts as an analog sound storage medium. These 'records' store the music on concentric rings of inscribed, modular, spiral grooves.

Archaic, right?

Hipsters, though, LOVE these vinyl records. Its retrograde chic is practically a sex pheromone to them. One might even make the bold argument that the hipster movement alone was responsible for the resurgence in the production of vinyl records in the early twenty-first century.

Given this, it will probably come as no surprise that a number of record stores still existed in 2005, and Simon living above one was not one of the great coincidences in the Universe. In fact, Simon was one of the daily visitors that walked around pretending they were there to buy something, but instead only had conversations with other patrons about the evils of the modern digital music age.

Ugh! We almost want to go and shower just talking about this guy.

Don't worry though, Loyal Reader, he'll be dead as a doornail before too long.

Simon's apartment was, as expected, just horrendous. He had taken one of the brick walls adjacent to the kitchenette area and had it covered in a series of broken pieces of black slate that he found at a landfill.

Gross.

A local school had been demolished and there were loads of these irregular slate pieces just ripe for the picking. Simon had affixed them to his wall and used the opportunity to write hipster motivational quotes.

We're not kidding, Loyal Reader; that's just how much of a self-absorbed douche this guy was. Stay calm, though. As we've said already, Simon's perfectly executed hipster demise will be arriving soon enough.

Though it might actually make us vomit in disgust to type these out, here are the actual quotes that Simon printed on the slate that covered his wall:

> - *Don't worry, just breathe. If it's meant to be, it will find its way.*
> - *Life begins at the end of your comfort zone.*
> - *Don't compare your beginning to someone else's middle.*
> - *If you ever find yourself in the wrong story, leave.*
> - *Doors are just barriers to the future.*
> - *One's destination is never a place, but a new way of seeing things.*
> - *Sometimes there is no next time, no second chance. No time out. Sometimes it's just now or never."*

See, Loyal Reader?

221

Painful, right? To make the above even more gag-inducing, Simon had bought old, faded, and cracked picture frames. He went on to affix them around the quotes to give them the 'look' of actual paintings.

For full hipster effect, on the top right edge of one of the more faux distressed wood frames Simon had hung a vintage K1000 Pentax camera.

As if to illustrate the point we've been making these past few minutes, Loyal Reader, Simon had never taken a picture with a camera that required film, but he whole-heartedly believed that film was immeasurably better. If one were to count, and we most certainly did, just how long his hands were in physical contact with the camera he draped on that frame, it was a grand total of one minute and six seconds of his life; long enough to buy it at the thrift store, place it in his reusable shopping bag, take it out of his reusable shopping bag when he got home, and spend more time than necessary to affix it to the frame.

Soon, Loyal Reader ... he is going to die soon.

Other than the camera, Simon had also attached a variety of dried leaves and flowers to the edges of the frames. In fact, the only thing missing was the cultural appropriation of a fucking dreamcatcher.

Wait ... it gets better.

On the brick wall above the head of his 'bed' (a futon he was gifted from his parents) were no less than 186 polaroid pictures.

Three years ago, one of Simon's fellow hipster friends (Truman was of course his name) had gifted Simon a polaroid camera for his birthday, fittingly wrapped in the previous day's newspaper, as is the custom for the urban douche. Since that day, Simon had made it his personal mission to capture life as he saw it - raw, unfiltered expressions of the people and places that surrounded him. While this makes for excellent hipster speak at the pub, what actually transpired are blurry shots of horrendous quality and composition, mostly of the sun rising and setting, trees being trees, low angle shots of way too many fences, and a variety of brooding selfies, blatantly meant to look like spontaneous captures of his mood.

Just like you, we too want nothing more than to vomit in rage, Loyal Reader.

There were other classic hipster décor elements that any man sporting a four-sizes-too-big beard must have - a pair of roller skates dangling by their laces from one of the pipes that ran across the unfinished ceiling and a large bird cage dangling in front of the living area window filled not with an actual fucking bird, but rather with arguably the greatest hits of hipster literature. Let's take a look at that wonderful, wonderful list.

- Sex, Drugs and Cocoa Puffs
- No One Belongs Here More Than You
- Eeeee Eee Eeee
- Infinite Jest
- IQ84
- How Should A Person Be?
- Open City
- As She Climbed Across the Table
- The Kraus Project
- High Fidelity

Please don't tell us you have actually read any of these, Loyal Reader. That would make us cry.

While the above items were standard issue for the laterally mobile hipster, Simon's greatest possession was a radio he found at a yard sale in Adelaide.

An old man's family was selling off his life's possessions in preparation for moving the poor fucker into a nursing home. Luckily for Simon, he had been in town that weekend visiting three friends that shared a house in the suburbs (birds of a feather braid their beards and armpits together).

That fateful morning, the four-person douche mob left the house on their trek to the nearby gastropub for brunch, and as they neared the end of the street, they encountered said yard sale. The Universe, it seems, was on Simon's side that day. The family was a tad bit late getting the sale started, allowing Simon and his gaggle of douches to be the first people to stumble upon its hidden treasures.

The band of dickwads recorded a few good finds that day, but none as magnificent as the Zenith 7S363 Floor Model Console Radio that sat beaming in front of the garage.

For Simon, it was love at first douche.

Not only was this radio one of the holy grail items for hipsters everywhere, it was in mint condition.

A radio like that you've gotta feed every day, Simon giggled to himself, impressed far too much by what he generously referred to as wit and further cementing in our minds, Loyal Reader, that he must die.

To make an already deliriously long story even longer, Simon bought the radio, and it occupied a position of glory and reverence in his loft. He loved it more than he loved most people. His hipster status was, as a result of

223

this find, legendary. The funny thing is, as you probably guessed by now Loyal Reader, Simon had no idea what brand or model the radio was; his only knowledge about the machine was an instant recognition that it was something that he must have. Simon had never turned it on; in fact, it wasn't even plugged in to the wall.

Simon was a legend indeed; a legend that was about to die.

And not a moment too soon.

As we were saying before you got us off-track, Loyal Reader, Simon awoke on October 15th, as he did most days, with a smile on his face, knots in his hair and beard, a heavy layer of residual patchouli scuttling through the air, and not the even the slightest clue that he would be dead a mere one hour, 24 minutes, and 16 seconds later.

The circumstances surrounding Simon's imminent demise might, you think, be convoluted, complex, and almost impossible to describe.

You would be wrong, Loyal Reader.

The circumstances were, as it turns out, quite simple to grasp and flowed logically from a knowledge of Simon as an exemplar of the hipster way - he loved music and he loved being one with the nature. For example, Simon would, without fail, listen to music whilst riding his vintage one-speed orange cruiser (an appalling excuse for a bicycle, in case you were wondering, Loyal Reader) to the local organic, free-range, fair trade, holistic, healing crystal-infused, GMO-free coffee shop every morning. This daily constitutional provided, in Simon's primitive primate brain, a great opportunity to really connect with the music he listened to. Well, as much as he could, anyway. Simon subscribed to the philosophy that true music was to be heard live; session recordings removed the 'feel' of the music and 'diluted the inherent meaning of the message.'

What a fucking douche.

As fate would have it, Simon planned on spending his bike ride to the coffee shop this particular day listening to a new album he had purchased a few days ago from one of his favorite websites for independent music. The album was called *Celestial Spheres* by a band named *Sacred Resonance*. Simon heard snippets of the music before, namely a few months prior whilst high as balls at the Adelaide Fringe Show. Though he couldn't recall too much about the music, he seemed to remember liking it so much that he wrote down the band and album details on the back of a napkin he found in his pocket the next morning.

Once awakened and showered, Simon would normally put on his usual hipster fashion - a t-shirt that would blatantly let everyone around him know that he was 'retro,' boxers, skinny jeans, a faded 70s light sweater, construction boots (perfect footwear for his bicycle), and a toque (current weather conditions completely irrelevant to this last decision).

The t-shirt for the morning of October 15th was yet another thrift store gem - a white cotton tee with *Pink Floyd's Delicate Sound of Thunder* album cover on the front. It didn't matter that Simon had never touched, let alone listened to the album and, if pressed, would say his favorite song, obviously, was the title track. It also didn't matter that Simon had no clue it was a live album, purportedly the confessed conveyer of this sacred musical message he would prattle on about at length.

Ugh.

This just gets more and more unbearable with every passing sentence, Loyal Reader, doesn't it?

Luckily for everyone involved, the end is near.

Breakfast consisted of Simon's own homemade granola (of course) topped with locally sourced organic strawberries. In Simon's own words, his granola 'filled the body while fulfilling the soul.' Had he any social media accounts, Simon would have undoubtedly professed to the world how much he thought of himself and his choices. *#eatorganic #eatlocal #foodforthesoul*

Or ... how about *#fuckigndouche?*

Seriously, how had someone not euthanized him before this?

Simon lived happily in his loft in a hipster-infused section in the south end of Brisbane. It was about a two-kilometer bike ride on the good ol' cruiser to the café in Paddington. Just enough of a jaunt, in Simon's opinion, to look active should anyone he knows see him, but not enough to work up a sweat and ruin a perfectly chosen outfit. Given he regularly biked at a top speed rivalling that of a three-toed sloth in heat, there wasn't much danger of sweat making an appearance, especially on this particular spring morning.

The first half of Simon's ride that fateful morning was perfectly uneventful. His vintage leather satchel hung perfectly across his left shoulder and his oversized headphones fit impeccably overtop his pastel grey toque. Notice the conspicuous and douchey absence of a bike helmet, Loyal Reader;

how was Simon to broadcast how perfectly unique he was with a bike helmet that interfered his with his headphones? The weather was sunny, the temperature moderately cool, and traffic was light along Grey Street and over the William Jolly bridge, the first of the two major thoroughfares he would traverse.

In fact, this particular bike ride might have even made Simon's list of the top 50 bike rides to the coffee shop except that he wasn't fully digging this new music. It's wasn't that the music was hideously atrocious or anything like that (we very much beg to disagree, Loyal Reader), it just wasn't complimenting his sunny disposition on such a correspondingly sunny day. As such, what could have been a truly stellar bike ride had descended into mediocrity about halfway through the voyage.

Simon had the album on shuffle, which, in retrospect was the harbinger of his demise. Had he simply played the album in order as *Sacred Resonance* intended, he would have stumbled smack dab into two roughly 12-minute tracks right off the bat, *Celestial Spheres* (12:56) and *Winds of Ascent* (12:38). Though they were, by intergalactic scientific estimation, the equivalent of harmonic miscarriages, Simon would have suffered through them and made his way happily, and most importantly alive, to the café.

Instead, Loyal Reader, the algorithm that chose the song order spit out *Calm Rain* (4:59) and *Expansion* (4:13). The former wasn't so bad, a bit soothing, actually, but the latter was beginning to tread into the territory of unlistenable noise as Simon approached the end of William Jolly Bridge.

Making his way from the bridge onto Caxton Street always did require a bit of finesse on Simon's part. The bike lane he rode across the bridge continued directly on to a small section of road called Skew Street. From there, he would be required to cross a major thoroughfare - Upper Roma Street. On the best of days, it's increased traffic, combined with the merging of the bike lane with the regular traffic more often than not made this a hairy pickle of a challenge to navigate.

Unfortunately for Simon, this was not the best of days. Not by a longshot

Simon approached the light at the corner of Skew and Upper Roma. Mentally noting that the light had just turned green, Simon mused to himself that perhaps things were looking up. As fate would have it, Simon's approach to the Upper Roma traffic light coincided with the beginning of Celestial Spheres' third track - *Interstellar Vortex*.

See Loyal Reader, we told you we'd get there in good time, didn't we?

Events from this point forward did not unfold favourably for our protagonist.

Simon didn't so much as listen to what we can only loosely describe as a song as he did get viciously assailed by it. By any sensible human's estimation, the song was at least an order of magnitude worse than anything the average person would have had experienced before, and Simon, interestingly enough, was no exception, having actually listened to the auditory sludge produced by The Dave Matthews Band on more than 354 separate occasions in just the past 5 years.

Having said that, it was only a meagre 16 seconds into *Interstellar Vortex* when Simon began to speed into the intersection.

At this point, Loyal Reader, Simon's fate was no longer up for debate; it had already been committed to the sweet strains of history.

Simon's racing onto Upper Roma with a fresh green light and at a good clip no less coincided perfectly with his unfortunately timed decision that he could take no more of this auditory torture. Regrettably for Simon and the four people that died along with him a few seconds later, he was so preoccupied with fumbling to access his phone and change the music that he didn't notice, a) the light very prematurely change to red, and b) an ambulance, lights flashing and sirens blaring, hurtling at top speed towards the intersection.

We take no pleasure, Loyal Reader, in having to inform you of what you most probably have already divined by now - the speeding ambulance is indeed what killed Simon Anderson.

Had he not been glancing down at his phone, Simon might have seen the ambulance's flashing lights. Had he not been wearing headphones with the music at a moderate volume, he might have heard the ambulance's blaring sirens. Sadly, none of this transpired. He was glancing down at his phone, he was wearing his ridiculously large headphones, and consequently, he most certainly was, a mere five seconds later, thrust 6 vertical meters into the air from the impact of the ambulance that struck him at 82 kilometers per hour.

Fuck you again, Imperial System!

We never get tired of that, Loyal Reader.

It is probably best for everyone involved if we save you from a detailed account of every nanosecond of the grizzly results. Instead, Loyal Reader, we shall approach the situation that unfolded with a cold, objective, and heartless review fitting of a computer-generated love song:

- *Simon's ambulance-induced flight ended abruptly when he collided with a large wooden telephone pole.*
- *Simon's upper torso struck the pole with enough intensity to immediately fracture a total of sixteen bones, four of them, unfortunately, were cervical vertebrae.*
- *One of Simon's left ribs (#4) pierced his pericardial cavity, skewering his heart's left ventricle.*
- *Simon's 4th cervical vertebra induced sufficient trauma to effectively render the remainder of his spine non-functional.*
- *Simon's limp body then descended said telephone pole and landed on the sidewalk.*
- *The force of this impact caused Simon's right shoulder to dislocate, his right clavicle to snap clean in half, and the right parietal bone of his skull to crack wide open.*
- *Simon Anderson died exactly 12.83 seconds later.*

In his defense, the ambulance driver, Clifford Lassiter, did his best to avoid hitting Simon. Clifford's best, however, was not nearly enough. Seeing Simon speed into the intersection at the last second, Clifford swerved hard to the left, but still managed to strike Simon dead center on the front of the ambulance. The hard swerve, however, also sealed the fate of Clifford, the other paramedic in the passenger seat (Katie Vickers), the paramedic in the back (Jason Taylor), and the poor individual laying on the gurney (Jessica Hawthorne).

Following the impact with Simon and his hipster bike, the ambulance vaulted across Upper Roma and smashed head-on into the brick corner of a building. Again, without going into the gory details, Loyal Reader, suffice to say that the four other deaths were, as was Simon's, not protracted.

Such was how October 15th, 2015 unfolded for one Simon Anderson and four other unlucky Australians. Though many factors appeared to have been in play that fateful morning, it can all be traced back to one singular appallingly unpleasant song. If Simon had just not listened to that bloody album, then everything would have been just fine.

It was, though, one less hipster that the world had to deal with, Loyal Reader, proving that if you look hard enough, every dark cloud does indeed have a silver lining.

With the story of Simon Anderson done with and safely out of the way, we can now focus our collective attention on who to hold responsible for this flagrant instance of musical misconduct. The answer, of course, lies with the two individuals who comprise what we have already opined can only loosely call the 'band' *Sacred Resonance*.

Like poor Simon, these men were Australian, but unlike Simon, they were not hipsters. Rather, they were something far, far worse. Their names were Darren Curtis and Bradley Pitt. Though we like to think that we could do justice to the complete nonsensical tripe they used to describe themselves on their blog, we can't. Nothing can compare to the actual drivel they produced.

With that in mind, let us use their own words against them. Below, Loyal Reader, please find this hot, hot mess, verbatim, and in all its glory.

DARREN CURTIS BIOGRAPHY:

> *- Darren Curtis is a futurist, composer, producer and spiritual teacher exploring the interconnection of science and spirituality. His background in Music Technology with honors from Adelaide University South Australia, explored sound waves and beat states to produce therapeutic effects on brain waves and mind-body states for altered states of consciousness.*
> *- Darren's main area of research also explores the science the 'Music of the Spheres'. This incorporates archeacoustics; which is the use of acoustical study as a methodological approach within archaeology (i.e., ancient pyramids and caves). Through this data and research, he*

> *produces music composition, live performances and presentations, recreating the sonic experience.*
> - *Darren is a strong advocate for disclosure by governments worldwide on higher realties. His background has been with Colin Norris from the former Australian International UFO Research Organization, one of the longest running UFO research Organizations in Australia and the world. His research on transformational musicology, ancient temples and 'initiating contact' has been presented at numerous conferences.*

BRADLEY PITT BIOGRAPHY:

> - *Bradley Pitt is a futurist and spiritual teacher dedicated to synthesizing science and spirituality, guiding us towards a vision of the new world. As an active member of the World Peace Prayer Society, and gifted visionary and spiritual communiqué, he promotes new peace initiatives and inter-religious harmony.*
> - *Bradley is particularly interested in the practice of vibrational medicine, which spans a broad spectrum of disciplines such as acupuncture, electrotherapy, meditation, sound therapy and psychic healing.*
> - *As a respected healer, psychic and trans-medium, Bradley delivers seminars and workshops on these topics to other practitioners and the general public.*

We challenge anyone of sound mind and body, Loyal Reader, to make it through the above compost and not want to go on a good old-fashioned killing spree.

And so concludes the only recorded presence of an *Interstellar Vortex* on Earth. It didn't take the shape of a whirling transportational void, but rather the hippy-infused auditory excrement of two unfortunate Australians.

230

You will take solace, Loyal Reader, to know that both Darren Curtis and Bradley Pitt are currently, and have been since *The Turning,* undead and trapped inside a depressing makeshift recording studio in Darren's mom's basement.

Perhaps there is a Flying Spaghetti Monster after all.

CHAPTER 27

SCOTT FUCKING BAKULA

And as we find ourselves once again smack-dab in the midst of yet another strange occurrence, Loyal Reader, you would think by now that everyone in our rag-tag group would be used to being pissed on by the business end of the regular SNAFUs that the Universe was oh so consistently throwing their way.

You would be wrong, Loyal Reader.

In fact, when the latest of the curveballs arrived in the form of a very loud bang, our heroes had no idea just how strange and fucked up things would end up getting.

For example, everyone in the cavern was blissfully unaware of the fact that a seemingly otherwise humdrum, double-barreled shotgun precipitated a series of events that led to:

1. The rather inopportune shredding apart of what is commonly known as the space-time continuum,
2. The subsequent arrival of a blinding, diffuse, blue light, and
3. The apparent instantaneous transport of Kyle, Chad, and their puppies to an all-too-well-known location - Kyle's hometown in the not-too-distant orbit of Nanaimo, British Columbia - on the evening of February 9th, 2013.

Like a zombie apocalypse, the space-time continuum is a funny thing, Loyal Reader. Lots of people have heard of it, and throughout history, a great many douchebags have professed to have an understanding of it, most of them at dinner parties hosted by that annoying tardfuck Bevin and talking completely out of their collective asses. Most people on the street, when asked to guess about the origins of the theoretical physics behind the concept of space-time will naturally gravitate to the grandfather of everything physics - Albert Einstein. That being said, as far as best guesses go, it's not a complete affront to science, just not correct. Einstein, to his credit, did many wonderful things, and his Special Theory of Relativity that he presented way back in 1906 remains the go-to reference for most people.

It was, though, Einstein's former college teacher in mathematics that got the ball rolling, as it were, relative to new and innovative ways for people to think about how space and time might need to be considered together in any fundamental understanding of the Universe. Just one year after Einstein published his above-mentioned work, Hermann Minkowski, in a public lecture on relativity, delivered his now famous quotation:

> *"The views of space and time which I wish to lay before you have sprung from the soil of experimental physics, and therein lies their strength. They are radical. Henceforth, space by itself, and time by itself, are doomed to fade away into mere shadows, and only a kind of union of the two will preserve an independent reality."*

Ugh! Even we fell asleep reading that passage, Loyal Reader.

Our point, however, very much still stands; even back at the turn of the Twentieth Century, physicists were beginning to theorize about the possibility that space and time not only exist in a continuum, but that this interconnected spectrum could be accessed , dare we say, even harnessed. The direct consequence of such theories is, of course the stuff of pretty much every science fiction television show and/or movie of substance that has ever been made; humans have always been fascinated with the possibility of being able to 'jump' through space and/or time.

Our heroes have been (un?) lucky enough to have witnessed, over the last hour of their lives, two such jumps. Most people never get to witness any, so one might consider this to be a pretty amazing by-product of the zombie apocalypse for sure.

Strictly speaking, Loyal Reader, the two vortexes that plagued our heroes fell into two very different categories. The first swirling vortex was interdimensional; it brought Ishitori and his Hentai Girls from a parallel dimension. It also had the secondary effect of plopping Ed, Vera, Harold, and Kumar onto the middle of Haiphong Road (incidentally, right in front of the Haiphong Road Temporary Cooked Food Hawker Bazaar) of that dimension's Hong Kong. We could go on and on about that particular dimension's unique traits, but we're in the middle of some pretty serious exposition related to our heroes' arrival in none other than 2013, so we've got no time for such lollygagging.

The second vortex that appeared did not return Ishitori and his crew back to his dimension, or back to Hong Kong, for that matter. Unfortunately for them, it was a textbook example of an intradimensional vortex - in other words, teleportation. The multicoloured swirling nature of the vortex lent a certain ethereal, alien look, but this was purely cosmetic coincidence. As luck would have it, this intradimensional vortex led directly to Hidden Hills, California, a lovely gated community outside Los Angeles and home to many a celebrity. As such, Ishitori and his Girls were essentially deposited into the middle of the zombie apocalypse where an epic battle ensued with the zombified members of the Kardashian family.

What a fabulous name-dropping opportunity for the Japanese crime fighter and his girls!

Einstein, Minkowski, and all the theoretical physicists that came after them never really thought that any of this was literally possible, just theoretically possible. The zombies that presently flooded the Earth were enough of a mind-fuck for most scientists, let alone the bending of interdimensional and intradimensional space. All of this was taken to a whacky and wonderful new level with the aforementioned arrival of a shotgun-induced tear in the space-time continuum.

In Kyle's hometown, at 6:41 pm on February 9th, 2013, epic things were afoot. Two days earlier was the 12th birthday of Kyle and Chad's nephew. To celebrate this occasion, Kyle's sister and her husband decided to stage a zombie apocalypse paintball party for their son and his friends. This involved a large number of moving parts, including the fathers of said friends dressing up like zombies and getting pelted with paintballs.

Every kid's dream, really.

Rather poignant amongst all of the details of that particular night was an intricate zombie apocalypse narrative that Kyle's sister had mapped out for the kids who participated in the paintball adventure. In this story, Kyle and Chad were two scientists working to find the zombie cure. At a rather pivotal point in the story, the kids, after dispatching of a zombie horde, would stumble across the scientists in a remote cabin and obtain the zombie cure.

That fateful evening, everything proceeded as planned. Carload after carload of kids arrived, duffle bags of paintball gear were assembled, fathers padded as best they could, and the birthday apocalypse unfolded with remarkable success. As predicted, and almost perfectly on schedule, the pre-teen troop arrived at an unfinished cabin (built by a cousin of Kyle's) where Kyle and Chad, dressed in lab coats and goggles, were patiently waiting to propel the zombie-laden narrative forward.

The scene played out as well as anyone could have possibly expected; shortly after receiving the cure from the two scientists (a small plastic vial Chad stole from his work and filled with water and green food colouring), the adolescent boys made their way to the next stop on their apocalyptic birthday adventure. As they left the cabin, Kyle's father added to the atmosphere of the night by making the aforementioned space-time shearing gunshot.

As Kyle and Chad would have told anyone who asked, nothing particularly exciting happened when the gunshot went off, with the possible exception of, a) various children screaming in delightful terror at the sound, and b) Chad worrying to himself that poor Bronx, safely tucked away at the cottage they were staying in on the family property, would be hiding behind the toilet and shaking in fear, as loud sounds tended to induce this behaviour in his little dude.

Post shotgun-firing, our heroes, if questioned as to how the rest of the evening's events unfolded, would have wasted no time in recollecting that they packed up their sciency props and made their way back to the cottage to await the kids' eventual return and enjoy some yummy, yummy birthday cake.

This eventuality, though, while representing what Kyle and Chad remembered of their experiences on February 9th, 2013, represents only one of an infinite possible number of parallel dimension trajectories of space-time. The shotgun blast, in one of those trajectories, for some reason unbeknownst to anyone how gave a sweet lick about such things, caused the fabric of space-time to rupture, and, as a cool and groovy side-effect of this unceremonious rupturing, instantaneously transported our heroes to that very moment and in their very bodies, but ... in a different dimension.

How almost very, but not quite ... *Quantum Leap*.

Let's be honest, Loyal Reader; Scott Bakula is no Patrick Stewart. Some would rightly argue that may be an unfair comparison, but our job, as you very well are aware by now, isn't to discuss the fair and unfair in this world. We seriously wouldn't get a bloody thing done if that's all we spent our time chatting about. For example, Loyal Reader, don't even get us started with people who park like complete and utter asswads - that discussion would take up the lion's share of a particularly spicy manifesto.

Rather, our job is simply to report the facts, and the fact of the matter is that if the good Mr. Bakula had ended his major acting roles with his delightful five-year portrayal of Dr. Sam Beckett, we believe, Loyal Reader, that his television legacy would have been set in stone. Everyone would look back and reminisce with bubble-gum nostalgia about his wacky weekly adventures. Sadly, this is not the case. For better or for worse, Scott Bakula was cast as Jonathan Archer, the original captain of the starship *USS Enterprise*.

Unsurprisingly, no one in Hollywood at the time envied Scott Bakula when it was announced he would be taking the lead role in *Star Trek: Enterprise*. By the time the show was set to premiere in 2001 (on Chad's birthday, if you are at all curious, Loyal Reader), there had already been four previous incarnations of the Star Trek Universe on the small screen - *The Original Series, The Next Generation, Deep Space Nine,* and *Voyager*.

Anyone who knows anything in the Universe, Loyal Reader is aware that Voyager was by far the best of the shows; every single intergalactic viewership poll that has ever been conducted in all of space-time soundly confirmed this to be a bona fide fact.

Further, the sad truth is that a large portion of the viewing public on Earth was ready for a bit of a Trek break.

Star Trek: The Next Generation appeared on television sets way, way back in 1987, much to the collective orgasm of nerds everywhere.

Those loyal to the late sixties and Captain James Tiberius Kirk were appalled at the presence of a proper British Captain who favoured diplomacy over schoolyard fisticuffs, but Jean-Luc Picard soon won over the hearts of even the most pessimistic of the Trekkies.

From 1987 forward, there was at least one *Star Trek* series on television right up until *Voyager* ended in May of 2001; that's a whopping 14 years, people. Needless to say, even the most nerdtastic of fanboys were a teensy-weensy tired of all this trekking through the stars.

Thus, it was with this waning public appeal for all things *Star Trek* that Scott Bakula and his steady troop of then (and still, we might add) unknown actors strode onto the small screen with what some reviewers called a 'bargain basement' *Star Trek* experience.

In the very beginning, though, reviews weren't universally all that bad. At best, though, they could only be considered tepid Viewership, as you know, Loyal Reader, is probably the most reliable metric for the viability of a television show from a network's point of view, and it started out respectable (12.5 million people watched the first episode), but very, very quickly began to fade. In fact, by the time the middle of the first season rolled around, viewership was down to a paltry 5 million viewers per episode. That's barely the population of Liberia. You remember Liberia, don't you Loyal Reader? They have yet to adopt the metric system. Poor fuckers!

In the end, the show concluded after running for a not completely disrespectful four seasons, with barely 3 million people watching each episode by that point. There is some saving grace in having lasted one whole season longer than the original series, but not much.

If we had to hazard a guess, there were actually so many forces working against the series, that it was somewhat doomed from the very beginning. Yes, it all started with the tepid mood of the viewing public about another *Star Trek* show, but there was also less of an emphasis on lighter storylines, and people had grown accustomed to this light-hearted approach to science fiction. It's as if the writers were trying to make a gritty, darker version of *The Next Generation,* but lacked the ability to do it well.

These issues aside, there was also the unflattering and inevitable comparisons of Scott Bakula to William Shatner and Patrick Stewart.

It was rather fortunate, from a purely academic point of view, that the two most famous *Star Trek* captains - Kirk and Picard - were such diametric opposites. This allowed for a remarkable dissection of the *Star Trek Universe's* fans into two die-hard factions. The average reasonable, carbon-based, bipedal, viewer was either on Team Kirk or Team Picard; there was no waffling on this particular issue. The two series that followed *The Next Generation* had sufficient differences in characters and structure, that harsh comparisons to the two icons were not a real factor for the shows' respective popularities.

Deep Space Nine actually overlapped with the last season of *The Next Generation*. It did, however, have its own unfortunate circumstance of being essentially a deathly boring soap opera set in space.

How utterly depressing, Loyal Reader.

They took the least likable characters from *The Next Generation*, combined them with a mish-mash assemblage of boring aliens and supporting cast, and the topped it all off with a Commander/Captain who basically just stood around and waxed on unpoetically about how uncomfortable he was with pretty much everything around him. This, of course, leads us to our biggest issue with this intergalactic turd of a show - pretty much all the episodes took place on the show's eponymous space station. This had the direct consequence of sucking pretty much every last ounce of fun and excitement out of pretty much every single unfunny and unexciting episode.

The only saving grace for everyone involved was that enough of the general lobotomized populace responded well to the soap opera approach to television, hence the reason it managed to stay afloat for seven very, very long seasons. So, Loyal Reader, perhaps in the end, it didn't really matter that the captain was, in reality, a walking piece of cardboard.

By now you have probably divined that we can't say enough good things about Kathryn Janeway. As the captain of the *USS Voyager,* her power bun became the stuff of legends in the *Delta Quadrant,* and being a female, any comparisons to other Captains in the *Star Trek Universe* were moot. Janeway was a force to be reckoned with; we could go on for much longer than you would care to listen about her many excellent qualities, but it is probably best for everyone involved if we stick to the point - for completely different reasons than for Sisko, Janeway's character didn't suffer from the potentially disastrous comparisons to Kirk and Picard.

Jonathan Archer, though, that was another story.

Though the producers and writers of *Enterprise* tried their best to make the series quite distinct from *The Original Series* and *The Next Generation,* it still remained a show revolving around the crew of the *USS Enterprise* and their adventures in space. It didn't help that Scott Bakula was portraying, with the exception of Zefram Cochrane, one of the most influential historical figures in the *Star Trek Universe;* a man described as the single greatest explorer of the 22nd Century - Captain Jonathan Archer. All of this led to an assload of expectations for the show, and, in particular, Scott Bakula's depiction of this great man.

To make a short story long, *Star Trek* fans were not kind to Scott Bakula, which is really too bad. The production company and television studio would have probably received at least a hundred role-craving actors to line up for the chance to play Jonathan Archer and of course, then the collective public vitriol would have been justified. But, c'mon, this was Scott Bakula; for five years in the late 80s and early 90s he was America's Golden Boy. Dr. Sam Beckett had become a household name and made goofy scientists everywhere collectively orgasm at the thought of people actually finding them cool.

For his legacy to be defined by *Enterprise* and not the cultural gem that was *Quantum Leap,* is nothing short of a travesty.

Travelling through time has been a staple for science fiction since, like, forever. *Quantum Leap,* though, provided and interesting take on the scenario. The lead character, as mentioned above, was Sam, a well-known scientist and lead of the government-funded Project Quantum Leap, where he worked on his theory that humans could travel throughout their lifetime. Faced with the impending news that the funding for the project was about to be cut, Sam took it upon himself to step into the Quantum Leap Accelerator to prove that project worked, consequently being thrust into the past.

But here's the kicker and the genius of *Quantum Leap:* Sam wasn't sent back as a younger version of himself, but instead inhabited the body of a completely different person. In fact, the remainder of the series focused on his weekly attempts to solve some overly dramatic and contrived problem so that he might somehow leap back to his own time and, hopefully, his own body.

Genius, Loyal Reader, pure genius!

However, what was never really addressed with any real detail was how the Quantum Accelerator actually worked. There was a bit of exposition about opening up a tear in the 'quantum fabric' of space-time, but nothing that actually would have made sense to anyone watching. At least, not anyone on Earth.

You see, unbeknownst to the writer of the first episode (and the show's creator), Donald P. Bellisario, he just happened to hit nail on the head with his description and depiction of quantum tearing. While he didn't provide any of the quantum mechanics to back up the bubble-gum physics, he thought he was writing, his treatment of the ability for a physical consciousness to pass through the fabric of space-time and temporarily hijack another consciousness was spot-on.

Well done, Donnie B!

Having said that, Loyal Reader, we are more than a bit excited to point out to you that everything else in the show is complete and utter nonsense. Totally fun and worth the watch nonsense, but still nonsense, nonetheless.

You see, the whole premise of the show was that Sam Beckett was jumping back and forth in time, but completely within his own timeline.

Complete garbage, Loyal Reader!

And ... Sam's trusty sidekick and friend Al just happened to have a machine that was tuned to Sam's brainwaves and could appear to him in his jumps as a hologram.

Utter bunk, Loyal Reader!

Anyone who knows anything about string theory, quantum mechanics, Norwegian basket-weaving, animal husbandry, and the space-time continuum will tell you that any rip or tear in the fabric of quantum space will automatically open up access to a veritable Pandora's Box of infinite parallel dimensions. In other words, the odds of Sam travelling back in time to inhabit the consciousness of someone in his own dimension's timeline were, to put it mildly, infinitely small. Then, every time he leapt to another time and another consciousness he would invariably leap to another parallel dimension.

Thus, are we to believe that Al's communication device was an interdimensional brainwave receiver?

In 1989, no less?

We think not, Loyal Reader!

But again ... we digress.

Scott Bakula's delightful performance in *Quantum Leap* was, as we are sure you already have concluded, a veritable small screen treasure. Just as his charming character Sam Beckett would often find himself confused as to what was going on every time he leapt, Kyle and Chad were similarly confused to find themselves in the midst of an underground cavern of mysterious intrigue one moment and then in Kyle's family's property an instant later.

CHAPTER 28

A CABIN IN THE WOODS

Blinding blue light began to fade away. Our heroes, basking in the final cerulean photons, once again assumed their standard confartled positions.

"What the fuck was that?" Kyle yelled, as the last photons of the blinding blue light began to fade away.

Chad was bent over and clutching his stomach. "I think I'm gonna be sick," he moaned softly as his eyes adjusted.

"You have weird hair," Kyle commented, a little too nonchalantly.

"You're wearing a lab coat and goggles," Chad retorted once his vision returned.

"So are you."

"Fair enough," Chad said, thinking that perhaps recent events had led to them both going completely insane. "But seriously, what the fuck is going on here?"

By this point, our heroes had begun to look around their surroundings. Though very dark, there was enough ambient light to allow them to notice the eerie familiarity of the room.

"What the fuck?!" Kyle exclaimed, "This is the river trail cabin." This cabin, Loyal Reader, built by Kyle's cousin, sat proudly just to the side of a trail that wound its way down to the Nanaimo River. The night of the zombie apocalypse paintball birthday party in February of 2013, this was the cabin in which Kyle and Chad waited for the intrepid pre-teen paintballers to arrive.

"What!? How is this even possible?"

"Really? After everything we've been through, you're just now having a hard time believing what's happening to us? You just had fucking laser beams shooting from your eyes!"

"Good point, but seriously, this is insane."

"Agreed."

Chad looked around the cabin's interior and took stock of the current situation. "So," he began, "the cabin isn't finished and we're wearing lab coats and goggles."

"And don't forget your hair," Kyle added.

Chad raised his hands up and patted the wig he was wearing. He removed it and looked at it. "Do you remember when we were dressed like this?"

"That birthday party a few years ago!" Kyle said excitedly as he began to put some of this together.

"Exactly. We were pretending to be scientists, hiding in the cabin, and waiting for the kids to arrive so we could give them the zombie cure."

"So, let me get this straight," Kyle added. "We've just been transported to," there was a brief pause as Kyle did the math, "four years in the past?"

"It would appear so," Chad replied.

"Fuuuuuuck."

"I know, right?" There was another brief pause, during which both men made a startling realization at the exact same instant and hollered in unison.

"The puppies!"

Panic began to set in. Kyle and Chad looked around the cabin, saying each puppy's name to see if they were somewhere in the cabin. The darkness, though, was being a righteous prick about the whole affair.

Out of habit, Kyle felt his front pocket and, much to his surprise, pulled out an iPhone.

His iPhone 4, as it turned out.

From 2013.

"Whoa," Kyle muttered.

Chad, still revolving around the orbit of *Panic Stations Alpha,* barely registered what Kyle was saying, but when Kyle turned on the flashlight on his phone, Chad's attention was squarely captured.

"You have a phone?" Chad asked in bewilderment.

"Yup," Kyle replied, shining his flashlight at Chad. "And it's my old phone from when we were here back when all this happened."

Excited at this prospect, Chad found his own phone right where he expected it to be (the pocket of his lab coat), turned on his flashlight, and began to assist Kyle is searching the inside of the cabin for any sign of the puppies. The search, however, only lasted for about 3 seconds - long enough for Kyle's brain to figure out that there were, realistically speaking, only two options available for the puppies' possible locations.

"Wait!" Kyle said hastily. "It looks like we've been transported here and are now occupying our bodies from a few years ago, right?"

"That would certainly explain why I appear to be 20 pounds or so lighter." Chad quipped. "I was hoping maybe time travel was just a phenomenally great workout."

"I know, right? So, if we're now occupying these bodies, then if the puppies got transported too, then I guess it stands to reason that they would be in the bodies of the puppies here, and they'd be at the cottage, safe and sound."

"But what if they didn't get transported to this time with us?" Chad asked, with more than a little trepidation is his voice.

"Then they're back at the cavern with our bodies, assuming, of course, that our bodies are still there. Of course, who the Hell knows what happened to our bodies when we came here."

"I hope no one else got transported, or at least not Suzie. I don't even want to think about the puppies all alone in that place."

"Well, there's no way for us to tell, and nothing we can do about it," Kyle concluded. "It sucks big time, but since we seem to be stuck here, let's figure out what we need to do, and we'll hopefully be back with them in no time."

"What if we don't *need* to do anything?" Chad asked. "It's not like this is an episode of *Quantum Leap*."

"Oh my God, I loved that show!"

"Right? Scott Bakula was *so* cute!"

"Totes! But, back to me; all the things that happened to us in that cavern seemed to happen for a reason. When the first vortex opened and that Japanese guy and his schoolgirl hookers came through, that could not possibly have been a coincidence. Then, after all the soldiers were dead, another vortex opens up and takes them away, and now all of a sudden we find ourselves transported here." Kyle paused and took a deep breath. "It all has to have some meaning."

"Okay, let's go with that and look around and see if there's any indication of what we should be doing." Chad looked at his phone. "It's February 9th, 2013; totally the night of the zombie paintball. So we were in an actual zombie apocalypse only to be transported back to when we were pretending to be in the in the middle of one? That's fucked up."

"I'll look around the inside of the cabin and you look around the outside. At least we don't have to worry about being attacked by any real zombies," Kyle said, while managing to crack a smile.

"I hope the kids have already been through here," Chad said while walking out the unfinished doorway. Shining his light on the grass and dirt, he noticed a number of spent paintballs. "By the looks of the mess out here, they've already made their way past."

"Good," Kyle yelled from inside the cabin.

Our heroes had planned on spending the next few minutes searching, taking notes of anything at all that might give them a hint as to why they were transported to this time, and then reporting back to one another.

This only lasted 12 seconds.

Chad managed to scan the remnants of the paintball carnage all over the ground and then raised his phone's flashlight to the front of the cabin.

"What the-?" he muttered and stopped in his tracks. Chad maintained a look of complete and utter confusion and began to make his way back into the cabin to report what he had seen to his husband.

"Chad!" Kyle yelled, just as Chad was approaching the door.

Chad, still fixated on what he saw, barely registered Kyle's exclamation.

"You are not going to believe what is on the outside of the cabin," Chad said as he entered through the doorway.

"Look," Kyle said, pointing at a bench lining the far wall of the cabin.

"Okay, my news is not *that* dramatic," Chad said, tilting his head to the side in a futile attempt to process what he was seeing. "Jesus," he mumbled, as he made his way across the floor. "Where did all this come from?"

Chad, much to his surprise, was staring at an incredibly elaborate scientific setup; it resembled the array of glassware, bubbling fluids, and technical equipment that one might see in one of those B-movies where a mad scientist is trying to take over the world.

To help with your understanding of just how exceptionally strange this scene was, we offer the following two pieces of information:

> 1. Kyle and Chad did not, under any circumstance, put together this contraption back when they were part of the zombie paintball experience for their nephew's birthday back in February of 2013.
> 2. The fabricator of the cabin, Kyle's cousin, was not in this, or any other parallel dimension (which is saying something, given that there are an infinite number of such realities), someone who would (or could, for that matter) come up with this setup.

Pretty complex, right?

"I don't remember any of this being here," Chad said, in awe of what he saw before him.

"Me neither. And look at this," Kyle said and pointed to the left side of the bench.

A large jug labeled *Uncle Fugly's Moonshine* was sitting to the left of a bubbling container. The rest of the stuff on the bench all seemed to stem from this beginning section and terminated on the right-hand side with a large glass flask at the end of the intertwining network of glass conduits. Positioned above the flask was a titration device, fed by a long, spiraling glass tube that contained a glowing, green liquid. The liquid slowly dripped into the flask, which was about a third full. On the bench to the right of the large flask was a series of 24 test tubes, neatly arranged in a metal rack, and all filled with the green concoction. To add to the incredulity of the situation, a small yellow note was affixed to the front of the rack.

Written in all-caps upon the square piece of yellow paper, in thick, crimson-coloured marker were the words "ZOMBIE CURE."

"It looks like you printed that," Kyle stated.

"That definitely does look like my printing," Chad responded as he steadied himself on an awkwardly placed supporting beam running diagonally through the kitchen area of the cabin.

Chad's printing was recognizable from up to a distance of exactly 136 miles away. The letters were printed with years' worth of Roman Catholic guilt drilled into the hands that crafted them and each capitalized letter was adorned with carefully positioned serifs - ornamentals that no other person in the history of life on Earth has ever added to a text that labeled a piece of scientific equipment.

While the perfectly manicured text was indeed the giveaway, Chad felt the left side pocket of the lab coat he was wearing and sure enough, inside was the crimson Sharpie he had apparently used to print the note. He took it out and held it up for Kyle to see. "Here's the Sharpie."

In case you were curious, Loyal Reader, and you probably aren't, Chad had a Sharpie problem. He owned hundreds of them; you name the colour, and you can be certain that Chad had it in Sharpie form. It was as cute an addiction as one could have and didn't really have a fiduciary impact on our heroes' lives. In fact, Chad was always in a very good position to whip up a homemade card for any occasion.

"Fuck. What's going on? Why is this different from what we remember? How can this be happening if we went back in time?" Kyle asked.

"I have absolutely no idea," Chad replied. "And what do we do now?"

"Good question. Maybe head up to the cottage, find the puppies, and see if we can figure what the Hell might be going on?"

"Sounds good to me."

Kyle and Chad exited the cabin and began walking up the trail that would eventually lead to the cottage. About 50 meters into their journey through the dark, a variety of strange whispering noises could be heard from the steep bank of trees to the right.

"Do you hear that?" Kyle said, as he stopped dead in his tracks.

"Hear what?" Chad replied.

Kyle held up his right hand, the universal signal for *be quiet and listen*.

Silence, nothing more.

Just as they were both about to continue up the trail, Kyle heard it again.

This time though, it was louder, but he still couldn't tell where it was coming from. Though higher in volume, the whispering was still ambient and incoherent.

Kyle turned to ask Chad if he could make out what it was saying, but to his horror, Chad was no longer on the trail beside him.

The sound came back again, louder now, and the words becoming clearer, speaking his name.

"Kyle?" the ethereal voice asked.

Kyle couldn't pinpoint where it was coming from, it seemed to be everywhere all at once. He looked around frantically, his brain trying to cope with the fact that not only had his husband vanished into thin air, but someone, somewhere was speaking his name.

"Kyle? Can you hear me?"

Those were the last words Kyle heard as he fell to the ground and the world around him faded to black.

CHAPTER 29

DALLAS ISN'T JUST A DREAMY TOWN IN SOUTH DAKOTA

Chi-Chi-Zeta-Epsilon is the only known Greek fraternity in the history of the known Universe to correctly deduce that the after-effects of knockout gas consistently places a respectable third in the *Kill Me Fucking Now* category of post-kegger hangovers.

Second place, in case you were wondering Loyal Reader, can be reliably achieved by consuming what frat boys lovingly call *Purple Jesus* - one example recipe containing an evil concoction of equal parts vodka, tequila, peppermint schnapps, and grape Tang.

Taking first place is an abomination of a drink whose ingredient list is so secret that only six living people on Earth at any given time possess the recipe. Its name? *The Bishop's Taint.* We pray, Loyal Reader, that you never experience its wrath.

Luckily for Kyle, it was a third-place kind of day.

"Kyle?" said the soft, reassuring voice. "Can you hear me?"
Is that a voice?
Everything was black and it seemed that concentration was a luxury Kyle could not afford.

I've heard that voice before.

Kyle's eyelids weighed a metric butt ton, conscious thought appeared to take more energy than could be provided by all the red-hot burning sons in the Universe, and his head hurt like a son of a bitch.

Like, really hurt.

Like, really, really, hurt.

Like really, really, really hurt.

"Are you there, Kyle?"

There definitely was a voice. Of that Kyle was certain. It was a woman. He knew that too. And not only was it becoming louder and clearer, but he had heard it before. He wasn't sure where or when, but it was eerily familiar.

I'm not going insane.

That's good.

I think.

Kyle tried to speak. Nope. That was most certainly not going to happen.

She sounds like a Cynthia.

Maybe a Dr. Cynthia Chalmers?

What seemed like an eternity of head-throbbing silence then followed.

It was, in actuality, only 18 seconds.

"Kyle. It's time to wake up."

The voice was gentle, but firm. In the background, Kyle could hear the rhythmic droning of a machine.

Beep. Beep. Beep.

Am I in a hospital?

This is too fucking weird.

Am I asleep?

I can't be asleep.

Chad and I were just walking up the trail to the cottage.

We-

"C'mon Kyle! Rise and shine," the woman said with a slight rise and fall of her tone.

Dr. Chalmers has a pretty calming voice. I bet she has blonde hair and it's pulled back into a tight bun just like Janeway's.

I miss Voyager!

If it were physically possible, Kyle would have smiled as he made that particular comparison.

252

Thoughts were coming faster now as the haze slowly began to fade away. Bastard that it was though, the pain just refused to leave his.
I'm lying down, that much I know.
Why can't I move my arms or legs?
Beep. Beep. Beep. The soundtrack to his environment began to speed up.
"There you go, Kyle. I can see you waking up. Good job!"
Wow, she's really excited for me to wake up.
Kyle's eyes began to race back and forth under his lids. His fingertips and toes began to twitch. Words, however, still wouldn't come, but they were getting closer. He could feel them wanting to form. Every now and then his vocal cords threatened to spark to life.
"Try and open your eyes. Don't worry, the lights won't be that bright."
Why would it matter if the lights are bright?
How long have I been asleep?
How bright is this place usually?
I bet Dr. Chalmers is tall.
She sounds tall, and she totally wears glasses, and she's probably holding one of those medical clipboard thingies like the doctors do on TV.
Kyle's mind began to race, reviewing all the possible scenarios of a) where he might actually be, b) who this woman actually might be, and c) where his husband and puppies might be. It was the third of those options that finally triggered the opening of his eyes.
The room is actually pretty dim, Kyle thought at first, as that was pretty much all he could make out. Everything else, though, was nothing more than a shadowy, opaque blur.
How is possible that my head is hurting even more now?
Beep. Beep. Beep. They were getting faster and faster as Kyle approached full consciousness.

Slowly, but surely, the blurriness continued its diminishing downward slide. If he didn't know any better, Kyle would have sworn someone was wiping Vaseline from the surface of his corneas. Words were beginning to signal their arrival too. Slow, guttural moans were all he could muster at this point, but it was progress, and progress was a good thing.
"Shh, don't try to speak yet. It's going to be a while before you'll be able to form coherent speech, but we'll get there. Maybe by dinner time."

Thanks, Dr. Chalmers! I didn't realize how hungry I was. How nice of you to bring it up.
Bitch.
I wonder what they'll be serving for dinner.
Kyle listened to her instructions and stopped groaning like a complete idiot.

"Okay, Kyle. I'm going to wash out your eyes with a bit of saline; they're a little bit crusty around the edges. It will help the fuzziness go away. And no, it won't sting."

At least it won't sting.

In fact, it didn't sting at all. Kyle found the process quite refreshing, actually.

That was actually quite refreshing.

In addition to the revitalizing coolness of the saline, Kyle's eyes were now almost completely blur-free. Now if only the good Dr. Chalmers could just give him something for this motherfucker of a headache that had settled into the front of his brain.

"Now that they're rinsed," the woman said, pressing her fingertips gently on his eyelids, "I want you to keep your eyes closed for two minutes."

Argh!

It might as well be a lifetime.

"After that, you should have your vision back to normal."

I better, Dr. Chalmers, or your Yelp review will be absolutely scathing.

Kyle managed a giggle this time.

"Someone's in a good mood. I'll start timing now and will let you know when you can open your eyes."

Kyle spent the entire two minutes refining the doctor's backstory. He decided that she worked in a secret government laboratory where they use time travel to solve major world catastrophes. Further, she was clearly in charge of the safety and well-being of unsuspecting time travelling agents.

Dr. Chalmers was married to a meek man named Jerry who worked as a financial analyst in the small town adjacent to the government complex. They had no children. The only pattering of feet around their two-story townhouse were the 8 paws from their cats Felicity and Finn. Misogynists would argue that Cynthia wore the metaphorical pants in the family, but she preferred a smart navy-blue business skirt, white blouse, ruby red lipstick, and a pair of don't-you-dare-fuck-with-me heels.

Men would wonder how a complete bore like Jerry could have landed a catch like that and women were immediately threatened by her combination of intelligence and ambition.

"Time's up, Kyle."

Whoa!

That went by fast.

Yay!

"Open your eyes and let's see how everything looks."

Kyle opened his eyes, was about to scan the room, but became distracted by three things: a) the 9.8 magnitude headache that violently erupted when light greeted his retina, b) not being able to move his arms and legs, and c) the woman standing to his immediate right.

What was previously a low, painful rumble in the front of his head was now announcing itself as a full-blown hangover.

Jesus Fucking Christ that hurts! Did somebody steal the Bishop's Taint recipe???

Instinctively, Kyle tried to bring his hand up to his head, a universally acknowledged pathetic attempt that everyone thinks will somehow contribute towards relieving the pain. His hand, however, would not comply. Kyle could feel the resistance of binding around his wrists and ankles.

What if my nose itches?

This is torture.

Luckily, the blinding pain and the fear of an itch were almost immediately overshadowed by the woman Kyle saw before him.

I am fucking awesome.

While the above conclusion could reasonably have been derived from any of a number of aspects of his life, this particular self-accolade arose from Kyle's realization that he had come up with a bang-on description of Dr. Cynthia Chalmers.

Tall? Check!

Blonde hair and in a bun? Check and check!

Red lipstick? Check!

Business skirt and blouse? Check and check!

High heels? Check!

Medical clipboard? Check!

The only blemishes in Kyle's appraisal of the good doctor were the colour of her blouse, light blue instead of white, and the fact that she was wearing a lab coat.

Dammit! That was a gimme!

Oh yes, Loyal Reader, and her name wasn't Dr. Cynthia Chalmers.

"Welcome to the world of the conscious," she said with a smile. "My name is Dr. Myrna Adamson, and I've been looking after you since you arrived at this facility."

Ouch!

Didn't even come close with the name. How could anyone have guessed Myrna? Lame.

Still, not too shabby.

As she spoke, Kyle looked around the room. It was, he noted, quite a bit larger than it needed to be. There were no windows, but there was a long, rectangular mirror along the wall opposite his bed. The mirror reeked of the run-of-the-mill, one-way variety.

Why else would there be a huge mirror in this room?

"My apologies again that you can't yet speak, I know how frustrating that must be. Also, I can tell from the wincing that your headache is still pretty bad. We've got you on some medication for that."

And yet it doesn't seem to be fucking working!

The room itself was also rectangular, with Kyle's bed positioned halfway along its length and directly opposite the mirror. A number of medical devices lined the left and right sides of the bed along the wall. The most prominent of these was a futuristic intravenous device that had no less than six bags of clear fluids dangling from various hooks. Who knows what manner of liquids they were pumping into his body? The beeping culprit appeared to be a monitoring device of some sort, although Kyle, for the life of him, couldn't figure out where the line from that machine attached to his body.

That's only slightly disturbing, I guess.

Where are Chad and the puppies?!?

Not only did Kyle's eyes convey the sense of urgency and panic flooding his mind and body, but the beeping machine sped up accordingly.

"Calm down, Kyle. There's no need to worry. Everyone you were with is safe and sound."

Everyone?

I was with Chad.

We were walking to the cottage.

That's where I heard her voice before!
Kyle's eyes lit up at the realization.
We were walking to the cottage and I started to hear her talking to me through the trees, and then I fell down and everything went black.
What the fuck is going on?

We challenge you, Loyal Reader, to guess just how many times our heroes have uttered that last phrase since the events of May 22nd, 2017. Guesses can be e-mailed to *howmanywhatthefucksaregoingon@gmail.com*. The winner receives a fabulous prize!

"You have to try and stay calm, Kyle. One of the unfortunate effects of what you experienced is not only the headache you are suffering, but also the heightened state of situational anxiety. Don't worry, it will pass."

Kyle was sure that Dr. Adamson thought she sounded reassuring, but she didn't.

"To ease your mind, let me explain. Your group triggered a self-defense protocol when you entered the underground bunker. A very potent derivative of methyloxyflurane - sleeping gas - was released. Our men retrieved you and brought you here to safety."

Methylwhatnow? Sleeping gas!?

In the back of Kyle's mind, a frightening connection had just been formed.

Smelly, smelly, toast and jelly.

Wendy knew, he thought, incredulously.

"I can see you have a lot of questions," Dr. Adamson said with Oscar-worthy compassion in her voice, "and I plan on answering all of them in due time. Right now, you need to focus on resting and getting your strength back."

She looked down at the clipboard, made a few notes, and placed a hand on Kyle's right shoulder and smiled just a little too broadly. "Everything is going to be just fine," she said and pressed a button on the big I.V. machine.

That's not good.

Dr. Adamson walked slowly to the door, opened it, and paused. "I'll be back tonight with some food. You concentrate on getting some sleep."

With that, she exited and softly closed the door behind her, still smiling.

Less than a second later, Kyle heard the distinctive click of the door locking.

That's never a good sign.

Kyle's mind desperately wanted to begin racing again, to sift through all the possibilities of where he was and why he was here. However, Dr. Adamson had clearly released a sedative into his system; his eyelids increased exponentially in mass as his mental faculties began to pack for a much-needed vacation.

Shit!
I don't want to go to sleep.
If we were knocked out by that gas as soon as we entered the cavern, did any of that stuff with the vortexes even happen?
Where are Chad and the puppies?
Where is Santa?
That was before the gas, right?
So, was that real?
Right?

Kyle's eyes began to close more frequently. It was taking all of his effort to keep them open.

It all seemed so real ...

Dead asleep. There's a reason why people use that term, Loyal Reader; a sleep so pure and so true that the person incapacitated might just as well be dead.

That is the kind of medically induced slumber that enveloped Kyle for the lion's share of six hours. It was such a complete, visceral rest that not even the four successive crashes against the door to his room woke him.

In fact, when Ranger Rod, once again beaten, bloody, sexy as hell, and sporting a white hospital gown, hurtled through the broken remains of the door, Kyle didn't even flinch.

It wasn't until Ranger Rod ran over to the bed and began to shake him and that Kyle finally managed to open his eyes.

For Kyle, confartlement initially abounded, but thankfully this lasted only a few seconds. The headache was pretty much gone, his vision was normal, and words finally made their appearance.

"R-R-Ranger Rod?" Kyle gasped. "What the fuck is going on?"

"No time for that!" Ranger Rod shouted as he pulled every last tube and cable from Kyle's body.

"Goddammit that hurts!"

"Don't be a pussy! We need to get out here. It's not safe," he said as he began to undo Kyle's restraints.

"Where are the others?"

"Alive and safe." Ranger Rod paused for a second and continued. "For now."

With the last of the restraints removed, Ranger Rod helped Kyle to his feet. "You okay on your feet?"

"I'll be fine. Where to now?"

"We go get the others and we get the fuck out of this place."

"Sounds good to me. Let's go!"

Made in the USA
Monee, IL
26 March 2021